AURORA METRO PUBLICATIONS

Founded by Cheryl Robson in 1989 to publish and promote the work of women writers and those under-represented by the mainstream, Aurora Metro Press grew out of a successful writing workshop programme run by our sister company, The Women's Theatre Workshop.

The workshops began at the Drill Hall Arts Centre in 1986, and the programme has now expanded to offer a wide range of workshops, across London, including video-making, scriptwriting, playwriting and directing, .

For her commitment to promoting and publishing women writers, Cheryl Robson received the Women in Publishing Pandora Award (1991), which she was enormously pleased to be able to pass on to Ros de Lanerolle, a generous soul and mentor. She also received the Arts Council's Raymond Williams Award (1992).

The important work of our editors continues to be widely acknowledged. They have been shortlisted for the New Venture Award : Marion Baraitser, *Plays by Mediterranean Women* (1994) and for the Raymond Williams Award: Kadija George, *Six Plays by Black and Asian Women Writers* (1993).

In this collection of 23 stories, only six are by established writers. The rest - and these stories were selected from over a hundred submissions - are by new writers living or working in London.

To the memory of
Ros de Lanerolle
1932 - 1993
endlessly interested in the stories of women's lives

how maxine learned to love her legs

and other tales of growing up

edited by **legs**

sarah lefanu

 AURORA METRO PRESS

LONDON
ARTS BOARD

We would like to thank the LONDON ARTS BOARD for financial assistance in the publication of this collection.

How Maxine Learned to Love her Legs
and other tales of growing up is the first in an occasional series of short story compilations, commissioned by Cheryl Robson and published by Aurora Metro Press. Contributions to future compilations are welcome.

Acknowledgements:
India by Ravinder Randhawa first appeared in *More to Life than Mr Right* (Piccadilly Press); reprinted by kind permission of the author.
Charity by Michèle Roberts first appeared in *The Seven Cardinal Virtues* (Serpent's Tail); reprinted by kind permission of the author.
Grandchild by Geraldine Kaye is extracted from a novel in progress.
Design by Suzanne Perkins, Grafica, 20 Gorst Rd, London SW11 6JE. Printed by Biddles Ltd, Woodbridge Pk Est., Woodbridge Rd, Guildford, Surrey. GU1 1DA.

ISBN 0-9515877-4-9

Contents

v

Sarah LeFanu was born in Aberdeen and grew up in East Scotland and East Africa. Significant moments from her early years: the terrible day when she and a friend, playing with some matches they had pinched, inadvertently set a cornfield on fire. He was beaten for his part in it, she was not. Various lessons were learned from this, and when, mucking about some months later with the lock gates on a stream, they inadvertently flooded several acres of land, they did not own up. From schooldays in Kenya she remembers the locust swarms. Some of the boys - and she has not forgotten their names - would stuff the locusts into the girls' desks, so that when lids were opened for the first lesson the locusts flew out into the girls' faces with wings whirring. She likes to think the girls kept their cool.

Introduction

One of the oldest traditions in storytelling, and one that is found over and over again in fairytales, folktales and legends, is the use of the journey as a narrative, with its movement from departure, through experience gained on the way, to arrival. Departure with its fond farewells to mother, father, hearth and home; or departure as the longed for escape from cruel parents or step-parents; whichever way it is, departure is a setting out alone to face the world. The core of the journey revolves around adventures met with on the way: meeting new people, tests of prowess, tribulations. And then journey's end: arrival. Arrival at some distant place where the mantle of authority awaits (you are the long lost heir to the throne), or marriage and riches await, or it could be arrival back home, a different person from when you set out.

The journey in these stories, and they are stories found in every culture and through the ages, is the journey from childish dependence to adult independence. These journeys illustrate, dramatise and illuminate the journey everybody must take, the journey of growing up.

The journey has inbuilt drama and tension. What happens next along the way? Will the protagonist reach journey's end safely? What will she, or he, find there?

In the widely disseminated collections of folk and fairy tales that were first published in the nineteenth century, of which the Brothers Grimm is now probably the best known, the protagonist was often cast as a boy: the prince who slays the dragon or wakes the princess or the seventh son of a seventh son who simply sets off to seek his fortune.

These compilers chose from a huge array of folktales, many of which had girls as protagonists: Mollie Whuppie and Kate Crackernuts from Scotland, Elena who defeats the wicked old Russian witch Baba Yaga, Rumanian Mizilca who fights in the Sultan's army, and the Spanish princess who kisses to wakefulness the sleeping prince.[1]

The compilers were men, while the storytellers who had kept these stories alive down the years were, on the whole, women. And not of course passive women like Snow White or the Sleeping Beauty, but working women, farmer's wives, shopkeepers, children's nurses, housekeepers. They were women, in other words, who led active lives and whose experiences of life were reflected in the stories they told.

All of these folktales and fairy tales are about growing up. The little girls and boys, the miller's daughters and the woodcutter's sons, set forth on journeys that lead them to adulthood. By the end of the story they have negotiated the witches and dragons and passed the tests set by wise old women disguised as beggars. They have reached their journey's end. They have grown up, and the story closes down with a formal 'happy ever after'.

In the course of the journey from hovel to palace, from poverty to riches, from being a daughter or son to being a wife or husband (or a queen or a king), what happens? Our heroine - or hero - has adventures, and through those adventures she learns all sorts of things about the world and all sorts of things about other people, including who can be trusted and who not to trust. She also learns about herself, she discovers qualities she did not know she had, such as courage or cunning or simply the ability to think quickly. The journey is a journey of discovery and self-discovery.

---

[1] I am indebted to Alison Lurie for her collection, and her introduction to it, *Clever Gretchen and Other Forgotten Folktales.*

Not all stories about growing up end with living happily ever after. Unfortunately. In the nineteenth century, while the Grimm Brothers and others were making their selections, and active heroines were being quietly put on the rejection pile, in accordance with conventional nineteenth century ideas about the role and place of women in society, writers such as George Eliot were exploring in quite different ways the stories of girls growing up. George Eliot was dramatising the struggles of her young female characters, Dorothea in *Middlemarch* for example, or Maggie Tulliver in *Mill on the Floss*, struggles to keep their souls alive as the world - men, marriage, social mores - closed in around them. In George Eliot's work, and in the work of many women writers who came after her, dragons can't be vanquished, and the old woman by the side of the road isn't there to help you on your way but is there to trip you up.

In the late twentieth century, what kinds of stories are being written and read about growing up? In this collection of stories about growing up female, the backgrounds vary enormously; different cultures, classes and countries are portrayed. But, as with the folktales and fairytales, there are many common crosscultural elements, for these stories portray the adventures of bold spirits in their journeys of discovery and self-discovery. They are also, some of them, stories of simple survival, stories of struggling against the world closing in. If girls in the late twentieth century do not follow the conventional routes to adulthood, then their fate is not going to be like that of one of George Eliot's heroines, disgrace or death or some other kind of disaster. But even so, not everything this side of the vote is rosy, and people's lives are as bound around as ever they were by economic circumstance and by the hierarchies of race and class. And girls' lives are still affected by ideas of what is suitable for girls and what is suitable for boys. One of the questions that this anthology raises for the reader is: do girls and boys grow up in different ways, do they travel different routes towards that nebulous state we call adulthood?

When indeed does anyone ever reach adulthood? Don't we end up with the trappings of adulthood (the palace and the prince, the bonny bouncing babies), while inside our hearts and minds we're still journeying? However old we are, we don't feel that the story is over, that we can retire into the happy ever after. There are certain points, common to various cultures, which are marking-posts on the way to adulthood, certain rites of passage: leaving home, first sexual relationship, the death of a parent, or the birth of a first child. More materialistic, more mundane even, but socially and culturally significant nonetheless, are learning to drive, getting a job, paying the rent. But none of these define the transition; they merely offer markers.

In the selection of these stories I wasn't looking for a representative range of rites of passage into adulthood. Stories can't be representative. They are, by their nature, idiosyncratic. And the stories that they tell are different from the kinds of stories you get in a novel. A novel can offer development and consequence, it can create a thickly textured pattern of event, motivation, circumstance, digression. In terms of growing up, a novel can show the whole journey, from departure to arrival, wherever that may be. A short story by contrast seizes an event, or a moment, and illuminates it, reveals its significance, its resonance for the rest of the story that remains unwritten.

The short stories collected here offer moments of illumination and revelation along the adventure-strewn path of growing up. Fleeting exchanges between mothers and daughters that encapsulate unspoken history, sudden outbreaks of hostility between siblings, or between girls and boys, a word, a glance, brief encounters that mark the movement from being just a child to being more than a child. There is a sense in these stories of familiar things being seen anew, of new questions being asked, of events no longer being taken on trust. The young woman no longer asks a girl's questions, and she demands different answers.

What I like most about these stories is the way they capture the atmosphere and feeling of growing up, an almost indefinable mood that isn't to do with events, or with other people, or with circumstance. Many of them capture a time when everything is burgeoning with significance, when everything is important, like the state of your stockings in Chrissie Gittins' story *American Tan*, or the dead woman lounging in the arms of the sea in the title story by Brigid Howarth, or Beacham's hair falling out in Ellen Phethean's *War Games*. The journey is a time of fluidity; it is only when you reach the palace that hierarchies of significance force their patterns on perception.

All the stories are about acquiring knowledge: knowledge of pain to come in *War Games*, in Sally Cameron's *Revenge*, and in Carolyn Partrick's *The Gulf*; knowledge of loss, that comes, as in Susanna Steele's *Long White Grass*, with the movement out of the eternal present of childhood into the world of change and decay and moving on; or the knowledge that comes later, too late to redeem it, in Michèle Roberts' *Charity*. In Mizzy Hussain's *Return to England*, the painful knowledge of difference acquired by the girl child separates her from her mother, as does the demon lodged in Yasmin's heart in Souad Faress's *The Lost Bus Stop*. These girls inhabit a different world from their mothers: the knowledge necessary to survive in such a world cannot be handed down from mother to daughter, but must be acquired independently. There are a lot of solitary children in these stories, solitary not because they don't have family and friends but solitary because they live in the head. Rites of passage have to be undergone alone, particularly if the rite of passage concerns a rejection of your mother, as happens in Daphne Rock's story *Jacey*. Part of the process of growing up is learning how to refuse, as well as learning how to accept. As the American writer Flannery O'Connor said, looking back at her life: 'I am much younger now than I was at twelve, or anyway, less burdened. The weight of centuries lies on children, I'm sure of it.'[2] Shrugging off the burdens of childhood leaves you free to face adventures, to step out alone and lighthearted.

Some of these stories dramatize anxieties and conflicts and dangers, but others dramatize the joys of new found independence, of choosing friends, of routing enemies and of cunningly sidestepping the traps set for the unwary girl. The protagonist of Máire Ní Réagáin's *Soul Mate* has no truck with victimhood - as her classmates discover to their disadvantage. Stella Rafferty's young woman, in *Last Night*, gathers up her courage because she knows what will happen if she doesn't make a break with the world of her childhood. She becomes, she turns herself into, a different woman, no longer awkward and silent.

Knowledge often comes obliquely: out of the ghosts and shadows of the past in Bonnie Greer's *God Don't Like Ugly* and Kate Pullinger's *My Mother, My Father and Me*; out of the casual chat of mother and grandmother in Vicky Grut's *She Loves Me, Yeah*; through the heightened senses of the blind girl in Kirsty Seymour-Ure's *Uncle James*. And it comes filtered through memory. Two other stories besides Vicky Grut's feature three generations of women: Elisa Segrave's *Mulberry Juice* and Kirsty Gunn's *Nona's Letter*. Both deal with similarities and differences between generations, and, like Hilary Bailey's story, *Two Women on a Bus, 1940-94*, with the patterns of women's lives in changing circumstances. In

---

[2] Flannery O'Connor in a letter to 'A,' 1956.

Geraldine Kaye's *Grandchild*, the older woman learns from the younger.

Sexual knowledge is often to do with knowledge of the other, the other's otherness you might say. Ravinder Randhawa's Inderjeet - 'India if you're a friend' - uncovers a boy's otherness with some pain; in Betzy Dinesen's *Ball Girl* it is another girl's otherness that Rachel discovers. But sexual knowledge can also allow for games of cunning and guile, as in Karen Whiteson's *The Chicken Thief*.

These stories offer glimpses of different instants along that journey from childhood to adulthood, from girlhood to womanhood. There is no pivotal point when the protagonist steps from one into the other, but each of these stories presents moments of insight, moments of realisation about the self, and about the self in the world, that illuminate that strange shifting intense time when we are alone, and yet ready to embrace the world. I chose the stories not in an attempt to define the process of growing up but because they seemed to incorporate in different ways a hard to define but familiar aspect of growing up, the mixture of mystery and of madness, of wariness and of wildness, above all the fluid sense of possibility, of dangers and the joy of overcoming them. It was only later that I saw common themes emerging, and began to think that in their very different ways these writers were all dealing with ways of knowing and of learning, of what you do with that knowledge and how you learn it. How, in other words, you face that series of adventures that structures our journeys of growing up.

Sarah LeFanu
Bristol 1995

Long White Grass

Susanna Steele

The grass is nearly white and it stretches over to the dark edge of Logan's Wood. Nothing, not even three months of continual sunshine has lightened that darkness. It is as dense as ever. But the grass has lost all of its greenness. Of course that will return when the first rains come but right now the grass is blonde and nearly knee high.

George is all for cutting it down. 'He's got no thought for the way the sun could parch the roots,' my mother said. 'We might lose our chance of greenness come the autumn rains,' she told him. 'You nearly killed it off cutting it down last year. Let it stand, George, just let it stand.'

I couldn't tell him I wanted him to leave it alone so that it could scratch and prickle at the back of my legs when I walked through it. I couldn't say that I wanted him to leave it standing so that it would hurt me to look at it.

Just to see it brings me a sense of loss. I can describe it like that now, loss. But I've found it hard to give a name to this feeling, this hollowness, like a shell after the bird has hatched and gone.

The afternoon before Olga left we went up to the back of Logan's Wood. There was a bed of wild strawberries up there that we knew always ripened first and lasted longest.

This would be our last walk together before she moved away for good. Logan's Wood was the same dense green then

1

and the grass just as long and white as right now. Olga fussed a lot about the grass heads scratching her legs. Only the idea of the strawberries kept her going. They grew right across the clearing, covering over the edge of the tree stumps, wandering right up to the edge of the woods and then stopping, as if they didn't have the courage to grow any further in.

And did we feast! We stooped and picked and picked until our hands were full, then we crammed the fruit into our mouths, filling our cheeks like pouches. The juice from the crushed fruit ran out between our lips and down our chins, dashing red against the front of our T-shirts. Again and again we criss-crossed the clearing as we searched the trailing plants. Flies buzzed around our heads and the air was full of the smell of sweetness. That was the afternoon of strawberries!

Olga called me away from the leaves. 'Come and have this,' she called. I looked up and saw her standing in the middle of the clearing, bright against the darkness of the trees. Her hands were cupped together and she was stretching them out towards me, offering me whatever they held. As I came closer I saw that her hands held a gift of red that I took to be a gift of strawberries. I stretched to reach them, cupping my hands under hers, thinking how I could bury my face in the bowl of her hands and scoop the berries with my tongue, licking her palms clear of the juice that would run between her fingers. But these berries shone in the sun and were linked with golden thread.

'It's my mother's. I've stolen it for you.' Olga drew the end of the necklace up until the whole of the chain of red beads hung in the air. I let my outstretched arms circle her waist and bent my head and rested it on her shoulder as she fastened her mother's red bead necklace around my neck.

'She'll never notice it's gone when we unpack and when you wear it you'll know I've never left.'

2

I had kissed Olga before. Once. Last winter in her father's greenhouse. We sat there sheltering from the cold air and talking of love, when it would happen and what it would be like.

'George wants to ask you to go out with him,' I told her.
'He asked me to find out if you would go.'

'Do you think I should go?'

'It's up to you,' I said.

She quizzed me about my brother and how he felt about her and I watched her cheeks flush as she talked about him, her eyes shining. Olga's head was on my shoulder, her hand holding mine, twisting my ring, squeezing my fingers between hers. She talked about how it might be if George kissed her.

'He would hold my face between his hands so gently and look into my eyes.'

She sat and turned towards me, she saw in me, maybe, a resemblance to my brother that allowed her to draw my hands up gently to her cheeks.

'This is what it would be like.'

My hands cradled her face and she smiled and called me George and kissed me. I was George for her but it was me that felt her lips.

In the strawberry clearing in Logan's Wood Olga kissed me and it was fearless. Under a halo of flies drawn by our sweetness we held each other and no one came between us. It was my name she called and my mouth she reached for.

Strawberries ripened around us and those green tendrils pushed their way closer to the dark edge of the wood. Everything went on growing and changing around us and my mouth on Olga's was the centre of it all and all of it was a kiss.

We walked back down the hill together through the hot white grass still surrounded by the sweet smell of

3

strawberries. Before we came to the house, Olga stopped and turned to face me.

'The necklace,' she said. 'Take it off.'

I bent my head and unfastened the string of red glass beads and coiled it into Olga's outstretched hand. She held them as she had before, cupped in her hands, brought them to her lips and kissed them.

'Here,' she said. 'Take it now and keep it safe.'

I put my hand in the pocket of my skirt and twisted the chain of strawberry beads around my fingers. Olga linked her arm through mine and we walked on down by the path by the edge of Logan's Wood.

That night I stretched the necklace along the table by my bed. I drew my pillow close to the edge of the bed and lay and looked at it, twenty two beads of red glass linked with golden thread, and thought of the strawberry clearing and Olga leaving in the morning.

George came in just as I was going to sleep. He asked softly if I was awake. Before I had even decided not to answer I heard him creep up to the side of my bed. I felt him bend towards me stretching out his arm. His shadow fell across my face and I could hear him breathing. I kept my eyes shut tight. I didn't want to see his face. But when I heard the necklace rattle as he lifted it, I opened my eyes and saw him standing in the middle of the room. He was holding my red bead necklace to his lips. Then I watched him catch each end of the golden clasp and hold it between outstretched hands. The beads hung in a glittering curve until George jerked his arms apart. Then the necklace burst all over the room, rolling and scattering until each bead found a place to hide. Then he left. He never once looked to see if this time I was watching him.

I picked my way around the room collecting as many beads as I could find. I stretched my arm under the bed, under the dressing table, through the narrow gap at the bottom of the wardrobe and felt in the dust and darkness for beads. But I never found them all. Seven have gone, rolled down between the floorboards maybe, beyond sight, beyond finding and the ones that are left no longer smell of strawberries.

The week after Olga and her family left I walked up through the hot white grass to the back of Logan's Wood and the strawberries. I reached the edge of the clearing and looked around. Flies gathered and the backs of my legs prickled from the scratchy grass. I wanted to smell how it was on that afternoon when we'd feasted there in that bright space, surrounded by the darkness of the woods, and imagine Olga again, caught up in my arms amongst the strawberries. The land had been stripped bare. Not one plant survived. The ground we stood on had been torn up by the roots and the leaves and berries had been left to wither in the heat.

This spring bindweed covered the clearing and the strawberries haven't returned. But the grass grew back and this long hot summer has bleached it white again. By evening it will glow against the dark edge of Logan's Wood. Long white grass, so bright in the sun that even when I close my eyes against the hurt I can still feel it burning through my eyelids, is all that's left.

War Games

Ellen Phethean

South London, Spring, 1959 is muggy and close. I am seven. Sydenham and Gypsy Hills look down on tablecloths of white horse chestnuts and pink and cream hawthorn, the roadsides are rural with waist-high cow parsley. Bomb sites our playgrounds, luscious with weeds, gaps in the brick terrraces exposing torn wallpaper from forgotten bedrooms hanging in the air, publicly intimate.

My brother gets the second-hand royal blue lady's bike because he manages to ride it first. I have to make do with the red tin pedal car, rusty and sharp. Sometimes we go up to the abandoned underground station at Crystal Palace, derelict and forbidding, daring each other to walk fifty yards into the palatial tunnel, uncertain whether trains still lurch along the grass tufted rails. Other days we go to the wooded slopes above Dulwich Golf Course, pedalling the estate road, guarded by the old white tollgate; on that route we stand on the bridge waiting for the steam train to pass underneath while we shout our heads off in the noisy smoke. I feel familiar with, and enclosed by, that seedy grandeur, a run-down theatre set of fifties suburbia.

In red dungarees and brown sandals with no socks, I like to feel my toes through the leaf pattern holes in the leather. My unbrushed hair is tied with a red ribbon that is always sliding loose. The boys from across the road have the biggest bikes, wear grey school uniforms and call each other Wentworth and

Beacham, they belong to school houses called Ojibway and Mohican. They let us play with them. We gather on neutral pavement between our houses, and Wentworth and Beacham decide if it is war or not today. War is intermittent but internecine, involving verbal catapulting, sometimes whacks with pieces of wood and occasional annihilation with bombs. To be on the wrong side of the war is to be German or The Japs. To be a girl is always being on the wrong side, war or not.

Beacham's sister goes to the local Secondary Modern: she wears a gingham frock and a simpering smile like her mother's. Her mother always wears red lipstick, even in the mornings, and she giggles a lot. She isn't frightening, but everyone is frightened of Beacham's dad. I think that's what makes Beacham's hair fall out, although we only talk of it in whispers, and never to his face. Beacham's contempt for girls is desperate, but I go along with it - I don't want to be responsible for greater hair loss. I know wearing a gingham frock to the Sec. Mod. isn't the same as grey flannels and being an Ojibway, and wearing red lipstick doesn't make up for it. My mother says 'Life isn't fair, darling', but that never seems to be an answer. Yet I understand the unwritten rules of War, the strategies for survival. Boys lose their hair if they don't win, girls are tolerated if they don't win. In possession of this knowledge, I store it up waiting. One day my secret information will turn the tide and it will be my turn to be Victor Ludorum. Beacham and Wentworth speak Latin, because they know the girls don't learn it at school.

One yawning Sunday afternoon, kicking forbidden laburnum pods on the dusty pavement, Beacham dares me to walk the Crystal Palace Tunnel. No-one else, just him and me. I know this is my chance; my throat is hard as we pedal up the steep hill, my knees powered by the knowledge of Beacham's eyes. The trees are still, the old station deserted, I can faintly hear the rumble of buses at the terminus above us on the Parade in this hot smothering afternoon. The tunnel is dark and glutinous as I step forward. My sandals make little sounds that echo back strangely. Beacham makes me go first, but he follows so close behind that I can hear him breathing. It occurs to me that he is frightened, so I step more boldly into the dark.

Fifty yards, he says. I count to a hundred in my head as I walk slowly, then stop. Beacham is breathing on my neck. As I turn he is silhouetted black against the light of the tunnel entrance so I can't see his face as I smile triumphantly. He doesn't say anything, and I feel my ribbon slip off my hair. Beacham's head grows as he bends towards me blocking out the light altogether. His hands grip my forearms. His lips are like a rubber ring - I have never kissed anyone before - I don't think he has. Our noses bump and I can't breathe. He presses so hard I can feel my teeth biting into my lip. I taste iron blood. His hands let go. 'I've dropped my ribbon,' I say as I bend down, spongy moss and slimy stones under my hand until I find the taffeta ribbon. I grin at the ground and, bobbing up, I run towards the light of the entrance shouting, 'I won, I won.'

God Don't Like Ugly

Bonnie Greer

As she sat on the hot cramped bus inching its way through the narrow back streets of Nice, Ida decided then and there that she would no longer call herself an African-American. The term with its kind of neat summing up, simply did not encompass everything she thought she was.

Not that she clearly wasn't of African descent (didn't her great-grandmother complain about her 'African' hair whenever Ida screeched during a typical combing session?).

She was too aware of her own parents' illustrious history in the Civil Rights' movement and the struggles and the joy and the heartbreak not to know what she was.

How could she help it? There were always people walking around the house dressed in dashikis and djellabas and boubous, expounding and bemoaning the current state of affairs.

She knew what she was. How could she help it?

Those strange survivors.

Her family - they sometimes celebrated Kwanza, the African festival that coincided with and replaced the Euro-centred Christmas. Then everyone dressed up more elaborately than usual. Then, even she exuded a kind of bizarre goodwill and calm instead of her usual cantankerousness.

No. She knew what she was. It was just that the term 'African American' reminded her too much of her Auntie Sylvia.

Ida glanced over at her aunt who was now in deep conversation with a greasy boy with deep black eyes and a nervous twitch. They were engaged in rapid French which sent waves of relief through Ida. She wouldn't have to listen to her aunt for a while.

Ida beat the mosquitoes away from her face as she thought about her Auntie Sylvia.

Auntie Sylvia had a stuffed-to-bursting pink and green bungalow. It was tucked away in a cul-de-sac in what was once a dingy Polish working-class suburb. It rather painfully evolved over the years into a shining model of African-American hard work and sobriety.

House-proud and lawn-proud and car-proud, these new occupants were just as harsh on the undesirables of their own race as any of the former occupants of the neighbourhood had been on them. Of course, this was minus the midnight semi-Ku Klux Klan raids Ida had heard about that had taken place in the early years of transition. No, things were better than that now.

It was just that Auntie Sylvia's place was so boring. It was filled to bursting with mementoes of Sylvia's various sojourns in Europe. These journeys occurred in the 'good old days' that her parents and grandparents and Auntie Sylvia herself always talked about. Those days when there was a 'real struggle' and things were as clear as could be and there was great solidarity, blah, blah, blah.

It all bored Ida to death.

Often as she sat listening politely to the umpteenth story about Dr. King, or Daisy Bates or some other pre-historic figure, Ida tried to imagine just what everyone's life would have been like if those 'good old days' had not occurred. Would they have been the dentists, and accountants, the funeral directors, and the owners of beauty salons, cleaners and minor officials in store-front churches that they were destined to be?

It didn't matter. For Ida had made up her mind that whatever happened she was going to be 'normal'. A normal woman with a position and a quiet life, anonymous, small, insignificant. None of this madness was going to rub off on her. None of this need to stand outside the normal run of things, as her parents and grandparents and her Auntie Sylvia had done.

Even if she had been named after a character in a James Baldwin novel.

Baldwin. Ida could once again see that picture of him among the African masks, strange things with grass thing-ma-jigs surrounding them like haloes, and seemingly endless photos and the snapshots of Auntie Sylvia with every black ex-patriate who had ever lived in the latter half of the twentieth century.

This is what the term African-American meant to Ida and she decided then and there on that hot bus to Cannes that she would have none of it.

Her older brother, Michael, all of twelve and already a Master of the Universe, explained to her once that adults have to have things to cling to, especially black adults because times were so difficult. So many promises, so many illusions had been destroyed.

Michael explained that Italian-Americans called them-selves Italian-Americans because they were proud of Italy, Jewish-Americans because they were proud of being Jewish, etc. Of course she understood that. Sometimes Michael treated her as if she were brain-dead just because she was ten years old.

Ida listened, but none of the things that had happened had been her fault. People had to just get on with their lives. They had to forget what hurt them, what troubled them inside. Keep your head down and your nose clean. Stay in your own back yard. Play safe. That was her motto.

Never mind, she thought as she settled back in her seat and listened to her aunt chatter away with the French boy. It was all too boring anyway.

Poor Auntie Sylvia with her strange, bizarre, wandering life. And it was bizarre the way she carried on about that photo she had of James Baldwin. It was as if he had been the centre of the earth. Jimmie this, and Jimmie that. Jimmie did this, or said that. Well, he was dead, wasn't he?

Ida thought she even heard his name now mentioned in conversation with the French boy. Well, this Baldwin was dead, right?

Right? she yelled inside her head.

Once, at her aunt's suburban paradise, Ida took some time to look at the photo of James Baldwin that was kept in pride of place in the middle of the cluttered mantelpiece.

In the photo he was standing by the side of the road. It was clear from the picture that it had been a hot day. Ida could almost see the waves of heat shimmering above the dust.

Baldwin was dressed to kill, her aunt would say, his ensemble completed by a smart jacket and cravat. A cigarette dribbled from his hand. But what she most remembered was his sad-happy smile and the big eyes which seemed to look beyond the picture and out at something else.

Ida had tried as hard as she could, but she could not forget that sad-happy face with the big eyes. She could not forget it at all.

She pressed her nose against the greasy window of the bus as it made its way along the winding Corniche up towards Monaco. She and her Auntie Sylvia were to have lunch there and afterwards meet one of Auntie Sylvia's friends.

Auntie Sylvia had wanted her to come along on this trip because she felt that it was 'important' for Ida. And Ida had decided to humour her aunt. After all, she was almost fifty and that was ancient.

But in spite of herself, Ida smiled now. The Corniche, the blazing sun that sparkled like diamonds on the deep blue sea, it was all very beautiful. And in that blue beauty, she could see Baldwin's face once again, now floating mirage-like above the sea, a great cartoon bubble full of light, a special light, just as her aunt had said Baldwin's face had been when she knew him all those years ago.

When they reached Monaco, Ida walked too slowly. On purpose. Auntie Sylvia was being boring again. She was flapping around like some wild bird talking about the time she knew Ava Gardner (whoever she was) and Princess Grace (she'd been dead for a thousand years) and parties and jazz and all that old, boring stuff. Again.

Monaco was like a tomb. The streets were too clean, the policemen smiled too much, there were no McDonalds and everyone was blonde, wrinkled ... boring. Ida wanted to escape, plop herself down in front of her computer back home, anything.

Because now that face with the sad-happy eyes seemed to fill her entire mind's eye.

Near the Casino, which looked like something out of a fairy-tale, Auntie Sylvia suddenly said right out of the blue: 'God don't like ugly.'

Ida straightened up and tried to compose her face. She must have been frowning the entire time. She could have explained that this was the way she looked when she was thinking, or when something extraordinary was happening and her face could not contain the tumult inside.

'God don't like ugly.' That had always been said to her, and hearing it now made her want to screw her face up again. If God didn't like ugly, he must have hated James Baldwin because he certainly was ...

13

Yes. He was ugly. She finally said it. Couldn't those people who worshipped him see that? She knew something they didn't know. She knew this deep down inside herself. No matter what he said, the reason he had fled America was because he had been too ugly to be there. That was it. She knew it. That was why he had left. And even Auntie Sylvia, even with her make-up and clanging jewellery, even she wasn't smart enough to know what she, ten year old Ida knew.

Suddenly, she wanted to go back to America, back to her room. Hide. Maybe if she turned back, maybe, Baldwin's face would go away.

But that was stupid. No. She just had to make the best of it.

Auntie Sylvia sat down on a stone wall halfway near the top. She was out of breath. Ida thought for a moment that she might run up to the very top, leave her aunt behind. Just do something unboring, something really ugly that would make Auntie Sylvia know what ugly meant.

Didn't Auntie Sylvia understand that she had only consented to come on this trip because she had been bored, that she had felt sorry for her nostalgic old auntie? Maybe she should tell her, even though it would be disrespectful.

But if she opened her mouth, her aunt would yell at her in French or something. It would be too embarrassing. So she said nothing and sat, too. Just as if she were as old as her aunt.

Later on, they had lunch at a restaurant in the grounds of the palace. Auntie Sylvia chattered away in French (once again) to a young couple while Ida gazed over the edge of the mountain fastness, down into the valley of high rises and shrubbery and flowers.

She saw herself floating above it, floating free. And beautiful. Beautiful. Now she had to admit it. The beauty of the place forced her to. Ida felt deep down in her heart that she was the ugly duckling of the family, gawky, bespectacled, cantankerous and odd.

And that Baldwin face which would not go away was so much like her own. She, too, was tiny and dark and bug-eyed. She understood him. She wanted to be seen all the time, even when she wanted to hide. Vanish.

That was the truth of it.

The absolute beauty of the place made her own ugliness stand out to her. All the radiant, tall, sunny images that bombarded her every day seemed to dance around her like demons. She knew now that every moment of her young life had been spent in fighting them.

Yet there was something laughing inside her even as she sat at the table in the shade of a great tree. Laughing because she recognised something. The delicious, all too rare sense of freedom.

This place was different from the ones she had known, different from the ones she would have chosen for herself. Different from the safe life, the predictable life she wanted. This was exile and this was freedom. Freedom.

This strange freedom allowed her to sit through lunch listening to her aunt's reminiscences. She listened to her aunt in a new way, a polite way.

The same old stories took on a new life of their own in this place. Ida could see her aunt as she must have been then at the time of the stories, her tall, slender body gliding effortlessly through the salons, the nightclubs, the cheap hotels and love-affairs of her youth. Her bright, sparkling eyes, eyes which never aged, danced and sparkled now as they had never danced and sparkled before.

Or was this sparkling essence inside Ida? She could not tell.

They met a woman after lunch. The woman was white with white-blonde hair and white super-clean diamonds with white clothes and too much perfume. Her jewellery clanked like broken church bells as she and Auntie Sylvia made a great deal of noise kissing and hugging. Then Auntie Sylvia retreated back into her old boring self.

But Ida had changed.

They were driven in the woman's great car to Cannes. The highway there was like any other highway, but Ida felt as if the entire world were about to open up. Open and spill its secrets to her, open up and tell her that she was indeed beautiful.

They drove up a winding road to a house above the sea. At first it was not possible to see it nestled among the trees, but as they came closer it rose from its hiding place like a sleepy white giant and seemed to go on forever. A man at the top of the drive waved at them, his skin brown and leathery.

Ida was kissed and passed around a great deal. She endured it, but all she wanted was to find a way to be alone.

She could feel that something was about to happen.

When she was able to escape, Ida walked down the winding stone staircase to a little area where strange looking plants were growing. They were placed in careful rows and stored in a greenhouse. They had gnarled shapes and strange growths. They were ugly, she thought, like something out of a book about a haunted house.

Just beyond the greenhouse was a barn filled with ten puppies. They scrambled to the edge of the barn but came no further. Their faces looked as if someone had taken a great pan and smashed them with it one-by-one. They were ugly, too.

She knelt to pet them. And from ground level she could see a barren, burnt-out landscape that didn't seem to be part of the Riviera at all. It was ugly. Yet she thought that she might like to stay here forever.

When she stood up there was a man standing behind her. She could not see his face in the twilight. Yet she knew that he was not one of the kissers and huggers from the house. For one thing, he didn't seem to be as old as the rest. But then he had to be because he must have known that James Baldwin, too. After all, this was a reunion of those who had known him. That's why she and her Auntie Sylvia had come all the way to the South of France, all the way from America.

That's why the white woman in the white clothes with the white hair and the white diamonds had come. He must have been a friend, too. Why else would he be here?

He didn't say a word as he knelt and played with the puppies. They licked his hand and nibbled at his shoelaces. Some climbed up on his shoulders, others curled up at his feet.

They seemed to become very beautiful as he touched them.

She could tell that he was black, but not much else. It was growing too dark.

He did not speak to her, but did make sounds to the puppies. She could sense a kind of stillness about him, a happy-sadness, too.

She knew instantly that he was dangerous, but not in a threatening way. And even though she could not see him, she knew that he was beautiful, too. He made the air crackle whenever he moved to smoke the cigarette that dribbled from his hand. He made Ida watch him, although the part of her that longed for a safe life did not want to.

He was like a Pied-Piper of the soft black Mediterranean evening. She could not resist him.

He finished playing with the puppies who instantly clambered back into the gloom of the barn. There was not a sound from them.

He had finished his cigarette by now and lit another. It glowed in the sudden purpleness of everything.

It was then that, although she really couldn't see him, Ida decided that she had seen the man before. She wasn't quite sure where. But it had to have been Auntie Sylvia's house. Where else? He must have been one of those survivors of the 60's who sometimes descended from nowhere into her life ... no. That couldn't be. She had seen him somewhere else. She had to have seen him before. That had to be true. Because she knew him.

She wanted to ask him if they had met before, but felt that she should not. He was lost now in the quiet of the evening and the voices above them in the big house, lost in the very swirl of life itself.

She followed him back up to the house, then out onto the path to the giant gate. He hesitated for a moment, but continued on, down the winding driveway. Ida followed him.

He walked down into the growing darkness. She stumbled on behind him, the undergrowth coming up on either side of the steps. She scraped her knees doing that, but it didn't matter. The night was falling quickly, swallowing up everything, but she followed the glow from the cigarette.

They reached the bottom which seemed to be a long road. For a moment, Ida looked back at the great house, now nothing more than a series of twinkling lights hidden among the trees. She could hear jazz in the distance and hear also some of the voices of the other people. But she didn't know where any of it came from. The house, her auntie, all of it seemed very far away now.

The man had not turned around and looked at her once. He did not even turn around to see if she was still there.

But none of that mattered. She just kept walking.

At the bottom of the road, they suddenly came into the city of Cannes. Yet even in the light of the town his face was still shrouded in darkness.

Suddenly he stopped and that was when she saw him. His small, simian face barely contained his large mouth and bulging eyes. It couldn't be. Wasn't Baldwin dead? Hadn't he been dead for years?

The man stood beneath an olive tree and smiled a great smile that seemed to contain all the mischief and beauty in the world.

He lit another cigarette. This time for her. She took it because when an angel gives you a present, you take it, she'd always been told. Her grandmother had told her once that in spite of her plainness, one day she would have a blessing and to take it with open arms. So she did. She took the cigarette, took a draw on it, coughed and felt very light-headed. But she liked it.

And with that draw, she suddenly felt a wildness open up inside her. The wildness that truly made her her parents' child, her auntie's niece. The wildness that had made all this that was happening right now to her possible.

This was what she had been fighting, not the boredom, or even her own plainness. This. This wildness. This need to break away, this will to be in the very flow of life despite what sex she had been born or colour or nationality. Despite all that. Her denial of this, this urge to freedom, had kept her awake at night, made her mock her parents' history, her aunt's past. This denial was what was truly ugly.

Ida, standing under the olive tree in the sweltering Mediterranean high summer evening, knew that she would some day leave her home, leave to seek something else. She knew that she would find it, too, and that even after her death her spirit would continue on. This knowledge was the beauty inside that man smoking beside her, too.

She finished her cigarette and when she did, he turned around and they walked back into the darkness. She walked beside him, now, because although she did not know her way, none of that mattered. Not any more.

He walked part of the way with her up the stone steps, then disappeared down the path leading to the little dogs.

When Ida reached the top of the drive and the house, everyone was very drunk either on stories about 'Jimmie' or the wine. She couldn't tell which. It did not matter.

She went inside the kitchen and poured herself some of the red wine. She stood for a while in the cool stone room and drank her glass to the dregs.

She caught a reflection of her face in the shiny surface of a silver platter left on the counter. Her eyes were large and bulging, her small face could barely contain her too large mouth. This beautiful kind of ugliness was her destiny. And she would not curse it, but settle herself down with it. Fit the world around it. Love it.

She walked back to the top of the stone steps where she had left the silent man. He was nowhere to be seen.

It was pitch black now except for the great moon coming through the trees.

Soul Mate

Máire Ní Réagáin

I heard him nervously clear his throat. 'Good morning, Dear. Sorry to disturb you again but I thought you should know that it is now twenty past eight.' I ground my teeth with irritation. This was the fifth morning call so far. My eyes felt heavy and swollen. Digging my fingers deeply into the pillow I forced the expletive back down my throat. Dad hovered nervously in the doorway. Missiles were often hurled at this stage. Indeed, were it not for the fact that my torch was out of the span of my fingers ...

As he closed the door he added tentatively, 'Remember Dearest, it's your first day in the new school.' Big deal. I had had a few of those already.

As the door shut I considered my predicament. I had been reading a thriller under the eiderdown until six thirty in the morning. One and a half hour's sleep. The bed was suddenly deliciously snug. It seemed unbelievable, unbearable that I was to be wrenched from this cocoon, savagely torn away, like a sausage from a roll, and made to go back to school. Three long months of summer holidays gone in a blink. My rag doll was bent over my pillow looking at me sympathetically. I punched her in the stomach. I watched my toe nails, yellow and inviting, peeping out of the end of the eiderdown. They tantalised me. There was a time I was so supple I could bite them. Now I had stiffened up. The onset of age ... I was thirteen, unlucky for some.

I snoozed uneasily, lids suspended unnaturally, ready to spring back if the bedroom door opened. At half past I heard *bam bam* on my door. No niceties, no finesse, just furious thudding and I shot back the covers and threw my legs so high in the air that I landed on the floor, shoulders first. Mother was about.

It was a typical 'first morning', and typical of all mornings to come. It was ten past nine. I was due in school at nine. A steaming mug of coffee, made with the top cream of ten pints of milk and sweetened with three tablespoons of sugar was on the table just out of reach. An entire Vienna Roll, split in the middle, was bronzing under the grill. Dad was running around the kitchen, following my every command. 'No Dad, not raspberry jam, I want strawberry on my toast.' A pan bubbling with fat, full to the brim with bouncing bacon, and bursting sausages, was threatening to flood the entire cooker top. Dad was trying to turn these and my toast at the same time. 'Three chocolate yoghurts,' I shouted as an afterthought at him. In the middle of this Mother was doing my hair. Through teeth barbed and spiky with hair pins she was trying to hiss violent threats over the clatter in the kitchen. Occasionally she would grasp my hair in handfuls and shake my entire head in a desperate attempt to focus my attention. But even through blurred vision I could still concentrate wholly on my breakfast. Only when my mouth was blocked with buttery Vienna Roll and my stomach distended with coffee, bacon, sausage and chocolate yoghurt did I tune in.

'For God sake now, will ye stay clear of those trollopy brats of girls ye seem to be so attracted to. I'll swing for ye if I have to be ducking in supermarkets to avoid a new batch of incensed mothers. Don't forget, Madam, we're practically living on these nuns' doorstep, and if I have to start going to mass in Dunlaoghaire to avoid them I'll spifflicate you. Really I will.'

Dad was now running around getting my blazer and rubbing more polish into my shoes. I felt exhausted just watching him. I had to sit down to recover from my breakfast. 'Don't forget my lunch box!' I warned him. He didn't. Outside I heard Mother revving the engine. Now commenced the great battle of nerves. I put my feet up and listened. I heard her roar the engine furiously. I knew I was now entering danger zone. I started to count slowly to ten calculating that by the time I reached six she'd be in to get me. At three I heard the engine stop. I jumped up and hurled myself outside the hall door. Too late. She was out of the car and whack! across the head, and into the car by my ear.

I sat at my desk, legs sprawled and eyes alert behind my thick spectacles. I had been wearing the same pair since I was six. They were so small that I had to wind them round my face every morning, and they no longer reached my ears. They left red indents on either side of my nose where they pinched so much. They were useful. They gave my face a worried look so that even when I sniggered I looked anxious. It was my first class and it was a study period. Already I had won my first battles. I had outstared a girl with a white, dead fish face, and I had kicked the leg outstretched on the way to the desk.

A blonde girl with a dirty white collar was blowing saliva bubbles at me. I wondered how her collar managed to be dirty on the first day back at school. I decided I'd ask her. Later. When there were lots of people around. In the meantime, I sucked my braces down and chewed them slowly, staring at her all the while. Then I turned them upside down in my mouth with my tongue, opened my lips slightly so that the metal protruded, and smiled. She stopped blowing bubbles. Her gaze wavered. She nudged her friend. They both stared, then looked away.

Moodily I shifted my seat. I was so bored I chewed the end of my plait and tried to swallow it, imagining the scenario that would follow. I made some gagging noises and took half my plait into my mouth to make it look as if I had, but no-one took any notice. I stuck my hand in the air but the old nun supervising was blind as well as deaf and she just stared past my arm with red and misted eyes. I spat my plait out and looked for some other diversion. I plunged my hand down the back of my skirt. It was so large it barely hung on my hips. I could fit both my arms up to my elbows down there. I snapped my knicker elastic noisily and checked my nails to see if there was sufficient regrowth for a session. Near me, a girl was attacking her ear with end of her pencil. Her face was squashed into an expression of ecstasy. I dug around for my pencil only to find I had sharpened both ends. Decided not to risk it.

Gloomily I looked around. Goddamned twosomes. I hated them. Pairs of desks stuck together. Two by two friendships. Linking arms at lunch, going to sit on the steps of the prefabs together to whisper. Names always in twos. Erika and Sandra-Jane; Donna and Hilary.

I yawned. It wasn't really a problem. Soon I would spot my quarry. Like a cuckoo's egg landing in the middle of a snug nest, I would descend.

Suddenly, one day, I would shuffle my chair along pulling my desk noisily with it. I would then ram my desk to the side of the chosen pair of desks. There my desk would adhere like a large pimple. I would lodge mulishly, face set in concentrated stubbornness, ignoring complaints of teachers and victims alike.

At first the girls would do what they could to get rid of me. Steal my pencil, draw on my copy book, extend elbows to mark territory.

But I never failed. At lunch time I would pursue. Trailing ten paces behind. Voices squeaking with outrage they would turn on me and hurtle abuse.

But sooner or later ... oho! Sooner or later Mr Measles or Mr Chicken Pox or plain old Mr Common Cold would confine one of them and then swifter than a vulture I would swoop. Loneliness would make them vulnerable - for who is not lost without a mate? Then insidiously I would worm my way in there. Chocolate and charm and willingness to listen tirelessly to complaints, first about their families, and then in an inevitable pattern, progress to backbiting about the best friend.

By the time poor pox-ridden mate rushed joyfully back, my bags and baggage would be packed neatly in her space and I would be holding the fort.

Sometimes there would be a savage showdown. Fists and nails flailing. Sometimes there would be a huffy mortified retreat on the part of the abandoned one. Sometimes, short on pride she would hang on grimly, sitting in my now vacant desk and trying to woo the lost one back with invitations to tea at McDonald's. Hopeless always. My mother's cooking was unsurpassed and tea-time at my home was legendary, with chocolate crispies to boot ...

My present situation, however, was an unenviable one. For this, my first day, I had been placed in the only empty desk beside the school's version of the big world's bag lady. There was always one. In every school I had ever been to there was one who wandered aimlessly, forever alone. One who quietly sat in the playground's shadows. Inarticulate with shyness, she would be awe-stricken in the presence of the more popular girls. In fact, the degree of their awe was a barometer of social standing. Mine rated low. She breathed cornflakes and disapproval in damp sighs every time I rustled my papers or snapped my knickers. She had been to the toilet twice during the study period and each time she packed up her satchel and collected her outdoor shoes and took them with her. I refused to allow myself to feel depressed. This was a mere social limbo out of which I was determined to clamber.

The second time she returned from the toilet and unpacked there appeared to be a problem. Some disparity between the number of pencils she thought she had packed, and the number that she unpacked. She met my eye with an uneasy scowl. I leant across and burped in her ear, quite loudly. The reaction was pleasing. A few heads swung around. She, beside me, bristled delightfully. I let rip. I sucked in air and forced it out. The effect was electric. Pencils were dropped. All eyes focused. A barrage of abuse started. I was animated and happy, and I kept on burping.

It was fate. At the same time as I broke my all time record for an extended unbroken burp, I saw them. Eyes. Nasty glittering, gleaming black eyes. The eyes of a kindred spirit. I was so fascinated that I stopped burping and stared myopically at them.

Their owner was exotic. Gleaming white teeth bared in a malicious smile as her friend flicked bits of chewed up paper at seemingly random victims in an obvious attempt to entertain her. I burped hopefully in her direction. Our eyes met. We sent rays of antagonism across at each other. My adrenalin started pumping. I was completely and utterly smitten. How had I missed her? What other treasures had I missed in this sea of nonentities? I looked around with renewed excitement.

Ping! A wad of chewed up paper hit my cheek, then another. I turned round quickly and glowered menacingly. The Paper Flicker was grinning insanely at me, her eyes anxious. I stared fixedly. She tried to grin wider but her mouth drooped slightly. As yet I was an unknown quantity, but the indications so far did not bode well. 'She made me do it,' she mouthed, pointing at Black Eyes beside her. Black Eyes sneered provocatively. Clearly she did not like my attention being on anything other than her. Paper Flicker was unwittingly being made cuckold. I knew the signs. Black Eyes was mine. All it would take was time. I just had to relax and wait ...

Two days later, and wild excitement. The manic Paper Flicker's granny had died. She was being taken up North to the wake. 'You'll get to kiss the corpse' screeched Mary-the-Ghoul. (Mary collected obituaries like some people collect stamps, and bunked off lessons to go to funerals.)

Very unreasonably, on the same day, Black Eyes had apparently grown yellow-eyed and was diagnosed as jaundiced. I cursed. It would have been a simple exercise to heap the fires of indignation, comparing the sorry lot of Black Eyes to that of her glamorous mate. I ate my pencils as I stared at that gap in the row of desks. Mirthlessly I plotted and planned, my enthusiasm fanned by the Bag Lady's bad breath and disapproval.

A day later, as a practice run, I moved in on another couple, one of whom I noticed had a promising sniffle. The day after, Sniffles foolishly took a day off. By lunch time I was firmly ensconced.

My prize was Miriam. Bow legs. Pale soapy skin which flaked on the forehead. She had thick straw textured plaits and very small round eyes, a tiny mouth, a brown moustache and little grey teeth. Her only claim to fame was her ability to draw. Lewd and lascivious was her style. With a few strokes of her pen, rapid shadings and obscene bubbles from mouth she could excite and titillate. She was a regular attender of the Legion of Mary, and there followed those awful boring Wednesdays when she returned to school, piety renewed after the Tuesday meeting and simper at my lustful beggings. 'Stop it, Máire,' she would say.'Jesus doesn't like it.' By Thursday she would be bored, by Friday she'd be again drawing.

But while I was waiting for Black Eyes, Miriam sufficed. Her ghastliness, a refined and subtle art: she creeped. She creeped to teachers to the extent of reporting me for copying her homework. (It took two foolscap pages of drawings and several pencil sharpenings later to appease my wrath.) She crawled to classmates she considered to be superior mortals. 'Nelly Kelly,' she would shriek aloud, and clamp her chunky fingers around her mouth as if to contain the cry within. Nelly would turn her crimped head in Miriam's direction. 'What?' she would drawl in her most bored voice which would excite Miriam wildly. She would go into paroxysms, swinging her fat little legs and squealing like a slit pig. 'Oh,' she'd say, cringing with obsequiousness. 'I was just thinking to myself who the prettiest girl in the class is and then before I could stop myself I shouted out your name.'

Her treatment of the lowly was just as frank: 'You know the boy who lives next door to me who you said is really nice looking?' she squeaked, twisting her fingers as though in an agony of indecision. 'He says you're a dog,' and she bit her lip, looked sad and wrung her fingers some more. 'Miriam,' I said gently, baring my chops in a yellow leer. 'Don't worry about being short - if your legs were straightened you'd be a good six feet tall.'

Shortly after this, the unexpected happened. I found I had to compete for Miriam's attentions. My rival was a tall, strangely shaped girl with dead white, almost luminous skin who stooped as she walked. Her chief lure to Miriam was religion. Jean's mother was, Jean claimed, 'a-Virgin-like-Our-Lady.' Miriam told me this, and severely miffed, I scoffed this idea. My unassailable logic being that no-one, not even Jean would dare ask her mother such a thing. Miriam just smirked and added the final pencil strokes to her picture of Our Lord in His final agony on the cross, folded it up and passed it winningly to my rival. My rival received the note, looked joyously over to Miriam and blessed herself and Miriam blessed herself. All the while they gazed deep into each other's eyes. I ate my nails and felt depressed.

That night I had a prophetic dream. I dreamed that I was running across a huge graveyard. Part of me was really angry about something, and part of me was really frightened and lonely. I ran and ran but wasn't moving fast. Suddenly I saw Miriam and Jean. They were behind me wielding giant crucifixes. They were dressed in white and had haloes on their heads. I was terrified. Just when they were upon me I heard a voice call out to me and suddenly Black Eyes was running beside me. She had long nails and a serpent's tongue. She had turned and was scratching the air. Miriam and Jean started to scream and run away. Suddenly Black Eyes and I were chasing them. Then I woke up, and Dad was 'aheming' nervously at the door, holding a dustbin lid for protection.

When I arrived at school Jean was loading her final items into my desk. Miriam was pretending to look guilty and licking her lips with excitement at the prospect of a showdown. But I barely noticed. My attentions were elsewhere.

'You can come and sit by me,' said Black Eyes. Then mistaking my state of suspended animation for reluctance she added, 'I'll even show you how to make your eyes look jaundiced.'

Even before I lowered my bum into the seat covered in thumb tacks, I knew I had come home.

India

Ravinder Randhawa

Inderjit is the name. In-Der-Jit if you're English. Intherjeet with the double *ees* dragged out if you're Punjabi. India if you're a friend.

We were having our first row. He wanted to pay for our meal but I said no, that I should pay because he paid last time. He said he never had been able to stand those Indian scenes where everyone insisted on paying for everyone else and argued for hours before paying the bill. 'We should do what the English do and just pay for ourselves,' he said. I said that's right, so I'll pay this time.

'Women don't pay,' he replied.

'Well this one wants to.'

'This one is soft in the head,' his hand ever so gently brushing my hair away from my eyes.

'It should be fifty-fifty,' I insisted. 'You shouldn't pay all the time.'

'I only do it because I know I'll make a profit on it,' and the look in his eyes made mine look away and tighten every muscle in my body to stop the red blush spreading over my face. Oh God! He'll think I'm really naive. What was the saying? '...be as bold as brass'. 'I think everything should be shared,' I said, looking him dead centre, straight in the eye.

'If I pay for this you can pay for the video film.' His grin spread all over his face.

We were going out together. At last! If you could call meeting in the back part of a café, walking 'together' on opposite sides of the street, pretending great surprise when we happened to be at the same place at the same time, 'going out'. We'd say wasn't it a small world and for the benefit of anyone eavesdropping we'd talk as though we hadn't met for years and years and exchange all sorts of news and ask after all sorts of people we'd never met, giving them names like 'gangrene-ganges-wallah', 'nose-picker-nosy-parker', 'Nina-never-been-kissed'. Stupid and childish? Yes it was, but it was a crazy time, a technicolour time, a shifting from black and white to colour TV time, from living in whispers to talking out loud time. I'd read about how love makes people think they're walking on air, sing about stars and sunshine and go around with perpetual Cheshire cat smiles on their faces. Goofy I used to think. Round the bend and bonkers with it.

I wouldn't say I'm in love like, wouldn't use that word, don't care for it. Feels like it's been through all the second-hand shops in town; you never know whose grubby hands have touched it. Even if I can't bring myself to say the word out loud I think I've got all the symptoms. Goldfinger said it to me, but I know he'd said it to all his other girlfriends too.

'You're different, Injun.' My heart used to go all soft and gooey when he called me that. 'I didn't feel like this for the others.'

Would you believe me if I said I believed him?

I'd had my eye on Goldfinger ever since last year when he'd had a big thing with Christine Chambers who sat two desks away from me. Christine was a cliché come alive: white, tall and beautiful with long blonde hair. The opposite of me you might say, if you were inclined to be that unkind.

'Thick as two planks,' my friend Suman used to say to console me. Didn't help. Christine had Goldfinger, I didn't.

I don't know when he first got called Goldfinger but it was on account of the amount of gold he wore; rings on practically every finger, chains around his neck, a gold watch and it was said even his cigarette lighter was gold. Those who didn't like him, like Suman, called him Fort Knoxious. Hurt me that did whenever I heard it. His dad was the richest Indian bloke in town, owning shops and property all over the place. My dad said you couldn't trust someone like that, they couldn't have made all that money by being honest. 'Why didn't you go to private school?' I asked him once.

'You don't pay for something you can get free. How do you think me old man made his dough?'

Christine caught me looking at him once, and smiled a horrible pitying smile. After that she started taking a really friendly interest in me: dragging me along with them, talking to me about Indian families, inviting me out with them.

'Why're you always with that gruesome two-some?' Suman asked.

'I'm tagged on for effect. You know, like you don't know what's beautiful until you know what's ugly. Right?'

'You're an idiot. You're a manic obsessive. Why don't you try a white boy? Boys are all the same. If you've had one, white or black, you've had them all.' Suman had done all her experimentation last year and was now a self-declared cynic. 'Super Cynic Suman. That's me,' she'd announced. I'd pretended to know what it meant. Wasted all my break searching under *S* in the dictionary didn't I?

I didn't agree with her. I didn't see how boys could be all the same. And it wasn't as if I had a choice. I didn't think I could ever love anyone except Goldfinger. Sounds fatalistic doesn't it? Like Karma and all that. My mum would really scoff at me if she could hear my thoughts; she says you've got to work for everything in life, things don't come from out of nowhere on a silver thali. OK. So how was I going to get him to stop loving Christine?

'Let's be honest,' I said to my mirror that night, turning my face sideways, up and down, around as far as I could. Eyes, nose, mouth, teeth, cheeks, chin, ears and neck. All the right things in their right places. Put them together and add them up and the total is ... wait for it folks ... you're not going to believe this ... the total is indisputably - Plain-Jane-India! Why didn't they total up to Beauty like Christine's? We do our job they said, we're functional, we'll help you eat, talk, breathe, look and sleep. What more do you want? I don't want you sticking out like the Rock of Gibraltar I said to my nose, trying to push it back, so the skin wrinkled like folds on a mountain, or these colonies of blackheads, I said, leaning forward and scratching at them. Suman had offered to squeeze them once and if she hadn't been my best friend for years and years I would have suspected her motives in mentioning them out loud in public like she did, just as we were queuing up for dinner.

I held my breath, sucking in my 'well rounded' stomach and, folding up the excess skin at the sides with my hands, I walked around on tip-toe, feeling tall, curvaceous and glamorous. By the time I'd circled back to the mirror, my breath had seeped out, my hands had loosened their hold and my stomach was back resting on its folds and my heels were on the floor bringing me back to my short square shape. The mirror doesn't lie, and I said I'd be honest.

At the Christmas Disco, Goldfinger was with Precious, her black fingers intermingling with his and I asked Christine what had happened. 'He's into multiculturalism.' She looked at me with another one of her awful pitying smiles, 'Hang around long enough and he-may-even-get-around-to-you.'

He did too.

Suman doesn't agree but I reckon it was going to India that did it. Mum got a letter from her parents saying that her younger brother was getting married. She read it and re-read it and tears started running all over her face and as she wiped them away with her chuni she saw me looking at her.

'Don't you ever get married and go away,' she said, 'thousands of miles away, not to see your parents, brothers and sisters for years and years.' She grabbed for her chuni again. 'Use these Mum.' I shoved a box of tissues in front of her. I know she would have liked me to go round and hug her and comfort her. But I wasn't like that. I was India born in England, ice running through my bones.

She did it when we were eating, that is my dad and I were eating and she was standing at the cooker making the rotis. Dad had tried to english-ize her and get her to make every-thing beforehand so's we could all eat together. Mum wouldn't have it. Said she couldn't have us eating stale food, only cooked us one meal a day and that was going to be hot and fresh. Slap, slap went her hands, the circular piece of dough growing between her palms, then a thump as yet another roti hit the tava. Sometimes I'd just want to sit and watch her, fascinated by her hands moving in a repeated rhythm, going through all the different movements in making rotis.

'I think I should go to India for Jeeta's wedding next month,' she said as she placed a hot crispy roti onto Dad's plate and continued before the strangled sounds in his throat could become words. 'He's the last one to be married and it's important that one of us should be there.' Her hands and eyes busy rolling out the dough, 'More importantly, it'll be Intherjeet's last chance to see a family wedding before her turn comes.' If Dad was surprised, I tell you, I was well and truly stunned. Didn't know what to take her up on first: missing school, taking me for granted, planning my marriage ... I was that astounded!

Things happened so quickly I don't think I found my tongue till the plane touched down on Delhi airport's sizzling tarmac. I never knew sunshine could be this hot!

I couldn't move, thought my dupatta (classier word for chuni) had caught in the door. It hadn't. It was caught in Goldfinger's hands. I swear he had even more rings on his fingers than before.

'Hello India,' my heart melted so soft you wouldn't know I had one, 'you've changed.'

'No, not really,' trying desperately to play it cool and wondering if Precious was with him.

'What's with all this Indian stuff?'

'Oh well,' hoping the wobble in my tongue wouldn't come through, 'I'm just India-returned, you see.'

'I see,' and there was a gap because I could see that he didn't really, so I blundered on. 'It's like foreign-returned! That's what people in India call people just returned from abroad.'

'Why don't we go and have a coffee and you can tell me more about it.' This was a chat-up line, a let's-get-together line and this time it was for me, for real. Of course I said yes.

I did tell Goldfinger all about my trip, my words tumbling over each other in my eagerness to share with him the excitement of finding a huge, new, ready-made family, of seeing the places my parents had always talked about, of seeing things being done in the real Indian way: like shopping for instance. It was great. You sit in front of a huge cloth-covered platform while they throw rolls of material whizzing across it and it all unfolds and flows like a river of colour in front of you. Getting all poetical I was when he said, 'Shall we go and watch a film on my video? We can get an Indian one if you want. That way we can see a bit more of India can't we Injun?'

I was speechless. It was like on a film when they're all chasing each other and everything starts going faster and faster, speeding up till you think they're all going to crash into one another, when suddenly they all stop, everything freezes. That's how I felt. Frozen. Cut off in mid-sentence.

Did things always move so quickly?

Thump, thump, said my heart, wake up he's asking you again. 'What about the latest Amitabh Bachan?'

'What about another coffee?' I suggested, stalling for time.

'I've got coffee at home.'

'I like the coffee here.' I didn't want to go to his place, it was all too soon, but I didn't want to drive him away. I didn't know how I could say *yes* and *no* at the same time. 'Anyway I'll have to go home soon.' It was going all wrong, and here I was making it worse.

'A right little good little Indian girl aren't you?' he said. Goody-little-two-shoes I thought. Yes sir, that's me. Step over the line? Not me! Won't even go near it. I didn't reply, concentrating on holding on to my tears, waiting for him to get up and leave. 'Want a sandwich with your coffee?' he asked.

I looked up. This can't be the same scene? He grinned his gorgeous grin and said 'Okay Injun?' before he went off to the counter and I thought it's happening, it's really happening and then the big horrible shapes of Auntie Bibi and Auntie Poonum came looming into my thoughts and I knew I'd have to be careful, plan my defences right from the start, make sure I had my alibis all worked out. I would want to tell my parents myself, when I was good and ready but I could just imagine how they would react to hearing from Auntie Poonum or Auntie Bibi that they'd seen me with a boyfriend, doing all sorts of things that girls like me weren't supposed to: 'Hand in hand sister. In broad daylight.' Auntie Poonum always thought things were worse when done in broad daylight. 'In front of the whole world, sister. Shameless!' Knowing her, she'd stir it even more and hint that I'd been seen with every bloke in town. '...with these very eyes sister,' opening them both wide in emphasis.

Love. Infatuation. Schoolgirl crush. Call it whatever you want but it really does do these funny things to you: everything's bright and sparkling and the dullest things become tolerable; life takes on an excitement it never had before and with each day there's something to look forward to. Mum couldn't believe it when I gave her a huge squeezy hug one day and she wanted to know what I was celebrating. I talked to Goldfinger like I'd never talked to anyone else, not even Suman. I felt I belonged with him. If our bodies were getting to know each other then how could our minds remain separate? We talked about white people, about our own Indian society, deciding on those things we liked about it and the things we hated about it. We played Indian music and watched Indian films and he said, 'It's such a relief not having to be a cultural interpreter,' and I said 'Wot's that when it's at home then?' and instead of giving me a sensible answer like any sensible person would, he started throwing cushions at me, but I tickled him into submission and extracted my reply, 'Having to explain every poppadam you eat. Now if you don't let me go...' I made a strategic retreat but still got drowned in the cushions that came hurtling behind me.

I felt whole and contented. All the different parts of me, the jagged ends that never seemed to fit, the bits that were English, the bits that were Indian, the bits that were just plain me, melted and fused together.

'I'm not going to have a dowry when I get married,' I said one day.

'Me neither,' he was laughing at me.

I wanted to tell my parents about him, to share him with them. Then, I thought, everything will be perfect. It was terribly important that it should be done properly, so I was patient, waiting to pick just the right moment. As I'd grown older Mum had tried to warn me: she'd said, 'Don't get yourself tangled up - our way is better - love should come after marriage - then you know it's forever; in this country everybody shops for love like shopping for a packet of cigarettes - before you know it you've finished the packet and got yourself a lung disease - but you're hooked so you have to run off and buy another one.' I didn't really understand all that. I wanted to say to her that when everyone else around you is trying out different brands you can't not breathe it in too. I had giggles when I thought of introducing Goldfinger to her as my personal packet of cigarettes and saying as I turned around, 'Look he's so safe he doesn't need a government health warning.'

Suman and I were laughing as we came out of Ms Missing-Something's class. Actually she was Ms Turnbull; you know the type: jeans, holey jumpers, skinhead hair and woman earrings. 'Needs to remind herself,' I'd whispered to Suman and we'd both giggled ourselves silly. She was Missing-Something because she used Ms and not Miss or Mrs. The boys had shouted it out at her when she first came. I thought it was unfair but she was one of them 'traditional' feminists, always wearing the uniform of the white feminist, she turned me right off. She held a discussion and debate class for us Young Women. We'd sit round in a circle (ever so trendy), clutching our cups of instant coffee and talk about 'relevant issues'. This time the talking had started off with social conditioning and moved on to the different roles of men and women; I can't remember who first introduced the words oppression and liberation into the discussion, frankly my mind was somewhere else (with Goldfinger), and I wasn't really paying attention. I sure woke up though when 'Dolly Parton' Donna started going on about Indian and Pakistani women (she really did say Pakistani and not Paki. Donna was a 'friend' you see). She gabbled on about how they were more oppressed than white women, kept locked up in their houses, shunted off into arranged marriages, having to sleep with men they'd never met before ...

'White women do it all the time,' I said interrupting her. 'Never heard of a one night stand?'

'Who'd stand Dolly Parton for one whole night?' Suman put in, and we were the only two grinning in the stony silence.

'Everybody knows Indian women aren't as free as us.' Parton was prepared to stand her ground, you had to give her that. 'I only wanted to help.'

'What makes you think we want your help?'

'Because I care for women. I only want Indian women to enjoy the things we do.'

'Oh yeh,' and I counted them off on my fingers, '...herpes...V.D....Cervical cancer...A.I.D.S...' I could see Ms Missing-Something looking awfully worried, her feminist and anti-racist badges jiggling on her shoulders.

'How many Indian women can choose their own husbands? You tell me that, and if they haven't got a dowry they can't get married at all.'

'It's like bribing someone to marry you,' said another brave spirit coming to Dolly Parton's aid.

'White women can't get married without they open their legs first.' Good old Suman. Ms Missing-Something stepped in and took over. She was upset though she tried to hide it. She didn't tell us off; we were all supposed to be free to express our opinions; so free that she made sure none of us could open our mouths for the rest of the session, spieling on generally about cultural diversity, respect for others' customs, equal rights, sisterhood and so on.

I guess it was poetic justice that Dolly Parton should inform me of the happy event. Came up to me after the class and asked if I'd received an invitation to Goldfinger's engagement party? I was a bit bewildered, thinking he'd got a cheek sending out invites for an engagement party without even having asked me if I wanted to; I'd imagined I'd make him get down on his knees and ask me the right and proper way.

B-l-o-o-d-y H-e-l-l! That really is taking someone for granted. Parton was rummaging in her bag. 'Me dad does lots of business with his dad,' she was saying, 'so they always invite us to their do's. Here it is.' She brought out a real expensive looking card. Covered in gold it was. Naturally.

'The girl's coming from India. Some millionaire's daughter. Fabulously rich. Did you know about it?'

'Course I did.'

I'd talked to him once about why he hadn't gone out with an Indian girl before, and he'd said they were hard work. They wanted to be dutiful daughters in front of their parents, but behind their backs they wanted to run around and do the same as everyone else.

'It's not our fault,'I tried to explain.'We love our parents, but we can't cut ourselves off from other people either. And we take all the risks, the boys don't.' He didn't agree, he thought the girls should choose, one way or the other. I talked about the parents and said how they were afraid to let their daughters go out because they felt boyfriends couldn't be trusted, a bloke can turn round and do the dirty on a girl anytime he wants to. He shook his head, 'Indian girls want to have their cake and eat it too.'

'I think they're special, they're risk-takers. Fighters. Anyway,' I asked, 'is that what you think of me?'

'You? You're my Injun warrior,' pulling me towards him. Corny maybe, but ever so tingling in my bones kind of thing.

My mind is saying something, saying it over and over again, saying to him all the time, saying:

'You want to have your cake and eat it too, too. Too.'

*   *   *

'Why do you Indians always end your names with *jit?*' The way it was said it could have been *git* or *shit*. He was shifting around behind me, sliding from one foot to another, shoulders twitching all over the place, hands and fingers moving on an invisible instrument. I turned back to my locker to finish putting away my books. 'It's a boy's name isn't it?' He'd shifted round to the side, the little stone in his earring winking at me.

'*W-i-c-k-e-d!* An Indianologist. My lucky day.' I closed the door, turned the key and bent down to pick up my bag, almost head banging into his yellow hair as he contorted towards me, his spiky eyelashes centimetres from tangling with mine. I gave him a look that should have blasted him through the wall.

'Why've you got a boy's name?'

'Unisex.' Hiking my bag onto my shoulders I made for the door. He was a kangaroo now, jumping from one spot to another following me.

'Since when did you lot get into the twentieth century?'

'Since about six hundred years ago.' I was at the door now, and trying to get through and close it all at the same time so's he wouldn't be able to follow me. Of course it swung back and nearly hit him in the face. 'Remember,' I said to myself, 'never say sorry.'

41

'*Miaow, Miaow,*' nails scratching at my neck. Slipping my bag into my hand I swung round, putting my whole weight behind it. I couldn't bear to be touched, it was like he'd pulled a light switch and lit up all the things I'd been trying to hide. My bag sliced through the empty air and he was laughing, leaning against the wall, hands in pockets.

'One day I'll let you hit me,' he said.

'Wouldn't want to contaminate myself.'

'Heavy doors, those. Could do someone a real injury.' He was walking beside me, human walk.

'I'm working on it.'

'Loveable bit of sunshine aren't you? What's with all this Indian stuff?' lifting my dupatta and letting it slip through his fingers. I tore the dupatta away from him, but suddenly I couldn't move, those words again, like glue on my brain.

'Just stepped off the boat have we?'

I turned and just walked on, and suddenly he was a dog, yapping round my heels, making pitiful barking sounds.

'Sorry.'

'People are always saying sorry. Sorry doesn't change a sodding thing.'

He drew his breath back in horror. 'Wash your mouth out! Detergent. Bleach. Fairy Liquid - softens the toughest tongue. Didn't mean that you know,' face wrinkling for forgiveness like a dog that knows it's done wrong. 'Just a joke.'

'You talking about yourself?'

'Actually,' straightening up and looking human, 'I'm terribly interested in Indian culture.'

I sighed. Should have seen it coming. 'Well I ain't.'

'Then what you wearing those clothes for?'

'Listen you reincarnated missionary. This isn't the tropics you know. Can't run around naked in sub-freezing temperatures.'

'Did you get them in Bombay or Delhi?'

Mi-gawd! A man of the world. I was overcome with admiration. 'Got them down the bleedin market - goin cheap.'

'Like you?' Looked ever so pleased with himself.

'Missionary turned flesh trader. Figures.'

'Only in female flesh,' and immediately did his kangaroo jump, way back, backwards. 'Only another joke. Didn't mean it,' eyes on my bag, hip-hopping out of range.

This time last year I would have walloped him one for saying that. Being older and wiser I thought, 'He speaks truth who speaks in jest.' (No. I didn't make it up, came from one of my Eng.Lit. books.) And now he's going to say sorry.

'Sorry. Hope you're not hopping mad about it. See you around,' hopping out of sight round the corner.

'Who's the boyfriend?' Suman had come up behind me.

'Clean out your contact lenses huh. That was no boyfriend, that was an animal.'

Suman shrugged her shoulders. 'Same thing. Fancy you?'

'Fancies himself.'

'Did he try the 'I'm really interested in Indian culture' line?'

'Yeh, and he slipped in Bombay and Delhi like he'd lived there all his life.' We collapsed into helpless giggles.

'Next time he'll talk about integration.'

'Soften me up.'

'Reckon he's a culture vulture? Collecting material for his dad's book on Asian girls.' That had actually happened to Suman. We laughed so hard our stomachs hurt.

'He's not even a culture vulture, he's just a filthy lecher.'

'*Wow*, now who's the cynic?'

Yes. I am cynical now.

Wouldn't you be?

Jacey

Daphne Rock

She threw the pen down so violently that it broke, the plastic casing splintering and the tube of ink poking out sideways. *Fuck, fuck, fuck.* Now she hadn't got a pen, and there was marge on her history homework.

She went over to switch the kettle on, threw a teabag at a mug, missed, tried again, missed again.

It would be history, wouldn't it? Mister bloody Jessel. He'd have something to say, like, 'Had a battle with the butter-knife Jacey? Perhaps you should try dry bread while you're doing your homework.' He was the one who had told them not to come the kitchen table sob-story, when he was a lad he'd had to work on the kitchen table and look at him. Look at Mr Jessel. Not if she could help it.

It didn't cross her mind to say they hadn't got a kitchen table. You didn't tell teachers things, not even the better ones. If she'd cleaned up the worktop instead of rushing to get through the homework ...

She poured boiling water on the teabag, and stood at the window, warming her hands on the mug. The sky was dark but a huge cloud was even darker, hanging out like half of an enormous moon. A few little puffs of cloud were being blown about underneath it. Jacey imagined she was one of the little clouds, trying to escape before she was blown into the heart of the huge mass of blackness. One of the little clouds went

44

suddenly, *pop,* it was part of the black moon and she dropped the mug, just as her mum came through the door.

Her mum leaned on the back of the chair, not saying a word. Jacey babbled in her anxiety.

'I'm sorry, I'll clear it up, I'll buy you another mug, I'll make you some tea mum.'

Her mum was tall and thin, pulling off the light mac she wore to work when really she ought to have a nice heavy tweed. Maybe, somehow, she could get her a woolly scarf for her birthday. Nick one if she had to. Jacey thought about it, scrabbling on the floor for bits of mug and mopping the tea and boiling the kettle again.

'I wish you'd think a bit Jacey,' her mum said.

What were you supposed to do, think about dropping mugs before you dropped them? She did think, mostly about how her mum looked ill and tired, as if they'd had to patch bits of her on to the other bits to get her all covered. Like Jacey did with the pastry when it wouldn't cover the tin. Jacey wasn't tall, she was a titch. That was another thing about her history teacher. Some of the pictures he brought in, houses in olden days, he said the doors were low and people were smaller then because they didn't eat well, not like the people today. He looked at Jacey and made a remark, like a joke, except she didn't think it was funny. Jacey's the only one who would get through the door now he said. So eat up your greens Jacey.

Her mum sat down on the kitchen chair and blew breath out of her mouth like she'd been holding it in all day.

'That Mrs Arbuthnot,' she said. Mrs Arbuthnot lived in Prince of Wales Drive looking over Battersea Park and Jacey could imagine the flat because her mum talked about it quite a lot. She had two bathrooms, one of them opening right off her bedroom.

'That Mrs Arbuthnot,' her mum said again.

Jacey pushed all the words about the pen and the marge down her throat. Maybe Mrs Arbuthnot had sacked her mum. She gave her mum the hot tea.

'She's going off to the Bahamas for six weeks,' said her mum. 'Only wants me in one day a week. We're just dirt to them, don't suppose she thinks about what I'm going to do without the cash.'

Her mum was picking at her cuticles, the skin was raw and red. Jacey turned her back on the kitchen window and sat down opposite her.

'Come on, we'll be all right.'

After tea she changed her clothes. Her mum liked to see her looking after her school uniform. Her white blouse looked dreadful lying on the bed. Much worse than when she was wearing it under her navy cardigan. Stupid, people who made school kids wear white blouses. She took it into the bathroom, scrubbed it and wrung it out. No way would it dry by tomorrow unless she put it on the back room radiator and she knew damp wasn't good for her mum who got a bad throat when the weather was wet.

School didn't ought to be about clean blouses. Mister Jessel said that when girls left school in the old days they went to work in big houses and they were treated very rough. He said things had changed and girls could go as far as boys now but everyone still had to be responsible and the changes in society didn't mean anyone could get away with sloppy work or sloppy clothes. Jacey reckoned that the teachers who'd been poor were the worst. She didn't think this Mister Jessel had been so poor, anyway. He just thought he had been.

She'd had a laugh with Julia about him. They'd managed to stay in at break, near a radiator, for five minutes anyway, before they got caught. She knew Julia wasn't a real friend. Jacey was just a sort of curiosity to Julia.

'You know what,' Julia said 'those girls in big houses they got caught for babies often as not. Young lords and things.'

'Yeah,' said Jacey. 'They got thrown out of the house. As if it was their fault.'

'Would your mum throw you out if you got into trouble?' Julia asked.

'We wouldn't have enough money,' Jacey said. 'She'd probably make me get rid of it. She tried to get rid of me. She told me. She said I'd cost her more in gin than I ever cost in baby food. Joke,' she added.

In the playground Julia wore a thick cardi which her mum had knitted but Jacey only had one of those acrylics which had stretched the wrong way so that most of it was in the arms. Her mum was knitting a new one now but it didn't grow very fast. Jacey shivered.

'I'd dump school,' she said to Julia, 'give me half a fucking chance. Long as I got money. All stupid rules, school is,' she said. 'Nobody asks us about the rules. Why do you think those girls let the lords do it?'

'Your mum let someone do it, didn't she?' said Julia.

She'd have to tell her tutor something about not wearing a blouse. Her tutor was Mrs Patel who was strict. Mrs Patel said she had one thousand saris in her wardrobe and none of the class would ever see the same one twice. Jacey thought she might, if she stayed at school, but it was hard to keep track. Saris weren't even decent, you could see all the skin round her waist when she wrote on the blackboard. Mrs Patel was bound to say something about the blouse, right in front of the whole tutor group.

Jacey reckoned she only went to school to please her mum, and because looking after her mum was the most important thing. She felt more like she was her mum and mum was her. A pity they couldn't swop. She'd be better at charring because she was strong and her mum would be better at dealing with

47

rules and bad days like when her homework was messy and her blouse dirty.

If she was her mum she'd do things differently. She couldn't start in now, she'd have to go back till her mum was her age. She lay down on the bed and started going backwards, making herself smaller and smaller until she got sucked back inside her mum's belly, turning into a little blob which kicked out at the fishy thing trying to stab into her and sending it back towards ... Jacey sat up clutching her arms across her chest, panicky, dizzy.

'Your mum let someone do it, didn't she?'

After a few minutes she got off the bed, still feeling dizzy. She would have to ask her mum for a bra, she couldn't go on without one much longer, especially in P.E. when everyone could guess she didn't have one. Her mum had thin little breasts but she wasn't like her mum. Supposing she got huge boobies so she toppled and bounced and couldn't see her toes. It was funny, hers being so fat. Couldn't be her dad she took after there, could it? Maybe her mum wasn't even her mum.

She went into the back room and sat on the arm of her mum's chair. Her mum had fallen asleep with the telly on. Jacey listened for her breathing. She fetched her mum's duvet and spread it over her. Tucked her up. Time to go out.

Times like this, she needed Number 25 badly.

She'd started window looking in the summer, during the long, light evenings when people were framed in their rooms like pictures on the telly. People who lived in real houses with front gardens and front doors, not like the flats where everyone lived down long corridors with no windows. Jacey got to know lots of families, the old couple, the blonde woman with the giggling baby, the place with squabbling twins. Only Number 25 became really close. At Number 25 they kept their curtains open even after dark. Number 25 felt like Jacey's real home.

She'd discovered Number 25 the day they'd moved in, the woman with long gold hair and the man with black eyebrows. You couldn't see the floor when you were window looking but the woman kept bending down and coming up with armloads of books and then laughing and dropping them again. She was wearing a black silky top, very low-cut with her arms bare except for strings of glinty bracelets. Jacey heard what she was saying. 'Double everything,' she said, 'double diction- aries, double Graham Greene, double maps of Paris. We'll never manage,' she said, 'we're too alike.' Then the man had grabbed hold of her and they'd both gone out of sight and left Jacey staring at the tops of settee and chair and a big silver lamp stand in the corner. She wished that her mum had someone to grab her. She'd told her she wouldn't mind boyfriends or even a stepdad but her mum wasn't interested. Probably men weren't either, now that her mum looked so miserable, with her hair stringy and her clothes anyhow. If only someone would take her off my hands, Jacey thought, we'd be a lot better off.

In October Number 25 had gone away for two weeks, and come back brown and shining. She'd been cross about that, just when she'd started the new school.

It wasn't as bad as the row, though. Last week they'd been shouting, she could hear them right through the window and her face was angry and his face had a silly sort of smile as if he was embarrassed.

'I'm not just a piece of furniture you can drag round with you,' she was saying, 'what about my job, my life, my career? This is 1995, you know, not the Middle Ages.' And he'd said, 'Honestly Meg, you're simply jealous because I got the promotion.' And she said, 'You patronising bastard,' and slapped him round the face before she walked out.

She knew she was daft, to be so frightened of them moving away, of having rows, and stopping being in love. She'd been down every night since, and the place had been dark.

Tonight the light was on and she ... Meg ... was sitting at the table with lots of papers round her. She put her pen down and stared straight out at Jacey, almost as if she could see her. Then she picked up the phone, but Jacey couldn't hear what she said. Maybe the patronising bastard had left and that was her career on the table. Perhaps she'd be better on her own.

When she got back her mum was wide awake and knitting. The duvet was back on the folding bed like Jacey had dreamed the time she was tucked up asleep. She measured the jumper so far.

'I can't wait,' she said.

'Never knitted you a thing when I was expecting,' her mum said.

Jacey shrugged. 'Didn't want me, did you?'

'Would have done if I'd met you,' her mum said. 'Trouble is, you don't meet babies till they're born.'

'And you can't get unborn, can you?'

Her mum stopped knitting a minute. 'What?' she said, then, 'Don't be so daft, Jacey.'

Jacey wished she could be unborn tomorrow, no pen, no blouse, no Number 25. Taken off the needles, unravelled like knitting, then knitted back again when she wanted. It was all right for some kids, they stayed off, their mums wrote notes and the ones who didn't got the welfare round. She couldn't worry her mum with that stuff.

'It's cold,' her mum said, 'and I've got first shift. Think I'll have an early night.'

When her mum had an early night Jacey had one too because they only had the one bedroom.

Have to ask about the bra soon. The day the giro came perhaps. There were so many worries when you had someone to look after.

In the night she woke up feeling sick. She knew what had happened right away, she had dreaded it long enough. Middle of the fucking bloody night, too. In the dark she went to the bathroom and fumbled around, trying to be quiet, unrolled yards of toilet roll, then back to her room to find the pants she had taken off earlier, put them on and stuff them.

She lay in bed, feeling messy, worrying. Her mum would be off early so she'd have to take some emergency money down to the chemist. There was a box of tampax in the bathroom and perhaps her mum would expect her to use those but it made her feel terrible, the idea of poking something up. She went to sleep for a bit and dreamed she was crawling down a tunnel and waves kept breaking over her and she woke up calling out, 'Come back you patronising bastard.' She didn't sleep much after that. In the morning there was less mess on the sheets than she'd expected even though in the night it had felt like spilling tea. She stood under the shower for a long time: she had to be careful. There was Lynn at school who smelt every month and the boys whispered things. One thing to be pleased about, she wasn't Lynn.

She found a white tee-shirt with a collar which didn't look too bad and she padded herself out again with toilet roll before she went down to the chemist. So much to do before school. She tipped some pound coins out of the emergency tin which had been her idea in the first place though her mum hadn't bothered when she mentioned it. Her mum wasn't bothered about much really. Jacey did the bothering.

'Suppose we need the phone, or to get a black cab to hospital or something,' she'd said. She hadn't thought about pads, then.

Everything was such a muddle, bleeding made her feel muddled too. She tried to make herself laugh. Let's hope we don't need a black cab. They never kept much in the emergency tin. She felt bad. She ought to have made sure she'd bought the stuff ready. Got to get a bra, she thought. S'pose I grow big really suddenly?

She was late for tutor in the end because she'd had to go to the toilet as soon as she got to school. Just to check. There was only a spot, which made her feel it was all gathering up ready to rush out in P.E. There was a biro lying on the toilet floor so that was a stroke of luck. She had a spare pad all wrapped up in her school bag. She thought it might fall out and kept the bag tight under her arm. Boys sometimes grabbed bags.

She went into tutor all mixed up and when Mrs Patel said with a sort of sneer, 'Late again Jacey Dixon,' she felt such a rush of anger that she went straight to her desk before the words came out. They got stuck inside her like the blood.

'You haven't brought back your slip about parents' evening.' Mrs Patel said. 'Bring it tomorrow Jacey please.'

She was even more angry. As if parents' evening was top of her head. Anyway, parents. She felt a stupid desire to shout at Mrs Patel, 'I haven't got parents. I'm the mum in our house.' Fucking monthly was sending her nuts. She pressed her knuckles against her mouth, just in case. Julia was whispering to that cow Jen. Some of the boys were looking at her in a funny way. She sat up straight and tried to act normal.

The pips went and she got to the toilets. First time she'd ever posted a dirty pad into the bag and then into the can. She wished she had a mirror so that she could check if it showed under her P.E. shorts. She'd got the runs too, sat for ages on the toilet. Did you always get the runs with a period? Didn't ought to be at school with all this going on. Not going to P.E. anyway.

She'd forgotten to make sandwiches and slouched round the playground. This was going to go on for years and years. Nothing better, she'd like to go out of the gate and home, into bed. Only her mum wouldn't like it, would she? If she was bothered. Maybe next month she'd let her stay off. This month, well, she'd got to manage.

Funny really. P.E. wasn't so bad. Not a word about her T-shirt. Mind, she'd worked hard on being invisible. Unborn herself. Turned herself into nothing. Sat on the edge, walked around the edges. It wasn't hard, making herself invisible. When the lesson ended she wondered if she was still there. No-one would miss her if she wasn't there. She'd even forgotten being on, until she stood up and collected her things and set off home. Then she felt the blood rubbing her thighs and blood sticking to her hairs. She tried to walk ordinary, going home. English homework, science project. She went into the shower and washed away what she could. The blouse was dry. Her pants were thinly lined with dark blood. She bundled the sheets and pants into the bath and washed out most of the marks. Then she took them down to the launderette, using the last of the emergency tin.

There was the woman from Number 25, doing her washing. You would have expected her to have a washing-machine. Perhaps the patronising bastard took it with him. She was doing towels and sheets. Jacey sat beside her, watching the tub whirl. Didn't seem right, that woman being out of the house. As if a picture had stepped out of its frame. Jacey hunched herself up and tried not to look.

Her mum was late. Jacey was going to ask her about the science project, but now she'd be too tired. And the bra. And the parents' meeting. She went out, down to Number 25. The house was dark. Jacey went up the path and close to the window, making out the rough outlines of familiar furniture in the gleam from the street lamp. They hadn't moved. Unless it was a furnished flat. She stared and stared, willing someone to come in the door, switch on the light, start up the peepshow.

No-one did. Instead there was a rough and heavy hand on her arm, holding it in a vice. 'Little bugger,' someone said. It was the patronising bastard. He pushed her roughly towards the door and she twisted and kicked but couldn't get away. Then she was inside the flat and he was shaking her.

'It was you, was it, little devil! Won't the police be glad to catch you?' Jacey didn't hear, she felt dizzy. She couldn't speak and he still had a grip on her when she slumped, passing out for a moment. She came back to consciousness being dragged over the floor.

'You won't get away with any tricks,' he said.

A real proper bastard. Where was the woman? She wouldn't let him do this. And, oh God, her mum.

She heard the door go and then in came the woman, holding her launderette bag.

'Christ,' she said. 'Max? What's going on?'

'Caught the little bugger just about to break in,' the bastard said.

'She's just a little kid,' Meg said. She sat down by Jacey, took out a tissue and mopped up the tears streaming down Jacey's face.

'Give us a few minutes Max,' she said. 'Go in the other room.'

'Don't let her out of your sight,' the bastard said.

The woman sat there, quiet. Silly cow, Jacey thought. Suppose I was the Boston strangler or something?

'Patronising bastard,' she said.

'I'm Meg,' the woman said. 'He's Max.'

'You called him a patronising bastard,' Jacey said between hiccups.

'Ho,' the woman said. 'So you listen at keyholes?' Jacey stopped crouching and sat back on her heels.

'I don't want my mum to know,' she said. 'I was just looking.' She measured the distance to the door.

'I don't steal,' she said. Then, 'So he didn't bugger off?'

Meg began to laugh. She laughed and laughed.

'He's thinking,' she said.

'He bruised me,' Jacey said. She rolled her sleeves back and there was her arm, all blue and red. 'I think you ought to see him off,' Jacey said. 'Unless you're pregnant.'

Meg's eyes went blank. 'No,' she said.

'You could be. You got to watch it, once you start,' Jacey said.

Meg was looking her over.

'I was just window looking,' Jacey said. 'I've done it for ages.'

'Get off home then,' Meg said. 'Window looking, it's not a good idea. You've got a mum to go home to. That's a good idea.'

She put out her hands and pulled Jacey to her feet. 'Out the door,' she said. 'I'll see to Max.'

'Patronising bastard,' Jacey said, rolling her sleeve down.

Meg made a funny face. 'Trouble is,' she said, 'trouble is, he's all I've got.'

She held the sitting-room door open and the front door open and Jacey scarpered, fast as she could go, down the road and over the crossing and up to the flat.

Her mum was sat in the back room, watching the telly.

'Hello Jacey,' she said.

'Hello mum,' said Jacey.

Nothing had changed inside the flat. The flat was stuck, her mum inside it, it was like some creature that never quite got born. And she was born, and fighting to get back safe and instead she was being pushed out further and further and further, and she hated it.

Her arm hurt a lot. No good saying anything, Her mum wasn't the sort to go steaming round and getting him charged for assault. She didn't think twelve year olds could sue either. She put on a long-sleeved shirt. Then she realised she'd got lucky because if it had happened before P.E. someone might have noticed and she knew what they'd think. You had to be careful, everyone knew that. You been battering your girl Mrs Dixon? Or maybe your boyfriend? Sometimes Jacey thought she'd die of problems. She had a pain but it wasn't a period pain. It was a bloody great hole in her chest because she'd lost Number 25. She looked in the mirror. Did she look like a burglar? What she did look was a mess. Her hair was all crumpled and there was dirt on her face. Fancy that man dragging her along even when she fainted. There was a little jagged tear on her jeans too. She'd bloody well love to break into that bastard's place and smash it up. Tip out all the wine bottles and all the sprays and shampoos into the basin and cut up the furniture. Find a nice china plate and shit right on it. Right in the middle of the floor.

She went back to her mum. 'There's a parents' evening next week,' she said, 'but I didn't think you'd want to come.'

Her mum looked up from the telly. Jacey could see that her eyes were far away, like they'd gone on a trip out of her head.

'You look funny, mum' she said.

Mrs Dixon began to cry, tears running out of absent eyes.

'I'm a bit down,' she said. 'Life's so ... so ... ' She didn't finish. 'There's no end to it,' she said. 'Nothing to look forward to.'

Jacey felt as if she had about one centimetre of care left in her. She dug about for it. Her arm hurt.

'We'll have a treat,' she said. 'Promise. A surprise treat. Next Sunday. Just you wait and see.'

'You're a good girl Jacey,' her mum said vaguely. 'I don't think I'm up to a parents' evening, really I don't. I'll come next time.'

'Okay, it doesn't matter, honest. And mum, I had to take some money out of the tin. I've come on.'

'Oh yes,' her mum said. 'It had to come, sooner or later. You could give my tampax a try.'

'And mum. I'll have to have a bra.'

Her mum started crying again.

'How do they expect us to manage? I ask you. Can you wait till Mrs Arbuthnot gets back? I'll get one then.'

Six weeks.

'Do they grow quickly?' she asked anxiously. 'You know, tits.'

'Sometimes,' her mum said.

'You're a lot of bloody help,' Jacey snapped. She walked out and slammed the door.

In the chill of her room she wrapped herself up in the duvet and got into bed. Was there a law said she had to do homework? She knew there was a law said she had to be at school. Didn't say she had to wear a white blouse did it? I'd like to be a law person, she thought. Stand up for kids rotten bastards drag around. Meg, she thought. Silly cow. Not even pregnant and she stays with him. And I bet my mum would have stayed with my dad if she'd had a chance.

Got to get some cash to take mum out on Sunday. We'll go to the zoo. That'll make her laugh. Got to get her on her feet again. So she can do without me.

She lay back on the bed, staring at the ceiling. Don't care what I do, she thought, so long as I get out. Parents' evenings and blouses and marge on my history homework.

The thought of not going to school was like jumping into the sea. Like a fish. Or flying over the sea. Like a bird.

The blood came bursting through, then, and she got out of bed, putting on a new pad in the bathroom. From now on, Jacey thought, I'll choose my own problems. It made her feel peculiar. No point in letting people choose for me. I'm not my mum, she thought. I'm not Meg. No dreams. It was like the blood draining out of her, giving up. I'll get something else she thought. Patronising bastard, she thought. I'm a woman now. Not a school kid.

She undressed and lay down under the duvet. She'd find a way. Perhaps she'd even track down her dad, sometime.

Mister Jessel, Mrs Patel. So what? Why be scared of them? It was exciting not to be scared. When I've got the cash for the zoo, she thought, after that, she'll have to manage. About time.

She had not drawn the curtains of her room and the sky was a wonderful dark. She remembered the little cloud that had been grabbed up by the thunderstorm. Jacey saw her mum had been grabbed up by a big black cloud. That Meg wasn't doing so well either. She wrapped her arms round her body and drew her legs up to her chin. I'm not going to let no man in, she thought. No lord of the manor. Not unless I choose.

She felt warm and confused, all wrapped up in her own arms, safe.

Last Night

Stella Rafferty

'There'd be just two of you sharing this bathroom,' said Mr Shannon as he pushed open the door. Susan only glanced into it, her attention being taken by a hair-piece hanging on the wall of the communal hall. Is that, she wondered, a decoration or perhaps kept there handily by the door for shopping trips and the like?

'This storage cupboard comes with the bedsit,' he said, trying an assortment of keys on the lock.

There was a dead bird lying on the bottom shelf. Susan waited for him to comment. He didn't. She didn't. She looked. He said: 'The main advantage of taking this bedsit is the woman next door has two rooms...'

'Oh,' she said.

'And being so close you'd be next in line...I'm not promising anything but she's 98.'

He locked the cupboard door. 'Mind you, she's lively.'

Susan asked for the grapefruit juice. It's not everyone, she reflected to herself, that can drink grapefruit juice - not in quantities at any rate. It's not like Pina Colada. Pina Colada's a common drink. Sweet and easy to like. When you want to be outside the vulgar herd, you must learn to like what is not easy to like.

She bent down to tighten the buckle on her start-rite sandals, hoping April would be served immediately and she wouldn't have to be by herself with Brian and his friend.

April rapped her on the head.

'Go on!' she said impatiently.

Susan moved off slowly.

'Hiya Susan, all right?' said Brian taking his sports bag off the chair next to him.

She gave a little nod and sat down. She took out her book thinking if she had to be out at least she could keep herself entertained.

'What you reading?' asked Brian.

Susan tilted the book towards him.

'Jane Eyre...any good?'

Susan nodded vigorously.

'What's it about?'

'Oh it's dead good,' said April, sliding Susan a grapefruit juice across the table and tossing her a packet of ready salted crisps. 'We did it for 'O' level...you'd have thought she'd have finished by now!'

She turned to Susan: 'I wondered where you got to, I've been looking all over the other bar.'

Susan was thinking of Mr Shannon. After he'd shown her the cupboard containing the dead sparrow, he'd tried to sell her a bit of old carpet for fifty pounds. She'd turned it down saying it would clash with her curtains. Now she wondered if he'd put that bird in the cupboard himself to test her temperament ... if she doesn't flinch at a dead animal in her storage space, I'll try flogging her this ...

She ate her crisps, noticing that April was favouring autumn shades that evening. Mossy green eyeshadow and brown lipstick, perhaps she hoped Brian fancied the rustic look. He certainly wasn't very taken with the pink and blue combination of the week before. The pink silk rose April had worn in her hair last Saturday was now pinned to the lapel of her dress. She should get rid of that rose, decided Susan.

'This is Ian,' said Brian, as he made his way over to the cigarette machine.

Seeing Brian leave, Ian jumped to his feet.

'Can I get anyone a drink?' he said.

'We've just got ours and so have you from the looks of it,' said April, laughing.

'I'll get another round in. There might be a rush later.'

As he left, April got out her lip gloss.

'Cherry...do you want some?' she said.

'No thanks, I don't want to spoil my crisps.'

'One crisp. Ten calories,' said April.

Susan passed her a leaflet she'd found on the floor. 'How many animals does it take to make a fur coat?' the leaflet enquired. 'Twenty, and only one to wear it.'

'You make me feel dead awful,' said April as her hand brushed her rabbit skin jacket. 'What's really cruel is somewhere in South America where they eat dogs.'

'It's only like eating cows,' said Susan.

'It isn't, it's barbaric. I worry about you. I expect when you get in tonight you'll be having your Fritz with chips.'

April leant over to slam Susan's book shut and put it in her bag.

'Right, when they get back I'll chat Brian up and you talk to his friend.'

Susan shook her head.

'Don't worry. Don't worry. If anything happens, I'll save you. Will you take that coat off ... people will start talking about you. Women don't wear Parkas.'

Susan shuffled in her seat.

'Well, just put your hood down. It's not raining in here.' She glanced out of the window. 'It's not even raining out there.'

April grabbed the edge of the fur and pulled it down sharply.

'You show me up,' she hissed and smiled as she saw Brian making his way back over.

'I was talking to your sister the other day,' April said, dragging her chair round to face Brian.

Ian came back from the bar. Seeing Brian cornered off he sat down next to Susan. He looked into his pint. Susan looked over at April who was giggling, acting thick. She tried to imagine April in her first job. Filing. Wasted. Being a clerical officer wasn't a bad job she thought, but April was a girl who at twelve years of age had re-upholstered a three piece suite - without a pattern. Susan's gaze drifted down to the floor where April's bag lay. She could see the impression on its leather made by her book and wondered if she dare get it back. 'The Yellow Rose of Texas' played in tinny little notes broke the silence.

Ian tilted his arm.

'Every hour, on the hour,' he said.

Susan raised her eyebrows and smiled.

'Birthday present,' he said, and unclasping the watch, handed it to her for her inspection. 'It's also a stop-watch.'

This, thought Susan, could be thought of as striking up a conversation. Although she hadn't said anything herself, a casual observer would no doubt construe at a glance she was indeed in conversation with another person who wasn't her immediate family or April. It's easier when people don't know you, she thought, like with Mr Shannon, yesterday. He didn't know she didn't speak - so she did. And then on the bus back she spoke for half an hour on the subject of colostomies with a woman from Halifax. It's funny how people are prepared to talk about their bowels to complete strangers. She supposed in some ways it was a perfect subject, highly personal and yet universal. It was a bit different here. People did know her, they'd look at her if she did start talking suddenly. Yet she itched to add something to the conversation herself.

Could she perhaps ask when his birthday was? No. Too personal and a leading question in some respects. How about, does it play other tunes or are you stuck with 'The Yellow Rose of Texas' until it breaks or the batteries run flat? Too negative. How much would a watch like that cost? Yes, that was O.K., she couldn't be misconstrued with a question like that. She felt giddy. How much does that watch cost? She wouldn't ask now, she'd wait till the conversation flagged and then pop in casually - save the day, so to speak.

Ian brought out an instruction book.

'You could get a watch,' he said, thumbing through it, 'that looks like this but cost a tenner, but this one cost fifty quid.'

Susan felt agitated. She took a swig of her grapefruit juice to hide her disappointment. Ian sensed he'd lost her.

'But it's worth it. You can go diving in this one to a depth of one hundred feet.'

'That's handy,' she said.

He smiled. She looked round quickly to check no-one had heard her speak. No-one was looking at her. She felt giddy with success. That little comment had popped out without any planning. If she put her mind to it she could have a collection of phrases like 'that's handy' for situations just like this.

'Right, I'm off,' said Brian, draining his second pint.

He asked Ian if he wanted a lift. Ian didn't, he'd stay and finish his drinks.

April's smile departed as she watched Brian leave the pub.

'Drink up,' she said.

As they emerged from the pub, Ian threw his arms into an extravagant stretch, as he lowered them his left arm came to rest on Susan's shoulder. She buckled slightly under its weight. She'd never had a boy put his arm round her before and to tell the truth she didn't think much of it. She felt distinctly unhappy. In fact the only consolation for having his arm round her shoulder was April having no arm round hers. She wondered if this would be the signal for April to come to her rescue, but observed April seemed more intent on making conversation than intervening on her part.

At the bus stop Ian barricaded her to the paint shop window. Susan decided this had gone far enough. She gave April a little kick. A reminder. April stepped out of kicking distance.

'Don't I get a good-night kiss?' Ian asked, stooping down. Susan considered her duty was done. A nod, a smile, yes. A kiss? Never! Now, she thought bitterly, she knew where all these social pleasantries led. All this nodding and smiling was bound to end in tears. She turned sharply to where April was examining the tins of emulsion through the shop window, causing Ian's lips to skid from hers across her cheek to her ear. Not one to ignore a hint, he nibbled obligingly.

'Do something,' she hissed at April.

'What?' asked Ian, a touch of anxiety entering his voice.

'It's a good job the bus turned up,' said Susan as she paid her fare and carefully avoided looking out the window to where Ian, confused by her sudden departure, stood noting the price of anaglypta.

April ignored her and went to the back seats and took her compact case from her bag and studied herself for a few minutes in its mirror, then she smiled at Susan slowly.

'I've never noticed before but you've got a big nose.'

Susan felt her nose tentatively.

'A huge conk and hands like chicken feet,' she said, fishing the silk rose from her cleavage.

Susan tried catching her reflection in the window, turning her head at various angles trying to ascertain the general impact her nose made. Then she looked at April who was staring out of the window, her face hard.

Susan tried to remember what it was like before she knew April, but she couldn't. She recalled the time when her then current best friends were bickering about who was to hold her hand on a school outing and when they'd demanded a decision, Susan had started to cry and April had stepped in and said she'd hold Susan's hand and said it with such authority that the other two had been forced to fall back and hold each others' hands. The bus stopped. April got up.

'Are you coming out tomorrow night?' she asked.

'No ... I can't.'

'Why not?' said April moving down the bus.

'I'm going to London.'

'You should have told me you were going. I wouldn't have minded a day out,' April shouted behind her as she got off the bus.

Susan wound down the window and shouted:

'I'm not going on a day trip. I'm going to live.' And she fell back into her seat as the bus pulled away from the stop.

My Mother, My Father, and Me

Kate Pullinger

When I visit my father I take the train. I leave home by eleven and catch the tube, the Northern Line, to King's Cross, walk across the street to St. Pancras, and take the Intercity to Market Harborough. If I get the train at noon, I arrive in Market Harborough just after one o'clock. I walk into the centre of the little town - I have got to know it quite well - and wander around. I tell myself I'm going to go into one of the pubs and have some lunch, but somehow I always feel too nervous to eat, too unsettled by the journey to sit anywhere for long. And, of course, I'm afraid that if I go into a pub everyone will look at me. Everyone will be able to tell. They will know where I am going and, in an instant, they will know who I am and what happened.

So, I avoid lingering anywhere too long, and just before two o'clock I go to a phonebox and ring for a taxi. The local firm are usually prompt, they drive up the hill out of the village in the rapid, neat manner of rural taxi-cabs. They too are accustomed to this journey.

The prison sits on top of a ridge, the highest point in the area. In winter after the sun drops away and the yellow dome lights come on, the prison glows malevolently, casting shadows over the countryside like a ghastly carved pumpkin on Hallowe'en. The ridge catches the worst of the weather, a breeze becomes a squall, drizzle becomes hard, piercing rain.

Once there, I wait with the others, all the parents, lovers, children, and friends, everyone's face taut with the same mixture of apprehension, longing, and shame. Here I have nothing to hide. In the queue for the visits room I can feel that no one will judge me, or my father.

The security procedure for the visits room, which is on the boundary of the prison, not really inside the prison itself, is complex and time consuming, even though in recent months the authorities have made an effort to make it easier. I thought the portakabins next to the prison gates were for the builders but it turned out - things do sometimes change between one visit and the next - that these low plywood boxes are the new visitors' facilities, the much heralded waiting room and advice centre. At least now we can stay warm and dry while we wait.

I don't get searched all that often anymore, which is the only sign that the pale-faced and nameless officers have ever seen me before. My father has been in this particular prison for several years, and I see the same officers every time I come, once a month, but they give no indication that they know me, not even the women, the female officers who have actually laid their hands on my body as they rummage through the folds of my clothes looking for contraband.

If I have brought presents for my father I hand them in to property. I never feel certain that everything I bring will get to him, but very little has gone missing over the years. My father doesn't ask for much, magazines mostly, paperback novels the library can't get for him. I always try to bring food as well, fruit mainly, some good quality tea bags. He insists that he can get everything he needs from the prison itself - meals, clothes, shaving gear, underwear. I once tried to replace the rubber prison slippers he wears with a pair of decent shoes. He sent the box back to me, unopened, with a letter demanding that I get my money refunded. He cannot support the idea of being a financial burden to my brother and me.

I've been coming on my own to visit for a couple of years now. Before that I always came with Auntie Ann. Auntie Ann is my legal guardian. My brother, Toby, and I lived with her after our father was sentenced. Uncle Greg lived with us as well, at first, but then they split up. Other relations worried that their divorce was hard on us, but I think by then Toby and I were immune. You could have hammered nails into our hands and we would not have felt them.

Ann is my father's sister and she has always been good to us. We didn't choose each other but, given the circumstances, everything has gone pretty well. I prefer being on my own, of course. But when you are young you can't just strike out on your own like in a children's book, you've got to be in thrall to adults for a while.

Toby used to tell other kids that we were orphans, but I've never had trouble telling people that my father is in prison. I find this information sorts out the meek from the strong.

When I was sixteen I had my first boyfriend. We met at a party, I thought he was very fine. He asked me to dance and then we sat in a corner and talked. Turned out we went to neighbouring schools in Tooting. By that time I had no trace of my old accent - Auntie Ann lived in London which was miles away from Durham, where Toby and I were born. We danced and talked and had some beer, smoked a spliff together - he was seventeen, almost eighteen. I could tell he was look-ing for a girlfriend and, as I was looking for a boyfriend, we got along well. We liked the same music, which is important. He liked to talk and I liked to listen to him, he liked to swear and boast and, in his way, he was charming. When I told him my father was in prison a certain look came into his eyes, a look I was familiar with. He didn't ask a single question and I guess he invented a father for me then, a bank robber most likely, maybe even a drug smuggler, or - yes - a spy. He found romance in the fact that my father was a prisoner. I didn't particularly care where it came from, any romance was enough for me.

Ann was very good at helping me buy clothes and shoes, she had a quick proficiency with make-up and hair. I don't think my own mother went in for dresses and high heels, at least not that I can remember. Sometimes when I go into department stores and walk through the cosmetics section I come across a perfume that will bring Ann to me immediately, but I have never found a scent that makes me think of my mother. I don't have any photographs of her, I don't have any of her clothes, the police confiscated everything personal and it was never returned to us. I don't imagine that we thought to ask for it back. Last Christmas Toby told me he could not remember our mother at all.

Once I am allowed through to the visits room I find a table and sit down. I like to try to stay away from the large family gatherings and the young women who have come to visit their boyfriends. I find the smoking and the noise get to me, the children always cry and end up running in and out of the room. Some afternoons the young couples will spend the whole time sprawled across the table in each others' arms and my father and I find this embarrassing. As I wait for him to arrive, I wonder how he will look, hoping I appear healthy and cared for. My father and I both spend a lot of time trying not to worry each other.

Doors bang, keys and key chains clank, officers shout, and eventually my father comes through the door. He keeps his prison blues very smart. He irons his prison jeans and shirts and he always wears a blue woollen prison tie for our visits. Every month I think he seems thinner, dimmer somehow, more and more faded, but this must be an illusion, he would have disappeared completely by now. He looks a tidy little old man, shrivelled and ruined.

Our visits go well, the two hours pass too quickly. I buy cups of tea from the canteen. My father drills me, and I attempt to prise information from him, what he needs, how he is coping. Sometimes when I talk to my friends about their fathers the irony catches me up and threatens to trip me - I know my father much better than they know theirs. They don't spend two hours together every month, two hours that always have and always will feel like the last two hours we may ever spend with each other. I try to bring photos or, at least, news of Toby - my brother does not visit our father himself. And my father tries to make himself understand that I am a grown woman now, that I am not a little girl, I am no longer the child witness.

That first boyfriend did not last long, first boyfriends rarely do. I was a morbid little soul and he wanted to have a good time. So did I, really, but things got in my way. I used to dream that I was in prison, that it was me alone in a cell, not my father. This dream got in our way.

My second boyfriend, a year later, was much more serious. Auntie Ann made it clear that if I was going to sleep with boys I had to take precautions, and she made this easy for me. She would not let Dorian stay the night but then, while Toby and I lived with her, she never brought her boyfriends home either. Dorian, well, Dorian was wonderful. He and I had rapport. We shared tastes and desires, our bodies rolled together like we were in the centre of a big, soft bed. When I told him about my father he did not make assumptions. He once asked if I would like him to come on a visit with me, and he understood when I explained that visits were just for my father and me. He didn't ask any more questions. Like most people, he could probably guess what had happened, and he saw it was not something I could discuss.

We went away together, stretching our student grants to trips to Amsterdam and Malaga, once as far as Morocco. After two years we decided to share a flat. Ann was very good, she made us curtains for our bedroom, drank a bottle of wine with us to celebrate the day we moved. Toby had already left - he was younger than me, but always quicker to do things - and I think Ann was not unhappy to be on her own after her years of sudden, unexpected, child-rearing.

Things began to go wrong in our third year. I had become more absorbed in my studies, I was always an earnest student, while Dorian became more and more disenchanted. He said he was not happy with the system, with the fact that the progress of his life seemed almost inexorable - college, work, pension, the rest of it. He wanted fresh excitement. I felt the opposite, I expected complete disaster and so was quite happy to be confined by routine.

My father and I are very similar. I don't know if this is because of the years we spent together, or the years we've spent apart. We are both easily embarrassed - our cheeks grow ripe and red for no reason. We share moods - when I am low, so is he. We are happiest when our lives are calm and plain. We have an uneasy relationship with the world, we do not trust others lightly.

During the day I mark the time when my father's cell is unlocked. 8:00 a.m., his door is opened, he washes, has breakfast. 8:45 he is locked into the plastic injection moulding workshop where he is employed. 11:45 he picks up lunch and is locked into his cell between 12:30 and 1:45. 2:00 is back to work, 4:30 he gets his tea and is locked up again from 5:00 till 5:45. In the evening he can go down to watch television if he feels sociable. 8:00 is bang-up for the night. Twelve hours he spends alone in his cell with a bucket to piss in.

It is the night-time that I like best. After 8:00 I know where he is, I know my father is safe. I know he is listening to the radio I bought him, quiet music, or a play. Perhaps he is writing to me, or to Ann. Perhaps he is thinking about when Toby and I were small and he worked in an office and stayed home on the weekends. Maybe he falls asleep and dreams of my mother. Or perhaps my mother keeps him awake.

Dorian began to have an affair. He deceived me as though we had been married for fifteen years and had nothing left to our relationship except wedding rings, children and contempt. He was abrupt, and indiscreet as well, perhaps as indiscreet as my mother had been, I don't know. He was always late. He worried about his appearance. He whistled tunes I had never heard.

I was paralysed by his behaviour. I could not speak to, nor move away from him. I could not confront him. I could not admit to what was taking place. I stood absolutely still, and let rage entomb me.

One night he came home about eleven o'clock. He was a little drunk. I was standing in the corridor just outside the sitting room as he came through the front door. He greeted me with happy insouciance and put his arms around me, embraced me, kissing me. I loved the feel of his body next to mine. I knew where he had been but, with his touch, I was willing to forget it.

I leaned back against the wall as we kissed. He pressed his palms against my breasts. I slipped my fingers over his belt and undid his flies and reached inside his trousers. His underwear was wet, not just damp, but wet from fucking her. I withdrew my hand sharply, but Dorian caught my wrist and pulled my hand to his groin. It was awkward, he took a step toward me, the rug slipped, we twisted around trying to stay upright and slid roughly toward the floor. I was on top of him. In fact, I had him pinned down. I sat on his legs, undid his trousers and pulled them open. He smelt very strong. I looked at him and he could see that I knew. He began to speak but stopped when I struck him across the face. Not a slap, but a punch, my knuckles stinging. I moved forward and sat on his chest, catching his arms with my legs. I hit him again, as hard as I was able. I thought if I could lift his head and knock it against the floor and ... I looked around for something to hit him with but he was struggling against me, pounding his knees into my spine, rocking back and forth. I hung on. Then he raised his hips off the floor and threw me over onto my back, landing on top of me, forcing all the breath out of my lungs. He grabbed my hair with his hand, wrenching my head to one side, pulling my neck taut, my cheek scraping hard against the rug, my back curved unnaturally.

From where I lay I could see into the sitting room. I could see the settee where I had been watching television and I could see myself there, twelve years old. From where I lay everything was sideways and up-side down and this is what my mother must have seen as she laid on the floor that day, my father on top of her. Her head was pulled back just like mine, her gaze wild and afraid. My father did not realise I was there but my mother saw me watching. She looked at me as I watched her die.

I don't remember my mother's character. I don't know how she ended up on that floor. If she had lived perhaps I would not be who I am. There would be more to the equation than just my father and me, our visits, our dreams, our failings. Auntie Ann tried hard, but she was only Auntie Ann. In the end, we are our parents' children.

Dorian did not hit me. He only pulled my hair to stop me from scratching him. Neither of us was very strong, but he

73

was bigger than me. He got up and left me there, my head craned around, my mother, my father, and me.

It is always difficult when the visit ends. The officers start to call the time, they walk up and down between the tables rattling their chains. My father bows his head and thanks me for taking the trouble to come to visit him. I ask how much longer he thinks they'll make him serve and he says he has no idea. He doesn't want to give me false hope.

I think my father would like to die in prison. I don't know if he could survive if they let him out, if they gave him a freedom my mother will never have. But he won't die, and one day he will get out. But not now, and at the end of every visit this bears heavily on me.

How Maxine Learned to Love her Legs

Brigid Howarth

Maxine arrived in Bournemouth with a mouth stale from cigarettes. As the humming electrical train pulled into the station
she was in the toilet pulling on a pair of sheer tights straight
from the packet. She had arranged to meet a friend by the
town clock, a friend who said that Maxine could sleep on her
sofa until she got herself sorted out. Bournemouth was a good
place to be in the summer. Maxine walked through the sloping
tree-lined streets with guest houses and car-parks to the centre
of town. She found the clock, set on the middle of a
roundabout at the very heart of the resort, circled by wheeling
buses and department stores. A gleaming white tower, the
Disneyland clock was topped with a pale blue and gold roof.

Maxine stood under the clock for an hour in the hot sunlight. Vague thoughts patterned her mind. Maxine's mother
had told her once: 'At least you've got good legs.' Two lovely
legs. They were quite perfect. Now she was nineteen, women
said that she would wake up one day and, like witchery, they
would go their own way, dimpling and sagging. So Maxine
often examined them in the bath or in front of the mirror, en-
gaging in complicated muscle exercise programmes. They
supported the rest that was more or less cobbled together with
bits of her grandfather and an aunt's chin, but the legs ... well,
if you've got it, flaunt it. When she was little and still read
books, her favourite one had been the story of a girl whose
eyes were so beautiful that they created light in a world where

the sun never rose, and huge alien flowers turned to face the visible beams from those optical jewels.

Maxine left the clock and went in a darkly carpeted coffee-bar in one of the department stores. She chose a fruit salad covered with clingfilm stretched so tight that the slices of orange were squashed flat like pinned butterflies. On the table next to her sat an Indian woman in a hot pink sari. Maxine tried to figure out what to do. The friend worked in a kiosk down by the beach and she was supposed to have met Maxine during her lunch hour. She had said that she wanted to show Maxine, who had hardly been out of Tooting, the beach and the kiosk. She had an idea that Maxine could get a job too and they could have a laugh. Maxine decided to head down to the beach to see if she could find her.

Freshly painted signposts directed her through a rhododen-droned park crowded with people. Old women in summer frocks that tightened across protruding bellies sat on benches with their legs akimbo. Families straggled and shouted and the heat made Maxine tired. She felt as though perhaps she was still on the train and this was a fuzzy and strange dream. She was wearing a new bra which pinched. A group of adolescent boys in trainers, jeans and T-shirts slouched past her, glancing at her legs and grinning like nervous dogs.

Maxine approached an ice-cream booth called the Kids Kabin that overlooked a wide plaza and faced towards the sea, a polished presence that banded the concrete edge of Bournemouth, filling the horizon. The kiosk appeared to be empty. A till sat on the counter with some stacked polystyrene cups. If she leaned over she would be able to open the till very easily. She would pretend to be trying to see if anyone was there and act cool and relaxed -

'Do you want anything? Or just trying to make up your mind?' somebody said from below the counter.

'I'm looking for a friend, 'answered Maxine.

'Ah-haa. She isn't here. Sure wish she was though - if she's a looker, that is.'

A scrawny man dragged himself up from the ground and straightened his shirt. He had dark skin, like an Italian, Maxine thought, with a wide slack mouth that was out of proportion with the needle-twist creases at the corners of his eyes. He was too old to be wearing his Bournemouth Leisure Staff cap at such a jaunty angle. He looked at her and she saw his eyes roll over her; a gold necklace (eighteenth birthday), white shirt, a black lycra skirt.

'You probably know her,' Maxine said. 'She works in one of these places, selling ice cream. Tanya.'

'Yeah, yeah, yeah ... Tanya,' he nodded but didn't continue. Brown sauce smeared the breast pocket of his tan shirt.

'So? Where is she?'

'I couldn't tell you. Bournemouth's a big and busy place. And since we're talking about names, what's yours? On holiday, or do you live here?'

He lapsed into his chat-up posture and Maxine tried to find a way to manoeuvre herself out of the situation. He appeared to be the relentless type.

'Look, I can't keep standing here. It's too hot. Where can I find someone who knows where Tanya is?'

'Slow down! There's no need to get stroppy. Come on, have an ice-cream,' he turned round and opened a chest freezer that stood to the left of the counter. Half his body disappeared into it as he scrabbled about at the bottom. He called back to her, 'Zoom? Double Choc Bonanza? Banana Dazzle?'

'Okay. I'll have a banana one.'

He turned round, holding a brightly coloured wrapped object and peeled off the paper for her. When she opened her purse to pay for it he shook his head and said that any friend of Tanya's was a friend of his. The ice-cream was banana-scented in an unnaturally strong way. She bit the top off with her two front teeth and tasted the smooth coldness. It was delicious.

'Thanks for the ice-cream. I'm off to look for Tanya now. See you.'

'Wait up! What sort of thanks is that? You haven't even told me your name, sweetheart. It's my break now - we could go and sit on the beach or catch a drink in the 'Smuggler's Cove.' I'm sure your friend can wait. Look, I'll tell you what. Why don't I walk you down to the front and we'll look for her together?' he spread his hands. 'I can't say fairer than that. Anyway, you owe me something for the ice-cream.'

Maxine screwed her mouth up, then assented. She was in debt for the ice-cream and now she would have to talk to him and make an effort. She wouldn't have minded if he was half-way good-looking, it could have been some sort of fun, but he seemed like a no-hoper. He opened the till and took out two notes.

'What are you doing?' she asked.

'Can't go short can I?' and he shrugged his shoulders. After all, he wasn't taking it from a person. Maxine shrugged hers too. He pulled down the hatch of the cabin and appeared out of the door at the side. He still had his hat on and was even shorter than he had seemed behind the counter. Maxine trailed along beside him. He pushed his hands into his trouser pockets and his fists strained through the material. One of his feet was twisted at a right angle to the other one. He had probably taken the job in the cabin so he would look taller and be able to hide his problem. They walked in silence across the concrete plaza and then he asked her for her name again, like he wanted to read a label around her neck. He sounded less confident now, as the relationship had changed and the status of the Kids Kabin had been taken away from him.

'Maxine,' she replied.

'I've got a mate with a dog called that.'

'Really.'

'Yeah. Nice dog though. I'm Rick.'

Rick Prick. Maxine finished her ice-cream and threw the stick into a wire bin that overflowed with burger wrappers and cans. Wasps hovered over it. She wished Rick would push off.

'You didn't read the joke! What a waste,' Rick said.

'Sorry.'

'Do you want to go down the pier?' he asked. 'You can't come to Bournemouth and not visit the pier. It's famous.'

'For what? Famous for what?'

'Who knows. It's just famous.'

'Do you think Tanya might be down there?'

'Could be,' though Rick didn't sound as if he cared much.

They reached the edge of the plaza and paid a pound each to go through the turnstile onto the pier. The structure stretched across the iron sea that churned heavily and Rick pointed through the cracks where the corrugated water was visible. They moved slowly along the walkway. All the time Rick was folding and refolding one of the notes he had taken from the till. Maxine stopped and turned round to look back towards the beach that was plastered with towels and bodies. She shaded her eyes and saw empty beaches further along, dark pine trees that hunkered down on the cliffs and beyond, the white hotels and watered parks. When she turned back to Rick, who had also stopped, she saw over his shoulder a delicate construction standing in the sea a distance out.

'What's that?' she asked, pointing.

Rick turned round, 'An oil rig.'

'Down here? I thought they were only in the North Sea.'

'Then you made a mistake, didn't you?'

Rick's chat had become more subdued the further they had moved along the pier and the twisted foot seemed to burden his body like a heavy and awkward bag. Out on the pier

79

Maxine felt as though she had stepped off a ledge at a great height but gravity was having no effect. She was suspended in a stratosphere of bright light. When she looked through the cracks of the pier the slits of deep green water appeared to be miles below her and she experienced a flush of vertigo that tightened her stomach. Then Rick took her elbow and propelled her forwards.

At the end of the pier the Showtime Pavilion was covered with flapping fluorescent posters advertising singers and comedians. When they reached it the promenade narrowed to a metal platform that stood out from the main body of the pier, held aloft by thin steel cords that were bolted to the walls of the Pavilion. There was a white sign on the rail that read 'Please Keep Dogs and Prams Away From the Edge', painted in swirly black lettering. A breeze from the sea pushed at them and threads of Maxine's hair blew across her face. A pale boy clattered towards them across the metal grill waving his arms and shouting.

'They've got someone's gran'ma round there!'

He barged past them to pass on his message. Maxine continued to walk around the edge with Rick behind her, relieved when she rounded the edge of the Pavilion and saw a wider space with a small group of people. There was only a rail now between her and the blank sky and sea with the oil rig. This rail was broken at various points where ladders ran down to the sea and when Maxine peered over the edge she saw two battered rowing boats tethered to pier posts. Rick had wandered away from her and hovered around the gathering of people leaning over the rail near one of the ladders. They were absorbed in whatever they were looking at. A man was holding the end of a rope that trailed over the edge.

'Hey Maxine! Come and have a look at this!' Rick shouted, although there was no need because she was only standing a few feet away from him. Maxine walked over and the people parted to let her join them. Maxine smelt the perfume of one woman and the cigarette smoke of an old man who leaned over the rail with his arms crossed. She opened her handbag, took out a packet of Silk Cut and lit one. Then she peered over the rail too.

Far below a man in a tight black T-shirt clung like a bat to the ladder with one hand reaching out, trying to grab hold of an object that circled slowly in the water, moving with the eddies and whorls that reflected off the pier supports. The object was recognisable as a body. It had a pearly sheen and a piece of cloth was stuck across it. She realised that Rick had come to stand next to her and she asked,

'Who's that?'

'Stupid question. How should I know? Someone's just told me it's some old woman. She doesn't look like she's got any hair.'

Maxine drew on her cigarette and watched the man in the T-shirt grappling to gain control of the body. He jumped into the green swell to tie the other end of the rope around it. A man next to Maxine muttered, '... must be a good swimmer...'

Then the fat man who was holding the other end of the rope gave a shout and a couple of on-lookers, including Rick, trotted over to join him and started to pull on the rope. Maxine asked the woman with the perfume who stood behind her,

'Has anyone called the police?'

'I don't know, love. I should think so. I arrived after it all started.'

'Is it an old woman?'

'So they say. My money's on her stepping out of her hotel and getting mugged. Bournemouth's like that in the summer although you wouldn't have thought - ' the woman paused and shifted a shopping bag from one hand to the other before continuing. 'Her handbag would've been pinched and what with that and a knock on the head she probably got lost and fell right into the sea. Poor old dear. What I'd like to know is how long she's been bobbing around? Just imagine if she'd floated in towards the beach and given one of the kids a fright!'

An old man in a pale blue and white checked shirt said portentously, 'The cadaver will be in a poor condition.'

There were grunts and straining noises from the men pulling on the rope. The sun was hot, but a spray scented with the cool depths of the sea touched her face. The woman leaned companionably on the rail next to her.

'Here it comes!' A ragged shout went up from the struggling men.

The body suddenly flopped over the edge like a slippery seal and with the weight suddenly gone, the team fell back in a mess of arms and legs. Maxine expected a rush to examine the corpse but a feeling of delicacy made the group hang back for a few seconds. Maxine flicked her cigarette over the edge of the pier into the sea and as she did so, the thin old man was the first to move towards the body. He moved mechanically like a crab, waving his ancient pincers before him. Once he had broached the barrier everyone else scuttled forward together, including Maxine. Rick removed his cap. Through the silence the sound of a siren threaded across the water from the town.

It was indeed the body of an old woman, and despite its immersion it resembled the ones Maxine had passed in the park. But the skin was bleached white like a bone and there was not a spot of dirt or a smear of sand. A delicately arranged frond of emerald seaweed tattooed an upper arm. The legs, which were luckily only exposed to mid-thigh, were shaped in soft curves. Maxine was fascinated. The two limbs were like a girl's, while the body, swathed in some geometrically patterned material, was more of a potato shape.

'It's a shame,' the perfumed woman said, pointing a foot towards the body, 'to be reduced to this.'

But Maxine thought the woman looked lovely, laid out as she was in the nourishing rays of the sun, washed clean. Instead of being shrunken and wrinkled and rigid with age the sea had rested her limbs, massaging them with pulses of cool water as she had lounged in its arms. Maxine also wanted to be unclothed in the breeze, round her stomach out and let go of the muscles that always dragged her body along beside her. She bent down and touched one leg with a fingertip, where whorls of salt that had already dried across the face were spreading like frosted sugar.

The Lost Bus Stop

Souad Faress

It was a cold wet winter night. Well, perhaps not night. Perhaps in the manner of British winters, it was really afternoon. Who could tell without a watch? We know it was dark and cold and wet. We also know it happened in a small seaside town in the North of England. Whatever time it was and wherever it happened, it certainly started at the Bus Stop.

Now the Bus Stop was one of the lost kind of bus stops. You may know the type. Imagine you are in a dark wet winter windy seaside town. Perhaps in an unfamiliar place. There is not a sound. No traffic to be seen or heard. People may be indoors but equally they may not even exist. Maybe the light from a shop pretending to be open reflects false hope in the glistening black pavement.

You turn the corner into a wide open black road, one way rivers into Infinity; the other, by all the normal rules, takes you home.

As you look into Infinity, your imagination tries to place the image of the squat, welcoming warmth of a red and white double decker bus onto that road, but the image is blown away by the wind. There is no evidence of man's hope as you look. You turn in the direction of your instinct, which may be wrong, and an avenue of Trees Which May Go Somewhere and start to walk home.

Well that is exactly what our little girl, Yasmin, did - turned down the avenue of Trees Which May Go Somewhere and started to walk home.

Understand that as she walked, every single warning her mother had ever given her went completely out of her remembering. Every single one that is except for 'IF YOU ARE WALKING HOME ALONE AT NIGHT, IN THE DARK, WALK IN THE ROAD *NOT ON THE PAVEMENT*.' Understand that her mother had not actually said this in Capital Letters but that was the way they appeared in Yasmin's head at that particular moment. As it was very dark, Yasmin could not actually remember the reason given by her mother for this. 'But ...' she thought, 'if I walk in the middle of the road and *not on the pavement*, when the bus comes it will run me over and anyway I want to be at a Bus Stop or then I will miss it and then I will feel worse.' She was an optimistic child and very brave or very stupid, depending on whether you are a little girl or a parent.

So Yasmin walked on the pavement. On the pavement between the tall dark silent houses and the tall dark silent trees. But a strange thing happened, as she walked between the very tall dark silent houses and the very tall dark silent trees. She grew smaller.

She did not notice this at all until she came out of trying to remember her remembering and tried to see whether she had passed the Bus Stop or not. She walked back a little and then forward again, looking around the trees, but the Bus Stop was not there.

It was when she could not see the Bus Stop and stopped to consider this question that Yasmin noticed that she had grown smaller. She was not totally convinced but then she realised that the trees had become noticeably bigger and denser and darker. Now she knew that trees took a very long time to grow and so it must certainly be that **she** had grown ... smaller.

This seemed to have happened very quickly. So she decided if she walked slower she might just get bigger again and she set off again, this time very, very slowly.

As she walked, slower and slower, another strange thing happened; the avenue ahead suddenly got longer and longer. 'It's going to take me Forever to get home,' she thought, 'and when I do I will be very very old and Mummy may not live there anymore.' Yasmin then had the very clear feeling that far from getting older she was getting younger as well as smaller. But she realised very quickly that the more she thought all this the younger and smaller she grew, and decided that she would not think this anymore so that it would not take her even longer than Forever to get home. As so often occurs when little girls stop thinking about Forever, something happened.

The Bus Stop arrived. It had not actually been lost at all. It had actually been only just around a tall dark silent tree; in fact the same tree it had always been around. It was just that the tree had got bigger.

It was a lonely Bus Stop so Yasmin stopped next to it. She was very pleased to see it, so pleased that she did stand very close to it and leaned on it.

It was odd that the Bus Stop also looked as if it had grown smaller like her, but as it was still bigger than her she felt better standing next to it than she had done walking down the avenue so she stayed there.

She faced back into the direction of Infinity because that was where the bus would come from but there was nothing to be seen except the wide black wet road edged by trees.

Suddenly, she heard a sound. A sound shattering across the keening of wind, dropping of rain and sighing of branches. A noise like a thousand blacksmiths hammering - it started far away in Infinity and came closer and closer. It echoed across the avenue, funnelled by the trees, darting round the trunks until it skidded up the wet roofs of the houses and flung itself up into the air.

Yasmin chose between the Bus Stop and its tree and took the tree. Crouching down in the muddy earth around its roots, she covered her face with her school bag and made herself invisible against the trunk. The noise passed her in seconds and behind it followed a cracking and a shouting and the sound of people running.

Yasmin got up and, hugging the tree, looked round in the direction the noise had passed. She thought that the noise would probably have its back to her and therefore it would not see her. In this case, she was right.

A herd of donkeys was galloping down the road chased by two men cracking whips to herd them. The noise should have been familiar - Yasmin could ride horses, but, she realised, she had never heard hooves on tarmac roads before. She had heard them on the flat red earth roads and the beaches of Africa she had come from just some long months before. This was her first British winter and, she was beginning to think, it could be her last. Already she was almost freezing with cold and almost frozen with fear. 'I suppose the men are exercising the donkeys,' as much to herself as to the Bus Stop. 'It's too cold for the beach surely.'

Actually it was not too cold for the English donkeys, but they had been born to the cold and the changing weather, just as she had been born to the heat and the certainty of sun.

The men, with their parkas done up over their heads, were as rugged and hungry as the donkeys. She wanted to run with them - they were going in the direction of home after all; the running would keep them all warm. But their backs looked fierce and mysterious and the capital letters came back, this time 'DON'T TALK TO STRANGERS. ' So she did not run with them and instead watched the cracking whips and wet hooves disappearing into the black road.

The silence returned. Even though she had been afraid of the noise, the emptiness of the night now seemed even worse and Yasmin decided that she would take the chance of walking. Maybe if she ran as fast as the men, she too would get home to her dinner. She would pretend she had a herd of horses to protect her and she took her belt out of her mac pocket to use as a cracking whip. She hooked her school bag straps over each shoulder and cracked the belt experimentally.

It didn't sound like a cracking whip but it made her feel braver.

Her trainers on the wet pavement didn't sound like hooves either, horses' or donkeys', 'But,' she thought, 'it doesn't matter, I don't care, it makes me feel better.' She looked back in the direction of Infinity just one more time, just in case, just to see if the bus was coming. Nothing.

Yasmin set off reluctantly down the avenue of trees, cracking her whip and trying to hear her galloping trainers keeping her company over the wind and the rain.

With dragon's breath, the bus threw its lights against the darkness. Yasmin ran back to the Bus Stop and commanded it to stop. It slid to a standstill and, sides shuddering, it waited for her to mount.

She jumped on at the rear and sat immediately on the long seats, grateful for their rough surfaces, always a surprise, drying the backs of her legs and hands.

Comforted, she took off her satchel and searched for her purse. The bus conductor was content to wait. She twisted and watched the trees go past harmlessly, tracing her name as victor in the condensation that kept her safe.

There was only one other passenger. A woman sat at the other end of the bus, facing the dark through the front window.

The conductor guarded the open doorway nonchalantly. He rang the bell and the diesel dragon set off down the empty road.

Yasmin held out her money to the conductor. 'Half to Hesketh Drive please.' She had never really understood this phrase. She must ask her mother. She was not a half, she was a whole. 'But,' she thought, 'it's probably 'cause this English is from England and my English is from Africa.'

She had been mystified when she had first arrived in this town, from home, as to why certain words there had meant something completely different here. In the end she had had to make a pact with herself that, in order not to feel left out at school, she would pretend she understood what they were saying. Really she would just watch them carefully to see if she could work out what they were saying.

'There you are chuck.' The conductor handed her the ticket. Well at least she knew what 'chuck' meant - little chicken - a brief image flashed across her mind. Of dusty hot red chickens pecking in a dusty hot pen. A pain shot from the base of her spine to her heart. Quickly she added up the numbers on the ticket to stop the tears coming - 13 - that was not so good. Maybe if she added the 1 and 3 making 4, she could change its meaning.

'I know who you are.'

Yasmin looked up. The woman from the front of the bus was standing now, in front of her. An old English woman, very, very fair, her hair peroxided against age, was bending intently towards her, her blue eyes watery behind her spectacles.

'I'm sorry?' Yasmin said politely, though her Capital Letters were repeating 'DON'T TALK TO STRANGERS. DON'T TALK TO STRANGERS.'

'I know who you are.'

Suddenly Yasmin felt all the cold in the world in her feet. She started to shiver. She shivered until she shook from her feet to her hands, from her hands to her teeth and then from her teeth to the top of her head. The very hairs on her head shook. Yasmin did not feel very well.

She tried to be polite. 'I'm very sorry but I don't know you. I am almost certain that we have not met.' Did I say also that Yasmin was used to being gracious; that is in a position of graciousness. She was not old enough to understand that it was not necessary on the Number 12 Bus on a cold, wet winter night in a small English seaside town. The bus conductor did not recognise it. It was not familiar to him, graciousness. He felt at once uncomfortable and awake. As though a lost wind of another time blew into his memory and took away the dust. He stood straighter in his duty of guarding the door, feeling inexplicably more responsible.

He watched the two females, staring at each other. One very fair and one very dark.

'Oh, but we have met. When you were very, very small.' The old lady swayed towards Yasmin, moving with the bus, and breathed out. At that precise moment, Yasmin breathed in. As Yasmin breathed in, she unknowingly breathed in a curse, a demon.

Of course Yasmin did not know that now she kept a demon in her body. She could not possibly know that she was cursed. She would not know for years and years. Even though she came from the land of curses and demons and magic and gods and spirits and cures and drums she did not guess. Who would expect to be cursed on a Number 12 Bus by an old mistaken woman with watery eyes and peroxide hair?

All that Yasmin knew was that the old woman's breath smelled. Strange.

'Oh, we have met,' said the old lady again insisting. Then she took a large breath and said, 'in fact I AM YOUR NAN.'

Yasmin was relieved. 'Oh that's not possible,' she said immediately, 'my nanny is still in Africa.'

'No, not that sort of nan.' The old lady looked angry. 'I am your grandmother.'

Yasmin didn't say anything - mainly because she did not really know what to say. She had no Capital Letters for this. And if the truth be told, she was not actually thinking at all. Her mind had stopped.

Luckily for Yasmin, so had the bus. There was a very long silence. Then the old lady said, 'Ask your mother,' and got off.

Although her mind had stopped, Yasmin knew one thing. That she would never ever ever ask her mother. That this would probably be the last thing that her mother would want to be asked. She did not question how she knew. She just did.

The bus conductor gazed after the old lady, then looked at Yasmin. He opened his mouth to speak but as he could not think of anything to say, he closed it again. He rang the bell instead. He felt it to be the only right thing to do.

The bus drew away with its shivering passenger. There was no whip to keep Yasmin warm now but her temperature rose. She lost track of the journey until the bus conductor touched her knee. 'Hesketh Drive love.'

Such comfort. She got off the bus. Walked the way to her house, not noticing the night or the weather - just fixing her tired, tired life towards the tiny front gate, the short drive, the porch, the bell, her mother.

Shivering still, Yasmin felt her mother taking her bag, her mac, taking her clothes; she felt warm water running gently over her body of ice. Gently, gently, slowly, slowly, she felt warmth starting to penetrate. Standing at last in her new home, in front of the open fire, in the darkness, in a bowl of warm water, a tiny demon sleeping in her heart, Yasmin felt her mother bringing her back to life.

Uncle James

Kirsty Seymour-Ure

I hear the car when it arrives, too fast so that gravel sprays up and falls back to the ground in a brittle hail. The car sounds small and powerful. I imagine it as bright red and gleaming in the sun, though of course I have no idea what colour it really is. The door opens and closes and I hear the gravel go crunch, crunch under uncertain feet. Then there's a pause and I imagine my Uncle James looking at the house, his gaze following the climbing roses up to the window where I am standing. Perhaps he smiles, or waves, I don't care: I just stare down blankly. From even a short distance, I know, I look like a normal girl.

I don't know why my Uncle James has come back.

Another set of shoes on the gravel, coming round the corner of the house: my mother.

'James!' Her exclamation is low, hesitant. I move back behind the curtain because I know she'll check to see if I'm there. 'You shouldn't have come,' she says. 'You know you can't stay.'

Crunch, crunch, he moves towards her with his light seducer's tread. She takes one step back, then stops. I hear a rustling of clothes, a pause - then my mother saying, 'Don't James, for God's sake, are you mad?'

For the first time my uncle speaks. 'You're as beautiful as ever, Rachel.' His voice is so soft I have to strain to hear it. He has an incredible voice, the only lovely thing about him, the only part of him that isn't ugly and scheming. It's a voice you want to trust; only my mother and I know he's not a man to be trusted. I wish my mother would send him away, but I can tell already from the calibre of her steps on the gravel that she will let him stay. He knows this too. He says, 'Just one cup of coffee, Rachel, and I'll be on my way.' It's a lie, but an irresistible one. 'You'd better come in then,' my mother says.

I go down to the kitchen. I want to be there. When they walk in, I'm sitting at the table casually, pretending to be engrossed in something on the radio. As soon as they enter I can feel the tension practically tangible between them. I feel James hesitate as he sees me, and I feel my mother's awkwardness. I turn my face to my uncle, fix him in the glare of my blue eyes: 'Hi, Uncle James,' I say. 'Long time no see.' I revel in his discomfort. He says, 'Hello, Kate. Er... how are you?'

'I'm fine, thanks,' I say, neutrally, though the goose flesh rises on my arms. 'I was just about to make some coffee. Would you like some? Mum?'

My mother says in a tired voice, 'Thank you, Kate.' Her weakness angers me. She and James sit down opposite each other; they clearly wish I wasn't there. I hear a tiny, soft, scraping noise near floor level. Are they playing footsie? A wave of disgust sweeps over me. I pour the coffee and shove it in front of them ungraciously. 'Here you are. I think I'll go to my room now.' I can't wait to leave the kitchen.

Instead of going upstairs I head for the garage. It's a very hot August afternoon but in there it's relatively cool. My beautiful cars give off the sweet, oily, fumy smell that I love. I climb inside the Sunbeam ... 1965 Soft-Top, British Racing Green, original spoke wheels and walnut dashboard ... The worn leather seat is soft against my skin. I put my hands on the tiny steering-wheel, taking comfort from its cool familiar feel. I will never drive this car. The sounds of summer reach me from far away, birdsong and the drone of bees, an aeroplane cruising high above, a combine harvester in a distant field. How long ago now since it happened? Seven, eight years?

I was eight. I was small and vulnerable, wispy and awkward. A shy little blind girl. But I was pretty and sweet and my eyes though useless are deep blue and have always had, apparently, a certain disturbing, penetrating quality. It was summertime, I was home from boarding school for the holidays, my parents were splitting up, and my Uncle James was staying for the month of August.

I hadn't met him before; he'd lived abroad since before I was born. My parents, oddly, hadn't warned him of my blindness, and I could feel shock waves of distress emanate from him when he realised, and then pity. Even at age eight I wasn't into pity. I remember maliciously asking him if I could look at the photos of his travels, and enjoying his unease. How can a blind girl look at photographs? But he had the grace not to ask; and, later, he showed them to me and I made him describe each one in detail so I could make a picture in my head. I see much more than people think I do.

I quickly began to adore James. He was kind to me, picking up on my unhappiness at my parents' fighting and making a lot of effort to amuse me. I shared my favourite places with him. We'd walk along the lane to the five-bar gate and I'd climb it, counting the bars, and sit on the top with my face turned towards the distant hills. 'There are sheep here now,' I told him, 'but it used to be a wheat field.' In the spring I'd been taken to a shearing and one of the men let me touch the thin, palpitating skin of a shorn sheep as it struggled in his arms, and gave me a hunk of smelly wool that left a residue of grease on my fingers. My Uncle James would listen and then I'd ask him to describe the view, the woods, the hills, the fields - the surroundings I couldn't see, but knew intimately. I could feel his pity giving way to admiration. Once I heard him say to my mother that I was marvellous, that it was amazing the way I roamed about on my own as if I could see. My mother said something for which I will always be grateful: 'I think she does see, in her own way. I think she sees a lot more than we do.' She didn't know I was listening.

It was James who instilled in me my love of cars. He started teaching me, that summer, about engines, communicating to me his own enthusiasm and skill. I was dexterous with my hands, and I found it surprisingly easy to feel my way around the engine of his old M.G. I usually have a pretty accurate idea, now, what's wrong with a car just by listening to the engine, and I'm the best blind, female, sixteen-year-old mechanic for miles around. Something that my expensive girls' boarding school hasn't been able to educate out of me.

My eyes are closed but I'm not even drowsy, despite the heat. I can't tell darkness or brightness, shadow or light. When I was very small, I could make out shapes, colours, movement. For a time, before the blindness became total, I could see objects as masses of colour with blurry outlines, moving or still. That's how I have, now, a memory of colour. Sayings like 'red sky at night' or 'the grass is always greener' do have, strangely, some meaning for me. The images in my dreams are always vividly coloured, and sometimes I wonder if that's why I wake up often feeling freshly bereaved.

I can hear from time to time my mother's and James's voices carrying from the kitchen. How can she bear to be with him? After a time I hear footsteps and I know that my Uncle James is looking for me. I sit very still, but it's only a few moments before he's here, I feel him in the garage, the weight of his presence looming above me. There is a tense pause, and I suddenly realise that I have been waiting for him to come to me. He says my name, and my skin prickles. I can't reply.

'Kate ... I thought we might be able to have a talk,' he says tentatively.

The hate I feel seems strangely mixed with - something else. Confused, I remain silent. What does he want? Do we have anything to talk about?

'This is a beautiful car,' offers my Uncle James, as if I care what he thinks is beautiful; my car; my mother; me? He pats the side of the car appreciatively and I flinch as if it's me he's touched.

Is he going to touch me?

'I don't want you here,' I say finally in a low voice. He hesitates and I turn my face away from him so he won't see my blind eyes crying.

He says, 'Kate, I - we - I never meant -'

'Never meant to hurt me?' I say with a sarcasm that I am unused to and that makes me feel strangely weary.

'It's true.' His voice is soft. The memory is there, in his voice. It is all contained in his voice, threatening to overwhelm me. Some kind of longing is growing inside me and I don't know what to do with it. I stammer, 'I was just a child back then.' And I don't know what I mean.

The car rocks slightly as James sits down on the side of it. I hear the rustle of his clothes as he moves, and my body tightens up. 'Katie, don't cry,' he says. 'It's all right.'

'It's not,' I say, remembering, wanting, scared. The petrol smell is strong. I feel dazed, almost high. He stretches out, strokes my hair, lets his hand come to rest at the base of my neck. I am trembling. I can hardly breathe. I catch hold of his hand, touch his fingers. From far away I hear my mother call.

She calls his name. Not mine. The connection between us is instantly broken, the tension gone.

'Ah,' he says, and at the same time I let go his hand. He strokes my hair, once, and says, 'You're still a child.' Does he remember what he did? Doesn't he see I'm grown-up now?

I can't bear it. I spit, *'Go!'*

He sighs heavily, then stands up and crunches back across the gravel; back to where my mother waits for him. I sit hugging myself, angry and aching.

Are they talking about the past, my mother and James? It hurts to think about it but, in retrospect, what happened half my life ago was not entirely unexpected. The signs were visible to all but the blind.

From the day my uncle arrived, I sensed something between him and my mother. He's her half-brother, they have the same father but a different mother. The blood tie is weak. I was aware of a strange sort of tension when James and my mother were together. The funny thing about it was, they were always happy, but underneath was a pressure, as if something was about to explode. I didn't understand it, but I didn't really worry, I was too young; and besides James had already captivated me with his interest and charm. I think I just assumed that he had done the same to my mother; what could be more natural? My father was out of the house a lot and it was nice to have James around.

But there were little things that made me uneasy, fragments of conversation overheard, for instance. James and my mother in the kitchen one evening, washing up, he saying, 'Come on, Rachel, you know we both want it. What harm can it do?' And my mother: 'Sssh, Kate'll hear.'

What was so terrible that I mustn't hear it? Then a time - the same evening? - when I wandered into the living-room thinking it was empty, to be instantly aware of their presence, an electric atmosphere, and my mother leaping to her feet and hurriedly switching on the T V; I could hear her brushing down her dress, and when she sat down it was not, this time, next to him. Or hearing, often, when they were quiet together, the soft repetitive stroke of his hand on her hair or skin. When this happened I would sometimes go and sit with them and take a nervous pleasure in feeling those caressing fingers shift from her to me.

My Uncle James and I spent a lot of time alone together too and he would say to me, 'You look so much like your mother, you know. She's a very beautiful woman.'

'Yes, I know,' I'd respond, dubiously. Did this mean I was beautiful? And how would I ever tell? I was always uncertain of what he was getting at; certain it wasn't straightforward. But then, after all, I reasoned, my mother was his sister, wasn't she? So it must be all right.

Even with the benefit of hindsight, such flimsy remembered scraps prove nothing. But proof isn't what I'm after; I have all the proof I'll ever need. If first-hand experience is proof, I have enough to condemn my Uncle James for ever. I can't understand why he's come back. Does he think he hasn't done enough? I think of him rolling up in his little sports car, his latest pride and joy, and that disturbing confusion of hatred and adrenaline wells up in me.

Because that's where it started that summer: The car. The memory breaks to the surface.

We'd spend hours bent under the bonnet in a strange intensity of shared experience as my Uncle James led my small hands around the engine, teaching them its intricacies and beauty. My fingers in his, stroking cold metal that warmed under our joint touch. Our mutual excitement as I learnt to recognise the parts without being guided. Certainly, a curiously sensual experience. And now, looking back, I shiver and want it again.

My mother was in the house. I don't know where my father was, but he wasn't at home, anyway. The day was hot again, and sultry, perhaps a storm brewing up somewhere far away. James and I were engrossed in his car; I think he was showing me how to clean the spark plugs, or something; it's not important, except that it meant my hands were in his. We were sitting on the drive, me in his lap, with the car between us and the house. I suddenly became aware of a change in the quality of his breathing, and at the same time a sudden sense of agitation. Uncomfortable, I tried to squirm away, but he tightened his grip, then twisted me round so I was half facing him. I dropped the spark plugs and turned my stare up to his face, not understanding what was happening, but knowing it was something dangerous and forbidden. 'Katie, Katie,' he whispered. My heart was beating fast, panicky and excited. I could feel his breath on my face, he was so close, and the extreme tension of his whole body. He said, 'Oh, God, look at you, just like your mother,' and then suddenly it was her name he was saying, my mother's name, over and over again. I started to struggle with more force. He let me go and heaved himself to his feet and I heard his footsteps across the gravel, rushing towards the house. When he'd gone I could smell the fumes of the engine mixed with some other, humid, human smell, and grass.

Slowly, without thinking, I went after James into the house. I don't know what I had in mind: nothing, probably; maybe I had a vague thought to look for my mother. I stood in the hallway for a short time, my senses alert and attuned to the smallest sounds. The grandfather clock tick-tocked solemnly away, somewhere a fly buzzed and batted against a window, outside a distant tractor droned. I could hear my own fast breathing, and then all at once I could hear what I had been seeking. The noises were coming from upstairs, my uncle's urgent voice mingling with my mother's.

I crept up the stairs, drawn irresistibly closer by the sounds and the feeling that what was happening - and I didn't really know what it was, except that it must be momentous and unforgivable - had something to do with me. I reached the doorway of my parents' room, my head filled with the inane creak of the bedsprings and the grunts of my mother and my

Uncle James. And then, abruptly, the fear hit me, and I turned and ran.

The memory is intolerable and even lying here in the refuge of the Sunbeam I find it hard to believe I have ever since found peace. It is not something we talk about, my mother and I. What would we say? They heard me as I ran downstairs, crying. Shortly afterwards, my Uncle James came outside, swearing as he tried to find the spark plugs to fit back in the engine. Finally he drove off with a screech and in my mind I followed the progress of his car through the village and down the long hill, before its roar became a moan and I realised that the sound was my mother's weeping.

James didn't come back, and, though I don't think the events were directly connected, it was not long after his visit that my parents separated for good. That's okay; I'm away at school most of the time anyway, and when I'm home I keep myself to myself. My mother indulges me, and I have several lovely old cars to tinker about with to my heart's content during the holidays. For that much, if for nothing else, I have to thank my Uncle James. What would I have done, without this ability to lose myself in the clean, pure, complex beauty of the machine?

But it's eight years on, and he has come back after keeping so long a silence. What does he want? Has he come for me?

Why not?

I can believe nothing good of him. And, in a kind of daze, I understand that I want him. I want him to want me. With slow deliberation I rouse myself from my Racing Green haven and saunter into the house, through the kitchen where my Uncle James and my mother, still as beautiful as ever if he is to be believed, are talking in low intense tones that cease abruptly as I appear. I smile at them and feel their smiles bounce back at me: I am the innocent, the one who must be protected. How true; only eight years too late, mother.

I stroll through to the front door of the house where that fiery red sports car is waiting in the drive. In the fields they have started mowing for hay and the afternoon air is sweet and heavy. I breathe in the smell deeply, feeling very calm and very concentrated, though the beating of my heart almost frightens me. Carefully, I open up the bonnet of the car and run my hands caressingly over the engine warm from the sun. As I lean over I am almost dizzily aware of my taut body, my new breasts, a slight scent of sweat rising from my skin. I straighten up and place my hands flat against my sides, my ribs, my stomach, and admire the strong feel of my leanness. I am fresh and young and powerful. I smile to myself. I drop the bonnet shut with a loud slam. Then I stretch myself out on the grass behind the car and bask in the hot sun, waiting.

Revenge

Sally Cameron

In the bluebell wood it was always cool and damp. The den, hidden by thick shrubs, was just far enough from the path to the old house to give a perfect view without being discovered. Passers-by often glanced at the dense, glossy leaves of the rhododendron bushes, perhaps sensing the four pairs of eyes within, but the lush green walls were reassuringly inhuman. No-one ever looked twice.

Katie was meeting the sisters to look at Margaret's breasts. The Doherty girls had extra homework so Katie waited alone in the den, lying on her back to watch the disappearing spring sunshine through the canopy of trees. She did not mind being on her own. Growing up without brothers or sisters had taught Katie the self-sufficiency of daydreams, but she was pleased by the noisy arrival of Margaret, Anne and Frances. Margaret, the eldest, was wearing a smug expression and Katie wondered if she had remembered her promise. She was eleven, a year older than Katie, and was already getting wolf-whistles. She had thick blonde hair and full, soft lips with which she had taught Katie how to kiss. Once, when Anne and Frances were not looking, they had pricked their forefingers with a razor-blade stolen from Katie's father and pressed the bloody wounds together.

'There now - you're my sister too,' Margaret had whispered. 'More of a sister than *them*.' She nodded over at where Anne and Frances were catching caterpillars in a matchbox.

'You're my blood sister,' she told Katie, her eyes shining.

Margaret threw herself down on the old tartan blanket with a sigh. Anne was on all fours, as usual, pretending to be a horse or a dog, and Katie noticed that little Frances' eyes were red.

'The bastard!' complained Margaret. 'That bloody bastard made me do my maths all over again - *and* he's given Frances another strapping.' Frances sniffed and smiled at Katie.

'Bloody bastard!' she said proudly, rubbing her fat bottom.

Katie tutted sympathetically.

'Let's have a look,' she said, and Frances happily pulled down her shorts to reveal four red weals across her dimpled buttocks.

'Gosh!' Katie looked at the marks. 'Did he do it on your bare skin?'

Frances nodded.'He made me bend over the bed and pull my knickers right down.'

Margaret snorted. 'Huh! You were lucky - at least he used the soft end of the belt. I always get the buckle!'

Katie cringed but felt a little stabbing thrill deep in her stomach. Whenever she visited the sisters' house she eyed the thick belt around their father's ample waist. Mr Doherty often appeared in Katie's daydreams, wielding his belt and grabbing at her pants, before her own father emerged at the last minute to rescue her.

'Well,' said Margaret. 'What shall we do tonight?'

Katie wondered if she was pretending to have forgotten. Margaret liked to keep people in suspense. Anne was jumping around on her hands and knees, whinnying and pawing the ground.

'Look at me! I'm a Palomino.'

Margaret aimed a vicious kick at her flank.

'For God's sake - cut that out will you!' She tried to grab her sister's hair, but Anne was already galloping off into the undergrowth.

'She's driving me up the bloody wall,' sighed Margaret, lying down and stretching her arms over her head so that her T-shirt rose temptingly above her cut-off jeans.

'Oh I'm so bored,' she moaned. 'What shall we do?'

Katie waited for a moment, trying not to sound too eager.

'I thought you were going to show us, Margaret,' she ventured.

Margaret raised her head in feigned innocence.

'Show you what?'

Frances giggled. 'You know.' Katie was embarrassed. 'Your - your bust.'

Margaret sighed wearily.

'Oh yes - I'd forgotten. We-ell, s'pose so.' She sat up, brushed her hair back and smiled at Katie. 'Mum's going to buy me a bra next week.' Katie breathed admiration.

'Well then - ' Margaret sat forward on her knees, forced back her shoulders and looked down, pulling the front of her baggy white T-shirt tight over the points of her breasts. Then she cupped one mound gently underneath.

'So what do you think?'

Katie could barely conceal her disappointment.

'Gosh,' she managed, before her impatience got the better of her. 'Well, you can't see that much actually. I thought - I thought you were going to, well, you know - show us properly.'

'I've seen them!' sang Frances. 'I've seen her in the bath!'

Margaret gave her a withering look then glanced slyly at Katie.

'Well,' she said. 'Okay, but don't tell anyone.'

Katie shook her head vehemently, and when Margaret pulled up her T-shirt she almost gasped at the transformation, not at the soft curves which she had already felt, pressed close to Margaret when they kissed, but at the new, swollen pink nipples. Katie was just about to think of an excuse for getting rid of Frances when there was a tumultuous crashing of bracken and Anne fell panting on to the blanket.

'Quick!' she cried breathlessly. 'Come quick!'

Frances slipped her hand into Katie's as they ran through the woods, her short, fat legs struggling to keep up with the older girls and dragging Katie back.

'Come on!' Katie hissed, but already Margaret and Anne had stopped far ahead and were peeping through the trees into the clearing beyond. Margaret had one hand over her mouth as if she was going to be sick.

'Oh Jesus!' she whispered as Katie reached them. 'Will you look at that!'

In the middle of the glade stood two boys, each with a handful of stones which they were hurling at the trunk of an oak tree. On the trunk was nailed a baby thrush, its wings pinned in crucifixion. Its head twisted and jerked as it let out shrill, rhythmic cries. Anne hung on her elder sister's arm.

'Come on!' she whispered urgently. 'Do something!'

But Margaret held her back.' Wait!'

Anne pulled at Katie's arm.'There's four of us - come on, Katie.'

Katie hesitated and looked at Margaret who was peering at the boys. 'No, wait will you? Look, they're going.'

The boys, growing bored now that the thrush had stopped moving, began to wander off towards the house. One of them turned, aimed a last stone at the bird and whooped with delight.

'Skill! Did you see that?' He jumped on to the other boy's back and wrestled him to the ground. They rolled around, squashing the bluebells for a while, and then the bigger boy jumped up.

'Race you to the gate!'

The girls crept quietly out of the undergrowth. Slowly they approached the tree in single file, Margaret leading, but they stopped some feet from where the bird hung, its head bent on its chest.

'Is it dead?' whispered Anne, 'Have they killed it?'

Margaret took a step closer and then looked around for a stick. Tentatively she leaned forward and prodded the thrush very gently. It managed to raise its scrawny head and Katie thought the bird looked straight at her before giving a choked cough. Blood poured out of its beak. Frances screamed, and Margaret turned her head away.

'Oh come on,' she said hurriedly. 'Let's go - it's had it anyway.'

In bed that night Katie kept seeing the thrush's beady eyes. She wished that they had killed it. That would have been the right thing to do, what you were supposed to do to animals in pain. Once she had watched her father kill a sick rabbit that they had seen in the countryside. He insisted on stopping the car, and told Katie not to look, but she could not help peeping as he raised his big shoe over the quivering animal. She had even glanced at the body afterwards, its red and white entrails oozing out of the split skin like a piece of squashed fruit and she had watched her father clean his shoe on a clump of grass, streaking the ground with dark blood. Katie wondered if the thrush was still alive. In her mind she took her father back to the glade where he knocked the boys' heads together and rescued the little bird, giving it to Katie for a pet.

'I've got a plan,' Margaret told them. 'I know how we're going to get those bloody bastards and make them sorry.'

They were sitting in the den trying to roast potatoes on a tiny fire.

'Not both of them at once - but we can get one of them easy,' explained Margaret.

Katie prodded a potato hopefully, but it was still as hard as it had been in the kitchen. Privately she was rather scared by the idea of avenging the murder of the thrush, but Anne and Frances were excited.

'Oh yes!' shrieked Anne, 'Four to one - that'll show them. How, Mags, how?'

'Sshhh.' Margaret put a finger to her lips and they all listened to the rapid footsteps on the gravel path. Four pairs of eyes watched, for the third time that evening, as the bigger boy raced past the den, shortly followed by his panting, red-haired friend. As they disappeared Margaret turned to the others with a superior smile.

'You see that?' she said. 'Now listen carefully.'

Katie and Frances sat in the den grasping one end of the rusty wire. Katie could not see Margaret and Anne but frequent jerks of the wire reassured her that they were still at the other end, hidden behind the bushes on the opposite side of the path. Katie ran through Margaret's instructions again, wishing that she had not been lumbered with little Frances who was sure to forget what to do, or lose her nerve, or giggle at the wrong moment.

'What are we going to do to him?' whispered Frances. 'When we've got him - what are we going to do?'

'Sshh - punish him,' replied Katie vaguely, keeping her eyes on the path.

'Will we kill him?' Frances' eyes were wide. 'Kill him dead, Katie?'

Katie wished that Frances was not there. She could feel a tingling between her legs and squeezed her thighs together hard.

'Oh no,' she told the smaller girl. 'Nothing like that - we're just going to make him sorry.'

It had begun to grow dark and Katie had cramp. She knew her mother would be starting to worry and she thought of shouting to Margaret and Anne, telling them to call the whole thing off. She rubbed her leg and brushed the midges from her hair and then, just as she was about to tell Frances to drop the wire, she heard the rapid footsteps. Katie's heart started to thump. She looked back at Frances' round eyes and tightened the grip of both her hands on the wire.

'Ready?' she whispered. 'Remember, don't pull until you hear Margaret.'

Frances nodded gravely.

Katie turned her back to the path and saw the big boy hurtling towards them. He skidded briefly around the bend but quickly regained his balance and shot past. He was out of sight by the time the smaller boy came running up behind in red-faced pursuit. Katie just had time for a moment's panic, to think that Margaret had surely left it too late, when she heard the shout and pulled as hard as she could, the wire cutting into her hands as she fell backwards over little Frances.

She did not see the boy smash to the ground with his animal yelp and she could hardly believe it had worked. Then she heard Margaret calling her name, and she was running to where the sisters stood over the body. He was only momentarily stunned and it was not long before he recovered, kicking and lashing out with his arms.

'Get a leg each!' cried Margaret. 'Sit on his chest, Anne!'

Anne was barking madly like a boisterous puppy and she leapt onto the boy's chest, growling enthusiastically. Margaret deftly slipped a length of wire around the boy's throat and pulled it tight so that his head jerked back suddenly with a rasping little cry.

'Now don't move, you bastard, or I'll strangle you!' Margaret tweaked the wire in demonstration and the boy stopped his struggling and lay breathing hard.

'Right, girls, get him into the den.'

With Margaret holding the wire noose around his neck they lifted him easily, for he was a skinny boy, not much bigger than Katie. As they laid him on the floor of the den they heard the sound of footsteps coming back up the path.

'Mickey! C'mon - where are you? Aw, Mickey, c'mon mate!'

Margaret tightened the wire around Mickey's neck.

'Not a word!" she hissed. 'One word and you've had it.'

Silently they watched the big boy march up the path, kicking at the gravel.

'Mickeee!'

He turned and stared into the undergrowth for a moment and Katie's heart seemed to stop as he screwed up his eyes. But then he sauntered off with a shrug, hands in his pockets, and his shouts faded into the distance.

'Okay, Mickey,'said Margaret. She savoured his name slowly.

The boy's face was pale beneath his freckles and his voice came out in a squeak.

'L - let me go.'

'Let me go - what?' demanded Margaret.

'Please,' squeaked Mickey. 'Let me go please.'

'No!' Margaret burst out laughing and winked at Katie.

'Not until we've finished with you, you bastard. You're going to be really sorry.'

'Beat him!' squealed Frances. 'Beat him like Dad does!'

'Yeah!' Anne shouted. 'You're going to be sorry, you bird murderer!'

She bared her teeth and gave a low growl before dropping onto all fours and sniffing at the bottom of the boy's trousers.

'Fucking hell!' cried Mickey, wriggling away from Anne's snuffling head. 'What's up with *her*?' He looked around wildly.

'Oh, she thinks she's a rottweiler,' Margaret explained. 'Unfortunately for you,' she added casually as Anne suddenly snarled and sank her teeth into Mickey's ankle, hanging on with clenched jaws as the boy shook his leg and yelled.

'For God's sake! It weren't me! It weren't - honest - it were Pete, not me.'

'Huh!' Margaret sneered. 'We all saw you doing it - so shut your face.' She squeezed the wire again and Mickey choked. Margaret smiled.

'Trousers, Katie,' she ordered.

'Nooo!' Mickey resumed his struggling but Margaret pulled the wire tighter.

'Silence, bastard!'

Katie could see red lines on the boy's neck. She took a deep breath and, crouching at Mickey's side, bent over the flies of his jeans, struggling with the button and sliding down the zip. She glanced up at the boy's face which was beginning to flush angrily to the roots of his ginger hair. Slowly Katie eased the jeans over his thin hips, sniffing the unfamiliar, slightly rancid smell, and then pulled to expose his hairless thighs. Mickey looked as though he were about to cry. He closed his eyes as the girls regarded the stains on his blue nylon underpants.

'Pants, Katie,' said Margaret.

The boy groaned and Katie hesitated, eyeing the bulge between his legs. At home, by the bathroom door, she had often tried to peep in at her father, but she had only ever seen his head and shoulders over the top of the bath. Suddenly Katie no longer wanted to know, but Margaret was fixing her with an imperious glare. To back out now would mean weeks of retribution. She adjusted her position and, kneeling, took a firm hold of each side of the nylon pants. She looked up at Margaret.

'Ready?' she managed.

Margaret nodded.

'Get 'em off!' roared Anne.

Katie closed her eyes and clumsily ripped down the pants, feeling her hand brush against something sickeningly soft and snaky. There was a loud scream behind her and she turned to see Margaret's face crumpling. Margaret screamed again, and then Anne screamed too, and Frances shrieked, and as Katie looked down the sisters shot out of the den and charged off through the woods. As the boy began to move Katie stopped staring and somehow remembered how to work her jellied legs. Then she threw herself after the sisters, stumbling and ripping her clothes on branches as she tore through the trees.

'Wait!' she heard herself crying. 'Wait for meee!'

When Katie reached the big gates to the old house the girls were slumped in a heap against the wall, panting. Katie fell onto Margaret, breathing in her sweet warmth.

'Yuk!' said Margaret. 'Oh yuk, that was really disgusting!'

'Yuk!' agreed Frances. 'Bleeahh!'

When Katie found enough breath to speak she turned to Margaret.

'Are they - are they all like that?'

'Like what?' Margaret sounded angry but Katie had to know.

111

'You know - like - like worms and boils and guts leaking out and...'

'Shut up!' Margaret put her fingers in her ears. 'Oh yuk! I feel really sick.' She pushed Katie roughly away and lay staring silently at the sky. Anne trotted up.

'Look at me - I'm a stallion with a great big -'

'*Shut up!*' Margaret grabbed Anne by the hair and punched her hard. Then she stalked off down the road. Katie knew it was no good trying to follow her. No-one could speak to Margaret when she was in one of her moods.

'C'mon,' she said to the younger girls. 'You'd better go home.' She gave them a push in the direction of Margaret's retreating figure. 'See you tomorrow.'

For a moment Katie paused and looked at her watch. She was going to have to think of a good excuse to tell her father. Katie glanced back at the dark trees swaying slowly at the edge of the wood. She did not think she would tell him about Mickey. Katie did not want to think about Mickey ever again.

The Gulf

Carolyn Partrick

When Pam woke, she knew instantly that she was in the car. Her parents were in the front, speaking low so as not to wake her and her elder brother Richie. Pleased that she'd woken before him, she scooted forward on the seat and put her mouth near her mother's ear.

'I'm awake,' she said. 'Are we nearly there?'

Her mother groaned. 'Please don't start that yet, Pam. Try and go back to sleep now, there's a good girl.'

Only a little deflated, Pam sat back, thinking how funny it was to go to bed dressed and then wake up in the car. She gazed sleepily out of the window. The sun was just coming up and Texas was beginning to steam as the dew burnt off. The land was flat, seemingly forever. In the distance, oil derricks pumped, black against the dawn sky, sucking like mosquitoes at the blood of the land. Every few miles her long distance view was interrupted by a string of single-store roadside emporiums - burger shacks, filling stations, 'nite' spots. Their neon signs were still on, glowing faintly in the strengthening daylight.

Soon the sun was up high enough for Pam to see the long shadow the car made on the road alongside. Their roof rack was piled high with camping equipment, and the sun's low angle made it look as though they were driving along under a small mountain. Pam waved her hand, in the car and in the shadow, and laughed quietly to herself.

113

'Please don't spoil everything, hon,' said her mother quietly, pleading. Pam was instantly alert.

'Please don't spoil everything, hon,' came her father's cruelly mimicked reply.

Pam watched her mother sigh and turn her head away. It only riled him.

'That's right, you ignore me, as per usual.'

'Dwight, please. We all needed a vacation. And now we've paid for it, we might as well enjoy it.'

He snorted. 'You've already paid for it, you mean.'

'Oh, Dwight. You know my salary is for all of us, same as it would be if it was you who worked.'

"Cept I don't, do I?'

'I wish ... ,' her mother began, and then stopped.

'Well, so do I, hon,' returned her father sharply, the 'hon' so twisted it was nasty.

Pam held her breath in the angry silence. After a moment, she reached out and tickled Richie's bare leg. He didn't wake. She brushed the flat of her hand over his crew-cut, loving the velvety feel of it. Then she pinched his nostrils together. His mouth popped open, but he slept on. While she was planning her next move, he woke up. She watched him realise where he was, answering his slow grin with her own. She put a shhh finger to her lips and inclined her head towards the front of the car. Richie understood. He pointed his index finger at his temple and made circles with it. Pam giggled. Hearing this, their mother turned.

'Oh, no! Are you both awake now? I thought you'd sleep hours longer than this. S'pose you want a drink and a bite to eat.'

She produced Fig Newtons and orange drink and passed them back, while their father growled, 'For Chrissakes don't spill it all over the place back there.'

Pam and Richie sat in quiet camaraderie, nibbling the outer biscuit off their Fig Newtons till there was only the tablet of dried fig left to be eaten all at once. Richie nudged her and pointed. There was an armadillo lying squashed by the road. They were always hoping, but had never seen a live one. She shrugged her shoulders and smiled, enjoying this wordless communication between them.

And then she remembered her secret. She'd brought something with her that Richie didn't know about yet. She slipped her hand into her shorts pocket to check. It was still there. She smiled to herself, imagining Richie's surprise when she showed it to him.

'Any more cookies?' Richie asked.

'Nope,' their mother answered. 'That was just a tide-you-over. We'll stop for breakfast later.'

And so, many miles later, they did - spotting a little diner and pulling off the highway with a crunching of gravel and a raising of dust. Inside, the staff were stifling yawns and rubbing their eyes as they cranked it up for the day, perking coffee, baking biscuits, filling cream jugs. Trays clattered, steam hissed, bacon sizzled. Everything was bright and polished, glass and chrome - right down to the maple syrup pitcher. Pam was delighted to spot the tiny juke boxes at each table, and rushed to get a place next to one. She sat, drinking in the scene, the red leatherette seat cooling her hot legs. When the tired-looking waitress came, her father ordered pancakes and bacon for them all.

Pam scanned the juke box choices as they waited. She felt Richie kick her, gently, under the table. He was only one year older, but he was always nudging her - see this, notice that. She looked. There was a huge man sitting across the room, dressed in farmer's overalls, his hair so short he looked like a convict. His fat red neck sat in a prickly roll over his collar. His eyes and hands were busy with a mountain of breakfast.

He hardly paused for breath as he pushed the food into his mouth. Pam pretended to vomit, for Richie's benefit. Her father's hand shot across the table and clipped the top of her head, hard.

'Just you keep your nose to yourself, girl.'

Pam ducked, too late. That wasn't fair - the fat man hadn't seen her, so it wasn't rude. She swallowed hard on the lump that came into her throat, and, tossing her head, went back to turning the pages of the juke box. The Everlys' *All I Have To Do Is Dream* vied for her money with *He'll Have To Go* by Jim Reeves. She decided on the deliciously low notes of the Jim Reeves song, and fumbled in her shorts for a coin.

'It's too goddam early for that,' barked her father.

When their breakfast came, they ate in silence. Afterwards, Pam tried to start a subtle face-pulling game, but Richie was too busy pretending to be grown up, leaning back in the booth and playing a toothpick around his mouth. If the back of the booth hadn't been so high, he'd have thrown a casual arm over it, like their father had. Remembering her secret, Pam felt half-inclined not to share it with Richie after all.

Her father sauntered up and paid the check, then turned and ushered his family out with an impatient gesture. They climbed reluctantly back into the car, wincing at the heat inside. As they roared off, everyone furiously rolling down windows, their father called over his shoulder, 'Hey, Rich! Did you see that waitress? She had legs all the way up to her butt, didn't she?'

'Yessir,' Richie mumbled, still trying to hold his own butt clear of the rear seat.

'Yessiree-bob!' his father went on, 'and a great big gap between 'em you could put the flat of your hand up to without touching the sides. Just the way I like 'em.'

Pam shot a look at her mother, and saw that she was, apparently, engrossed in the road map. Her father chuckled. It was the first happy sound he'd made all day. 'Well, lookey there, Rich, I guess your mother doesn't like me talking that way about other women...'fraid I might run off after one, hon?'

'It's you talking that way to Richie that I don't like,' she muttered.

'Oh, Richie's a big boy now, aren't you, Rich?'

'Yessir,' Richie said, looking pleased.

Pretending indifference, Pam began to hum quietly to herself. She found herself humming a tune her father liked to sing while they waited in the car to pick her mother up from the beauty parlour. The words came to her, 'Dance with the lady with the hole in her stocking, hole in her stocking, hole in...' Her father laughed, but not kindly.

'Girl, you can't sing that song,' he said. 'That's a man's song. Anyway, it's not nice.'

'Why?' Pam asked, surprised.

This time Richie joined their father in laughing.

'Don't you know what it means?' he crowed.

She frowned. 'No.'

'Well, never you mind what it means,' said their father. 'Just you don't sing it.'

Pam saw her mother's mouth open and then close again on a sigh. When her head turned, Pam followed her gaze - away, out of the car.

Richie scooted up behind his father and said, 'We gonna get some big fish, you reckon?'

'Well, I sure as hell am - don't know 'bout you. You haven't got the strength to pull a really big one in ... sit back now, Richie, you're bothering me.'

Hurt, Richie slumped. Pam shot him a sympathetic look, but he ignored her and pulled out a Superman comic. She tried to read over his shoulder, but he held the comic up so that she couldn't. After a moment, she made a grab for it - but he tightened his grip, the pages tore, and they were left holding half a comic each. Pam giggled, hoping Richie would giggle too, but he just said, 'Very smart,' in an angry voice.

'What are you two doing?' their mother asked.

'Nothing,' piped Pam, just as Richie began, 'She ... '

'Well, it had better be nothing. I've told you before, no fighting in the car!'

Richie was furious. 'Give it back!' he mouthed.

'Make me,' Pam mouthed back.

He made a fist and punched her in the thigh.

'Didn't hurt,' she mouthed, though it had.

'Richard!' said their mother, 'I saw that! Are you all right, Pammie?'

'Yes,' whimpered Pam.

'For Chrissakes, Pearl, can't you shut them up?' shouted their father suddenly. 'I'm trying to drive here, goddammit!'

'She ... ' began Richie.

'If you can't leave your sister alone, Richard, you can get out of the car and walk to the coast!' shouted their mother.

Pam stifled a snigger. Richie turned his back on her. She got bored and began to root around in her travel bag. She'd put her half of Richie's comic on the seat beside her, and now, seeing his chance, he swooped and snatched it back.

'Oooh!' she squealed.

'Richard! I've told you a hundred times you're not to hit your sister! Now get right over behind your father and stay there! Don't speak, sign, mouth or pull faces at her! Do you understand me?'

'Yes'm,' he mumbled, glaring at Pam.

But their father was pulling over to the side of the road.

'Get out, boy,' he barked, standing and unbuckling his belt. Richie went white and shrank back in his seat.

'Move!' came the command.

Reluctantly, the boy obeyed, blubbing, 'But I didn't do any...'

'Shut up!' shouted their father. 'Get round to the back of the car!'

Pam felt sick. Richie was going to get a whipping for sure, and she might be next - and it was all her fault. There was no one to turn to but her mother - and she was sitting as if frozen, staring blindly out at the scrubland. Pam pulled her legs up and sat with her arms around them, her fingers in her ears, and her eyes tight shut. It didn't work, though - it didn't ever work. She could still hear the terrifying thwack of the belt on Richie's behind, and his cries, and his hopeless, pitiable begging, 'Please Daddy, please don't hit me, no, please, please stop!' Then it was over, and he was being thrust roughly back in beside her.

Her father leant into the car, glaring at her. 'And if you want to feel my sting on your tail, girl, just you make one more peep and I'll be happy to oblige,' he threatened. Pam sat, motionless, reprieved, ashamed.

They set off again, everybody silent. When Pam finally opened her eyes, she saw that Richie's cheeks were streaked with tears. His fists were balled up and stuffed into his eyes. But gradually his ribs stopped heaving, his shoulders relaxed, and he sat staring out his window at flat, flat Texas rolling by.

Pam rummaged in her bag, and pulled out a Tootsie Roll. She nudged Richie's arm. He turned his head further away from her. She put the candy on his thigh. As she did, she saw an angry red weal snaking around his leg. She caught her breath and shuddered. Richie looked around at her, such hurt and anger in his eyes that she dropped her gaze.

'I'm sorry,' she mouthed.

He sniffed and swallowed and, taking up her offering, popped it into his mouth. Then he made the 'fuck you' sign at his father's back, his face ugly with hate as he jabbed his middle finger into the air.

The car bumped along, the sun continued to climb. They ate the tuna salad sandwiches their mother had packed. It was unbearably hot. All the windows were open, but the air that streamed in was hot too, and dusty, and hardly refreshing at all. Nobody spoke. The family sat slumped in their four corners, half-hypnotised by the rumble of the wheels and the relentless flapping of the ropes on the roof rack.

On and on they drove, south across Texas, down to Corpus Christi and, finally, on to Padre Island. All around them, the sparkling waters of the Gulf winked and beckoned, tormenting Pam and Richie, for they were still trapped in the car, only nearly there, not there yet. They looked out the windows and at each other with wide, excited eyes and fidgeted on the sticky seat. At last, in a swirl of powder-fine sand, they pulled up at an empty cabaña. This one was to be theirs for the two weeks. There were only three walls - you were meant to rig up an awning at the front, which would shade the bleached wooden picnic table that stood in the sand there.

Their father got out of the car. His shirt was stuck to his back and he pulled it off, exposing his hairiness and fat. Pam caught the look of distaste on her mother's face. Her father was struggling to get the tarpaulin off the roof rack. He was cursing already, and would surely have driven himself into a bad-tempered frenzy but for the sudden appearance of a stranger.

'Howdy,' said the man, holding out his hand. 'Name's Bud Halpern. Me and my family's staying next door. Need any help with that tarp?'

Pam's father shook the hand, saying, 'Name's Dwight, this here's my wife, Pearl, and these are my younguns.' He claimed them all with a wide sweep of his arm.

'Glad to meet y'all. You come far?'

'Just drove down from Dallas today.'

'No foolin? In that ole Ford? You made good time.'

Pam's father intercepted Richie, who was struggling to carry the cooler indoors.

'Here, gimme that, son.'

Opening it, he offered his new friend a beer, and they both sat down to drink, the tarp forgotten. Pam sighed and looked around. Her mother had flopped into a chair in the shade. Richie was standing out of his father's sight, behind the cabaña wall, and he was beckoning to her. She sidled away, nervous until she was sure she couldn't be seen, and then the two of them were free: running pell-mell through the hot soft sand, arms whirling like cartwheels, whooping and yelling down to the beach, jumping high over drift-wood and dead jelly fish and splashing into the Gulf of Mexico.

'It smells just the same!' cried Pam, taking deep breaths and throwing the water up around herself - and they laughed and kicked water at each other and rolled around in the surf. When they'd cooled off, Richie said, 'Race you to the pier?'

'Go!' replied Pam, and they sped off along the damp sand.

The pier smelt just the same, too, of salt water and sea-weed, of fish and rotting crab. Laughing, they raced up the steps and ran out across the weathered boards, weaving through the anglers and their catches. When they were about half a mile out, they sat down, dangled their feet over the side, and watched the gulls wheel and glide above the waves.

Then Pam remembered the surprise she had been saving. Now, right now, was the moment! She fumbled in her pocket, and pulled it out with a flourish. But Richie wasn't looking. He was staring down into the swirling green water below them.

'I wish I had a fishing line,' he said, wistfully. 'I'd pull me up one of those fish down there.'

'Da Dum!' trumpeted Pam, smiling broadly, holding out her hand to him. And there in her palm was a length of fishing line, neatly bound round a short stick, with a float, a weight and a tiny hook already on it.

Richie's eyes widened and his chin dropped, just as she had imagined. Laughing, she started unwinding the line, saying, 'We'll have to find something to use for bait ... '

And then suddenly Richie's hand was in the way and he was taking the line from her, saying, 'You go do that, I'll fix this up ... '

Pam tightened her grip on the stick and frowned at him. 'No! I'm doing this! You get the bait!'

Richie strengthened his pull, confident he could overpower her. Pam hadn't imagined this. 'It's mine,' she pleaded. 'I brought it! We can take it in turns!'

'You gave it to me! Indian giver!' Richie hissed. 'You don't know how to use it anyway!' He was trying to twist it from her grasp.

'I only showed it to you! It's for both of us!' Pam cried. But Richie forced her on to her back and straddled her, prising her fingers off one by one. Only Pam's fury stopped her giving in. As fast as he prised one of her fingers off, she tightened it again.

'Give..it..to..me!' Richie demanded.

'No!' she yelled, louder than she'd ever yelled in her life. 'No, No, No!' she continued, not noticing that people were looking. She was thrashing and bucking under him, her legs kicking out, her hands firmly clenched around the little stick, determined that Richie was not going to win. And suddenly he gave up. 'Okay, okay,' he said angrily, getting off her. 'No need to go crazy, cry-baby.'

Pam sat up. 'I'm not crying,' she shouted.

Richie was walking away. 'Yeh, yeh,' he threw back over his shoulder.

Pam flexed her fingers to let the blood back in and began unwinding the line. When Richie came back he threw a couple of shrimps down beside her. Steeling herself, she pulled a piece from one and pierced it with the hook. She'd never done that part before, and she looked up to see if Richie had noticed. But he was sitting with his back to her, sulking, spoiling everything. The way she'd imagined it, she would produce the line and Richie would beam at her and say, 'Wow, Pammie, what a neat idea!' Then they would take turns catching fish, with Richie saying over and over how smart she was and what a good surprise it had been.

She sat, disconsolate. When Richie snuck a look to see what she was doing, she handed him the line. 'Here - you can go first,' she said.

'Thanks,' he said, as if it was nothing, and took it from her.

He dropped the hook over the side and unwound the line until the float rested on top of the water.

Pam got down on her stomach and watched through a gap in the boards. They were silent for a moment. Then the float bobbed under and Richie gave a jerk and there was a tiny black and white angel-fish struggling in the air.

Hauling it in, Richie said, 'Wow, Pam! Did you see that? I got one in about ten seconds flat! I'm gonna try again!' Then he checked himself. 'Can I?' he asked, reddening. At last he was smiling at her.

Pam couldn't speak for the effort of keeping the tears in. She nodded and turned her head away, resting her other cheek on the decking.

'Thanks, Pammie,' Richie said softly. 'I'll only be a minute, then it'll be your turn, okay?' He dropped the hook back in.

Pam lay, looking sideways out across the Gulf. A big group of purple-pink jelly fish floated just off shore.

'Portuguese Men O'War,' she said aloud, wondering again why they were called that. She knew that underneath their delicate, iridescent bodies trailed a forest of tentacles, loaded with venom. The sting if one touched you was hot, and sharp, and kept hurting for a long time. Remembering the pain, Pam shuddered. She would stay well away from them this year, that was for sure.

Ball Girl

Betzy Dinesen

Rachel wound up the gramophone and inserted a new needle in the arm. The machine was an old one with a small horn to release the sound. It had belonged to her father before the war. He had had it when *he* was young, long before he was married or had even met her mother. When her parents got the new radiogram for the lounge, they gave the two girls the old gramophone.

'Might as well let them have it,' said her father. 'A clapped out thing like that would never have any second-hand value.'

Now the girls shared the old gramophone, each having it in her bedroom for several days before passing it back to the other. Rachel's sister, who was older, had laid claim to the newer records, songs from the hit parade by Dickie Valentine and Frankie Laine and Guy Mitchell, but Rachel preferred the older records anyway, the ones she had heard for years.

She put a record on the turntable, straightened out the jointed arm and put the needle on to the groove.

'Goodnight Irene, goodnight Irene
I'll see you in my dreams.'

She liked the coincidence of the name and hummed along with the tune. She lay on her bed on the blue candlewick bedspread, looking at old magazines. They were old school magazines, with accounts of school activities - the Christmas play and the

125

sixth-formers' ski-ing holiday in the Cairngorms - and lists of cup winners, G.C.E. results and sporting events. The four centre pages were printed on glossy paper and had photographs, mainly of school games teams.

'Irene Barnes, centre, captain of the school lacrosse team, with (from left to right)...' The picture showed a group of 17 and 18 year olds, holding their lacrosse sticks in a fan, with Irene Barnes at the centre. On the next page was a photograph of the school netball team, grouped in two rows. The front row was kneeling, with Irene Barnes again at the centre, her hand resting on a large ball. She was smiling at the camera, looking relaxed despite the contrived pose, with her long wavy hair tied in two bunches.

In the earlier magazines, a younger Irene was photographed as part of the teams but not yet captain. As young as the fourth form, she had been a reserve for the school lacrosse team. There were no photos of Rachel herself, but her name appeared elsewhere in the magazines. 'Lower School Work Cup: Rachel Mercer', she read, and, in a later magazine, 'Middle School Languages Cup: Rachel Mercer'.

But there were never any photographs of the winners of work cups; no-one except her parents cared.

'Antonia, Rachel. Supper!' called her mother from downstairs.

'Coming,' she called back, without moving. She was looking at a photograph of Irene in the most recent magazine. It had been taken at the end of the spring term when Irene had won the Victor Ludorum Cup for the second term in a row. She was holding it up and smiling: the perfect smile again, perfect features.

She heard Antonia going downstairs. She put on 'Goodnight Irene' once more and continued flicking through the old magazines. She looked at the G.C.E. results of two years ago and reread what she already knew: 'Irene Barnes,

English Language, Scripture'. Two 'O' Levels, and one of them scripture, which only the thick girls took anyway because no-one ever failed it. Since then, Irene had been adding, slowly and painfully, to her 'O' Levels in order to achieve the required number of passes to start her nurses' training at a London teaching hospital. She was taking biology 'A' Level as well, to avoid the disgrace of being in the upper sixth and not doing a single 'A' Level.

Rachel did not see any disgrace in retaking 'O' Levels. It was the need to retake that had kept Irene on into the sixth, where she had become captain of various house and school games teams. Her performance at athletics was so good that she had represented the school and county at White City in the high jump and the hundred yards. If she had already been a student nurse, she would never have achieved that.

'Rachel, are you coming?' called her mother. Rachel took off the record and went slowly down the polished wooden stairs into the dining room. As she and Antonia were eating, they heard their father at the front door. He came in to ask about their day.

'What did you get for your history prep?' he asked Rachel, interrupting her daydreaming. He grilled them both with gentle concern about their grades and then went into the lounge for a drink. Rachel returned to her daydreams.

A few weeks before, she had realised, in growing panic, that this was Irene's last term and that separation was frighteningly near. How could she contrive to meet Irene after she had left? The sixth formers witheringly referred to the middle school as the pipsqueaks. Antonia, though, in the lower fifth, was nearer in age to Irene. Could Antonia invite Irene to tea? 'I couldn't possibly,' Antonia had said, appalled at the suggestion. 'She's in the sixth form. I'm only in the fifth.' Then Rachel thought about asking her father to pay for tennis coaching so that she could join the tennis club where Irene was a member. Her father would almost certainly agree, but she doubted if even the most intensive coaching would bring her up to the required standard. Finally she wondered about becoming a nurse herself. In four years, *less* even, she could be a student nurse, at the same hospital as Irene. She saw herself as a junior nurse attending a dying patient under the supervision of Staff Nurse Barnes, a long night's vigil, a life saved, a look of gratitude in the eyes of the senior nurse.

She had mentioned the idea of becoming a nurse to her parents.

'Can't have a bright girl like you emptying bedpans,' said her father.'Much better to be a doctor.' Rachel had tried imagining the scene with herself as a doctor supervising the work of Nurse Barnes. But the spirit of humility and service was lacking in this version, the exhilaration of coming through an ordeal and so proving herself worthy of the good opinion of Irene. It disturbed her sense of an unchanging universal order to see herself as senior to Irene. Perhaps she should be something else entirely, an architect or air hostess. Both sounded glamorous. But would they bring her into contact with Irene?

On Saturday, she found instructions on how to make a picture frame in *Girl* and decided to frame the photograph of Irene holding the Victor Ludorum Cup. She needed passe-partout for the mount and took out her bicycle to ride down to the shops. She noticed the chain was loose and hoped for the best. It was an old bicycle, passed on from Antonia, dented and too small for her anyway. She longed for a brand new bicycle of her own.

She took a detour along Cedar Avenue in order to pass Irene's house. She had been making trips past Irene's house since the spring term. 'Barnes, A; Barnes, A.W...' She found that there were any number of Barneses in the phone book. She didn't know the Christian name of Irene's father, but she knew the road Irene lived in and needed only to find out the number. She didn't like to ride past too often in case she was seen. It was a winding road with large detached houses set far back from the road. The area had once formed the grounds of an 18th-century house, her father had told her, and there were a number of large cedars. When the old house had been pulled down at the beginning of the century and the land developed, the cedars had been spared. As she cycled along the avenue, her bicycle chain clicking threateningly, Rachel wondered why some streets were cut parallel in straight lines and others were winding like this. She might have to know about such things if she became an architect. Perhaps she might write about architecture in *Country Life* which she sometimes looked at in the doctor's waiting room. She could use Irene's house as an example of an important period of architecture, with a photograph of Irene at the front door. 'My thanks to Irene Barnes for her help while I was writing this article,' she would say in the acknowledgements. 'My *special* thanks ...'

She pedalled slowly past Irene's house. The house was of red brick, with the window frames and window bars painted white and big chunky chimneys. She slowed almost to a stop and looked up, wondering which was Irene's room and what she was doing now. She hoped her bicycle wouldn't pick this moment to break down on her.

The end-of-year exams came round and she did well. So too did Antonia. Her parents promised them both a surprise. The homework load was lightened as they went into the last weeks of term, and there were house and school competitions. It was hot and sunny on the day of the school swimming sports to the relief of those taking part: the swimming pool was out of doors and unheated. Rachel, a poor swimmer, had not been entered by her house for any of the events, and she watched the competition from the side of the pool.

'Oh *no,*' she groaned when Irene was just beaten in the senior freestyle by a sixth former who was built like an Olympic swimmer. Points gained were carried forward for the Victor Ludorum Cup. Rachel hoped that Irene would be the first ever to win it three times in a row. And now Irene was losing all these points - freestyle, then breaststroke and backstroke - to this beefy swimmer.

When the whole school gathered in the hall, Rachel was entered by her house for the middle school spelling bee. Each girl stood up in turn and the headmistress called out a word for her to spell. Scores were marked by the English mistress on a large blackboard.

'Anaemia,' said Mrs Davies when Rachel stood up. That was easy: she knew it was 'ae'. She hoped Irene was noticing her success. One girl was given 'qualm' and a gasp of sympathy went up but she managed it and got a round of applause. Another girl muffed 'retrieve' and members of her house sighed. There was even laughter when one girl started spelling 'awkward' with 'ork'. How had she ever made the team?

It was difficult to spell things right when the whole school was listening, thought Rachel resentfully.

But she got 'niggardly' right, adding to the score of her house, and 'diaspora' was considered difficult enough for her to win applause.

'Benefited,' Mrs Davies called out when Rachel stood up in the final round. The two top houses were close and every score mattered. Competition points were valued even if good spelling wasn't a real achievement, like sport.

'B, E, N, E,' Rachel began with confidence. 'F,' she added, more slowly. It was 'fitted' surely, as in the verb 'to fit'?

She was aware of the whole school watching and waiting. What would Irene think if she got it wrong?

'I,' she went on, trying not to lose her nerve. She felt faint.

It must be a trick question; otherwise it would be too easy. Suddenly she remembered. 'T, E, D,' she said in a rush. 'Benefited' didn't double the 't'.

There was applause and Rachel felt a burst of happiness. She was the only girl to have spelt all her words right. She turned to see if Irene was impressed. But Irene, although a sixth former and a pillar of the community, was simply chatting to her neighbour in whispers and seemed bored by the whole competition.

Her father, at least, was pleased. 'Good girl,' he said proudly that evening, and then, 'I think you should have your surprise present now and not wait until the holidays. It's hidden in the garage.'

Antonia had been in on the choosing. It was a new bicycle, full size and with gears.

'Thank you, Daddy,' Rachel called out, riding in tight circles round the lawn. It was the first time she had owned a new bicycle, having gone through Antonia's hand-downs from her tricycle days onwards. 'See you later,' she shouted, racing out of the drive and doing a tour of the neighbouring streets right up to Cedar Avenue in the hope of being seen on her new bicycle.

The senior tennis tournament began. Rachel followed Irene's progress which was charted on a large diagram pinned on the school notice board. Day by day, the dense crowd of names on the left thinned as the winners' names moved across the centre and towards the right of the chart. A group of Irene's fans could be seen at the board most days, predicting the results of the next round. Rachel never joined them. She didn't want them to guess her feelings about Irene.

* * * *

The English mistress announced in class, 'Rachel Mercer has been selected to represent her house in the senior school competition. This is the first time that a member of the middle school has reached the senior competition. Well done, Rachel.'

One or two girls whispered, 'Jolly good, Rach,' but most of the form stared in disapproval of her being different from them. At break she trailed downstairs after the others. Just beyond the cloakrooms, trays of milk had been laid out and she took a bottle and a straw. The milk had been taken out of the refrigerators too soon and was slightly warm. She drifted away from the crowd, past the school and house notice boards. A knot of girls from her form were standing in front of the 'New Today' board which was usually full of old yellowing notices.

'It's Latin last period on Tuesday. We'll miss Latin.'

'Volunteers! They should jolly well pay us.'

'What a nerve.'

'I'm not doing something for nothing.'

'Bully for you then. You should have more esprit de corps.'

'But if we volunteer, we won't be able to watch the match properly.' This was one of Irene's fans.

When the other girls had gone outside, still muttering complaints, she went up to the board.

SENIOR TENNIS TOURNAMENT
Final: Irene Barnes v Elizabeth Richards
The final of the senior tournament will be held on Tuesday 20th July at 3.30 pm. The middle and senior school will be excused their last lesson in order to watch.

She helped herself to a second bottle of milk from a tray of surplus bottles (there were always a few girls absent) and stared happily at the notice. Irene had made it to the final.

Elizabeth was also in the upper sixth and a good tennis player but Rachel felt certain that no-one could beat Irene. At the bottom of the notice was a final announcement: 'Volunteers for ball girls are required. Prospective ball girls should assemble by the tennis courts on Friday at 4.15 pm - E. J. Hopkins.' Hoppie didn't like her and shouted 'Butterfingers!' at her even before she dropped the ball at rounders. Did she stand a chance of being selected as a ball girl? She was determined to do her best at the trials.

Only five girls turned up to try out as ball girls on the Friday. Miss Hopkins looked them over like a bullying sergeant major trying to find fault and Rachel's heart was squeezed tight inside her.

Four ball girls were needed, one each end and two at the net. 'I'll give you all some coaching, and then pick four ball girls,' said Miss Hopkins. 'The fifth will be the reserve.' Rachel knew at once that she would be the reserve. They were sent on to the court where two seniors were playing. She was placed at the net, where she knelt with one knee on the tar-macadam surface, which left a textured mark on her skin. Then she was moved to the back of the court and at once missed a ball which hit the wire netting and ricocheted all over the court. 'Oh Rachel, *Rachel*,' called Miss Hopkins on a note that blended impatience and despair.

After the trials, the five of them were called together. 'Thank you for your enthusiasm," said Miss Hopkins. 'The results will be on the 'New Today' board on Monday.' She looked at Rachel who knew that the delay in giving the result was a form of cruelty.

All weekend she wriggled on a hook of hope.

On the 'New Today' board on Monday morning, Miss Hopkins had pinned a notice. 'Senior tennis tournament final. Ball girl selection. After the trials last Friday, the following have been selected as ball girls: Claire Barker, Gillian

Harrison, Sarah Powell, Diana Walker. Reserve: Rachel Mercer.'

Rachel turned away from the board and walked slowly up the stairs to her form room. She handed in her prep and sat at her desk, lifting up the desk top so that she could hide behind it. A flowing tide of misery was creeping up on her and she took a handkerchief out of her pocket to blow her nose. The bell went for prayers.

'I have several announcements to make,' said Mrs Davies at prayers, not that day, but the next. 'I will remind you, first, that prize-giving will be on Friday 23rd July at three o'clock. Would girls whose parents have not yet replied to their invitation kindly bring a reply tomorrow, Wednesday? Secondly, would Natalie Peterson stand outside my door after prayers and would Rachel Mercer see Miss Hopkins at break?' Natalie Peterson was a rather beautiful fair-haired girl, drawn to trouble like a doomed heroine of tragedy. Looking anxious, she and Rachel exchanged looks. 'Finally, we have had a blockage in the cloakrooms and girls are reminded that sanitary dressings must be placed in the containers provided and not flushed.' There were several titters in response to the euphemism 'sanitary dressing' for 'sanitary towel', which Mrs Davies ignored and went on, with no pause or change of tone to mark the transition to more spiritual matters, '... and we will now say the prayer of St Ignatius Loyola.'

'To fight and not to heed the wounds,' Rachel mumbled along with the rest of the school, wondering why Hoppie wanted to see her. What had she done wrong? '... save that of knowing that we do Thy will, Amen,' they all concluded in approximate unison, and then they were into the doxology and marched out of the hall while Mrs Saunders played a piece by Beethoven on the piano.

'Ah, Rachel,' said Miss Hopkins, when she went down to the staff room at break. 'You've heard the news about Gillian?' Rachel shook her head. 'She's gone down with measles. That means, of course, that she won't be a ball girl at the tennis final. You'll have to step in.'

Rachel ran upstairs, against school rules, singing silently to herself, 'Ball girl! Ball girl!' She looked out of the form room window, across the school grounds to the tennis courts, now empty. She imagined Irene smashing a final winning shot and heard the crowd roar. She saw Irene acknowledging the acclaim and turning finally to her, the humble ball girl, removing a sweat band from her wrist and handing it to her in front of the school as a gesture of thanks.

When the bell went at half-past three, her form put their books away. Only Natalie Peterson, who was not allowed to watch the match, stayed behind. She had been seen in the street eating a Mars bar in school uniform and had been reported.

'I hate boring old tennis anyway,' she was saying defiantly as she got out the Oxford Book of Ballads. 'I much prefer poetry.' She had been set eight verses of *Sir Patrick Spens* to learn by heart.

Rachel dashed down to the middle school cloakroom with Claire and Diana and Sarah to change into games clothes. She took a stick of Clearasil from her shoe bag and smeared a little on a throbbing red patch of skin by her nose. Until six months before, her skin had been clear. Then a first lone spot made its debut, followed by an eager cast of blackheads and pimples that seemed to have been waiting in the wings for this sign to make their appearance. Now her skin was never free of two or three spots in varying stages of development.

She smudged the brown cream around the spot that was forming to conceal it and combed her hair. 'Are you coming?'

called Claire and they all four went out together to the tennis courts.

There were three hard courts surrounded by high wire netting. The groundsman had erected raised banks of benches on the three sides of the furthest court outside the wire netting. Within the enclosure, the middle court had been cleared of its net and posts and a row of chairs had been placed there. This was the row of honour for the staff and prefects, with a large chair in the centre for Mrs Davies. The prefects were filing in to take their seats and outside the enclosure the benches were filling up with the middle and senior school.

Suddenly the crowd fell silent. Mrs Davies appeared at the entrance to the courts, followed by her deputy and the school secretary. The ball girls stood in a line along the court, in their pale green Aertex shirts and dark green shorts, their arms by their sides. It was like the Wimbledon finals in the Pathé News at the cinema, thought Rachel, where the ball boys from Dr Barnardo's homes formed long lines that the royal couple passed along before presenting the cup. With regal dignity Mrs Davies swept past the line of four ball girls, as though they were an imperial phalanx. The four girls tried to rise to the part, squaring their thin shoulders and holding their arms by their sides with a look of military alertness. Then Irene and Elizabeth appeared, wearing tennis whites. Irene's blonde curly hair was fixed back with slides and kerbigrips and her dress was edged with lace. As she walked past the ball girls, Rachel felt a sense of pride. The whole school clapped wildly.

'Good luck, Barney.'

'Come on, Richie.'

Rachel felt as tense as if she herself had been called upon to play.

'Rough,' said Elizabeth as Irene threw her racket. Miss Hopkins examined the catgut of the racket where it lay on the ground. 'Smooth,' she called out to the finalists, and Irene chose to serve first. Miss Hopkins climbed up to the umpire's chair.

'This is the final of the senior tennis tournament,' she announced. 'The winner will gain ten house points in addition to the senior tennis cup. The house points count towards the House Sports Cup. Macleod's stand at 82 points and Warwick at 80, with the other houses all below 75. As this is the last sports event of the term, this final also determines which house will win the cup.'

'Up Macleod's.'

'Up Warwick.'

The excitement in the crowd sharpened.

'Finally, the winner of the match will also gain points towards the Victor Ludorum Cup. Elizabeth is not in contention, but Irene is five points below the top score' - the top score was held by the muscular champion of the swimming sports for whom Rachel felt a rush of hatred - 'and so stands to win the Victor Ludorum for the third time.'

Mrs Davies led the applause. When the clapping had stopped, Miss Hopkins said slowly, with a sense of drama, 'The senior tennis tournament final. Irene Barnes of Macleod's versus Elizabeth Richards of Warwick. Play.'

Irene took up a serving position behind the line. Rachel stood at the opposite end of the court. Irene threw the ball in the air and brought her racket up through an arc. She threw the weight of her body into the serve and the ball was struck right in the centre of the racket. The catgut gave off a twanging sound and the ball flew over the net into the service court. Elizabeth swung her racket and missed the ball which came too fast and too low for her to return. Rachel sprang in the direction of the ball, caught it and rolled it up to the ball girl at the net. When she stood up again, she saw that Irene was smiling, ready to serve again, when the clapping stopped.

Irene took the first game and the players changed ends so that Irene stood at Rachel's end of the court, ready to receive serve. Rachel, standing a few yards away, willed her to play her best and win but Elizabeth played a good service game, and games went with serve. Rachel could hardly believe that anyone's service could be so accurate. At 2-3 down, however, Elizabeth opened her service game with a double fault, followed by a feeble serve. Standing behind Irene at the receiving end, she saw Irene swing back her racket, with predatory determination, to make a winning stroke. On the next point there was a long rally. Forehand, forehand, backhand, backhand (and Rachel admired the easy backhand of both players - *her* backhand went all over the place) until Irene placed a low forehand right in the corner of the back court which Elizabeth failed to return.

'Love forty,' called Miss Hopkins and there was tension among the spectators as Irene hit a volley to win the game. Everyone clapped.

'Liz'll try and break back at once,' Rachel heard a senior in the crowd whisper to a friend. Rachel felt anxious: the set was not yet won. She bounced two balls to Irene who was serving from her end. The girl in the crowd was right and Elizabeth attacked strongly but Irene won the game with a lob which bounced high and then took the set without difficulty.

'First set, Irene, 6-2,' called Miss Hopkins. A group of Irene's fans started up a chant of 'Two, four, six, eight,' in their excitement, but they were immediately hushed by a teacher. Shouting support was done in netball and lacrosse but not tennis.

For the next set Rachel was at the net, crouching below the umpire's chair. It was a good position for watching the match and it was easier work, with less risk of fumbling the ball as she had done several times. But she felt so far from Irene. Not that it mattered. She could see that Irene was going to win in two sets.

She was wrong. Elizabeth recovered in the second set, playing a game of attrition. Once she played a terrific smash that had Mrs Davies calling out, 'Oh, shot!' in her precise voice. In panic, Rachel saw the points and then the games slipping away. She wished she could help Irene. But how?

'Second set, Elizabeth, 6-3. One set all. Final set,' said Miss Hopkins.

She changed places with Claire Barker to act as ball girl in her original position at one end of the court. She bounced two balls malevolently to Elizabeth who was serving first. But the malevolence had no power and Elizabeth won the point with a wide accurate serve. She seemed to have saved her best tennis for the final set. And so had Irene, who won her next service game to love.

'Uh!' The crowd breathed in a sharp gasp as Irene hit the ball lightly so that it only just went over the net out of Elizabeth's reach.

'*Zing!*' Irene's shot, half-way between a forehand and a volley, was just out. Rachel didn't even know the names of these ambitious shots. Some went out, but surely they must win Irene the match in the end?

Two all, 3-2, three all, 4-3. Irene trailed a game in the set as she had served second. At 3-4 down, she served from Rachel's end. Rachel bounced the balls to her with the greatest care, as though she was sending Irene all her love. At forty-love, Irene turned to Rachel. As Rachel bounced the first ball, Irene gave a little smile, a smile of confidence and knowledge of victory, it seemed to Rachel. And as Rachel bounced the second ball, Irene met her eyes and included her in the smile, apparently noticing her for the first time in the match. 'Thanks, kid,' she said quietly to Rachel.

Rachel sprang after the balls, alert and hyper-tense, fired by Irene's thanks. She no longer fumbled the ball: she felt transformed. She had become the ideal ball girl. It was like a Wimbledon final, Irene a girl-wonder like little Mo Connelly, and Rachel her special aide. Irene ran back and forth across the court, her fair hair flowing.

At five all, Irene, once again at her end, tapped her racket on the ground, waiting to receive serve. One foot twitched on the tarmac, like an animal pawing the ground. Elizabeth served. A low shot from Irene, and everyone clapped the winning return.

Irene walked across to the backhand court and stood threateningly inside the baseline to take serve. She hit the ball hard and ran in to the net. Elizabeth tried to pass her but hit the ball wide. Rachel ran smartly to retrieve the ball.

Left, right, left, right: the crowd moved their heads in a synchronised movement at two long rallies that Elizabeth won.

'Thirty all,' called Miss Hopkins. But at the next rally, Irene moved in to the net again and hit a volley at an irretrievable angle.

'Thirty-forty.' Irene bent to receive serve, full of concentration. Rachel thought, this is it. If Irene gets this point, she's broken serve.

'Out,' called Miss Hopkins at the first serve and Elizabeth took her second serve. Irene returned the ball on her forehand, staying at the baseline as Elizabeth hit it back deep, starting another long rally. One of the players must make a mistake in a minute, thought Rachel, and at once Elizabeth's shot was on the line. The crowd went quiet. No-one shifted or whispered: there was just the rhythmic vibration of the ball hitting the catgut.

Elizabeth hit the ball wide to Irene's forehand and Irene ran across the court to reach it. On her next stroke Elizabeth hit the ball to Irene's backhand. Irene raced back from the forehand court to get the ball. The ball was hit a little high and from where she stood, Rachel could see that it was going to land wide. She shot forward to collect the ball as soon as it bounced and the two girls collided, Irene falling forwards into a crumpled position, Rachel knocked sideways, grazing her elbow and upper arm.

She got up slowly and noticed that rows and rows of tiny bubbles of blood were forming on her skin. Then she saw that Irene was still on the ground, holding her ankle.

There were angry whispers in the crowd. Rachel looked up at the little group of Irene's fans. One girl was sobbing; the others stared murderously down at her. She remembered a film she had seen about Wyatt Earp where a lynching mob had been held back by the sheriff only minutes away from hanging an innocent victim.

It was Mrs Wykeham, the biology mistress, who cleaned Rachel's arm and bandaged it. Irene was in the sick room, attended by Miss Hopkins. She had limped off the court, her arm around Elizabeth's shoulder, unfit to play on. Rachel stood by herself; the other ball girls kept apart. Then Mrs Wykeham took pity on Rachel and led her away to the staff room.

When nearly everyone had gone home, Rachel returned to her form room to fetch her satchel and went to the cloakroom to change. She put on her blazer and panama. A side door through the senior school cloakroom was used as a short cut to the bicycle sheds. As she went into the senior cloakroom, she heard someone talking from the far side of a free-standing frame with rows of pegs on it. Shoebags, games clothes, pullovers and laboratory overalls hung from the pegs, concealing her from the speaker.

'That bloody kid,' Irene was saying. 'If I live to be a hundred, I shall never forgive her.'

Rachel was trembling as she backed out of the cloakroom. She went out of the rear door to the bicycle sheds and clipped her satchel on to the back of her new bicycle. She looked at it, wondering why she had ever been so excited about it. She wheeled it across the orchard and out of the school grounds through the back gate. She pedalled along the road for a few minutes. Then she dismounted and propped the pedal against the kerb. She leant against a poplar tree as the shaking of her shoulders increased. She looked at the bicycle, the reward for her academic success. What did exam results matter? What was the point in being the star of the spelling bee? She had wanted to be like Irene and be good at sports. And since she couldn't manage that, she had wanted to help Irene be the biggest sporting star the school had ever had, a three-time winner of the Victor Ludorum Cup.

She pushed her bicycle with her foot and it toppled. Deliberately she pressed her foot down on it, deforming the bumper with satisfaction. Then she pulled her handkerchief out of her pocket, tears filling her eyes and her mouth, covering her face and spilling down on to her blazer. Above her, a July breeze shook the leaves of the poplars.

American Tan

Chrissie Gittins

For C.D.

Stockings never were long enough. I had the longest legs in
my year. I knew because we measured them in gym. We'd
huddle in the cloakroom before going next door to the window
bars, ropes and vaults. We stood side by side, lifting our
games skirts and aligning our thighs. But where did legs
begin?

The gap between stocking top and roll on put more strain
on the suspenders than they could take. Strands of vermicelli
elastic would escape from the silky bank at the top of the sus-
pender. They'd fray and come astray. I hated sewing and
mending, so I'd often risk going to school with one or two
suspenders missing.

If the remaining suspenders were at the front, the stockings
would gape down the back of my leg. I'd stand in the dinner
queue and yank the stockings up, pulling great holes as my
hands ripped through the flesh coloured nylon. *American Tan*,
thirty denier.

One Tuesday I sighed at having ruined yet another pair of
stockings as I stood in line for my portion of pink sponge with
pink icing and pink custard. Tuesdays started off well.
Bunty arrived in the morning. I relished the stories and
illustrations, but never got as far as cutting out *Bunty's* clothes
on the back cover. The clothes were meant to be attached to

Bunty's figure with fold over tabs. It seemed a precarious paper-thin way to dress her. And I could never figure out why the Four Marys were always in the third form at St. Elmo's. I always meant to write in, but never did.

Tuesday was also the day of my piano lesson. The thought made my stomach lurch. I enjoyed the theory. I liked to match the lines of words with the rhythm of the notes. I remembered the Italian instructions - *moderato, andante, allegretto*. But I hated to play in front of my teacher, Mr Hamer. And more than that, I hated to play in front of a stranger for exams. I'd sit quaking in the cloakroom of the technical college feeling sicker and sicker. I'd be called to sit at a grand piano in a vast hall while the examiner lowered his bi-focals and ordered scales and arpeggios.

I continued taking lessons, taking exams, sitting in Mr Hamer's tiny room with its white bust of Beethoven, and polished wooden metronome sitting on top of his upright. Mr Hamer was very conscientious. Even in a power-cut we continued with a candle lighting the keys. But he loved tennis, and when Wimbledon was televised he would slip next door to check on progress and scores while I prepared a piece to sight read.

I sat on the top deck of the bus. It took me past my stop for home. It was two extra stops to Mr Hamer's. I sat in my blue uniform with grey hat. The grey hat which at first I'd been so keen to wear. Some girls from the convent sat behind me giggling. Brown uniforms and berets. They placed some lettuce leaves in the rim of my hat.

The bus pulled up at the stop I needed. As I stood up to go down the stairs I could feel both my suspenders disengage. I stepped off the bus onto the pavement. Both stockings drifted down to my ankles, and sat on my outdoor shoes. I wanted to slide down a grid. I hurried across the road to a doorway and pulled off my shoes and stuffed the stockings into my pocket.

I arrived at Mr Hamer's with bare legs and the lettuce still in my hat. We played Scarlatti.

The Chicken Thief

Karen Whiteson

The girl saw the dog as she was making her way across the outfield, on her way to the woods' edge, to gather stuff for a salad. Still there, she thought; and it gave her a brief, exultant glance before bellying back down into the long grass.

An unremarkable looking creature with a slight, goatish frame, the stray had spent all winter hanging around Clochac, stealing chickens from the villagers' yards. Despite repeated stonings it had refused to be scared off. Clenched in its exhausted soil Clochac was not a village where the stray, whether on two legs or four, was made welcome: dogs and vagabonds were pelted alike. Then, as spring came, the dog had withdrawn into the field where it fed on rabbit, hare, field mouse and vole; the spring's vermin.

At the woods' edge the girl stopped and began the task she had come for, filling her basket with sorrel, asparagus, sassafras and dandelions. The herbs leaked their citric, urinous odours onto her hands. She was fifteen years old and spoken for. After the harvest she was to be married to their neighbour's son, a boy whose features were so familiar to her she had never even thought to ask herself if she found them pleasing or not. This was the last spring of her youth.

It was a year since she had been any deeper into the forest. She used to go every week, to take food to her grandmother, who gave her charcoal in return. But since the old woman's death the track from the cottage to charcoal shack had remained untrod. The shack stood out of bounds, visited by the girl only in her dreams. Sometimes it appeared as a burnt out waste; other times, a fertile wilderness with the woven branches of the shack wall so overgrown they entwined seamlessly with the surrounding trees.

What happened to Little Red, after her tale was done, and she returned from beyond the pale, from the belly of the woods, filled with its hungers? She'd wondered about that one's fate, having heard her tale told often enough.

She had in fact once asked her mother, the widow, who gave the terse-lipped reply - she let sleeping dogs lie - a thin veiled warning not to enquire beyond the field of the narrative.

Let Sleeping Dogs Lie. She thought of the one in the field, its patchy face floating before her as she recalled the look it had given her. As if it would know me the next time, she thought: as if it had marked me out. Where had it come from anyhow? Perhaps it was a dog of war.

For as long as she could remember France, that vast land that lay beyond the forest, had been at war with itself. The war had not passed through Clochac, for beyond its forest lay a labyrinth of muddy lanes, pocked with pot-holes deep enough to drown a grown man. The sheer exhaustion of the road had been known to swallow armies whole, before they even reached the battle site. Locked into geography Clochac was immune from history: the eternal village, sealed within the jar of the cosmos.

She decided she would gather some clayweed, that grew a little further in, beside the stream. (Its roots, dried and hung by the door, were good for keeping gnats out of the house.) This errand would allow her to delay her return across the outfield. She was wary of crossing paths with the dog twice in one day. Fear, which kept her for so long from the forest's interior, now began to drive her in; the dog in the field behind her, following her with its look. Its look that bored through the back of her head and gazed out, clear from her skull; so she was afraid to look square at any tree or bush - for all her eye fell upon went through her gaze and into the dog's. And the forest, in its triumphant new-sprung growth now seemed a quivering mask of green. Behind the twinkling leaves the predator lurked. In the breakage of twigs underfoot she heard its abrupt bark. In the symmetrical gaps between the leaves she glimpsed the triangle of its head. In the vapour rising from the muddy earth she whiffed its liverish, doggy odour. She recalled how her mother, once finding the devil in a lettuce, had summoned the priest to cast it out. Now the entire vegetable kingdom seemed bugged by that diabolical presence.

Once the vastest in all France, the forest had been left untouched by Caesar. Accustomed to the open plains, the Romans couldn't hack such dense terrain. They feared the Germanic tribes it harboured within, the Goatpeople of Gaul. It was the Celtic monks who'd cleared the site where Clochac stood, and built its church. Its massive bell-tower that dominated the village was pierced with airholes to give less purchase to the ferocious coastal winds. For though too far inland for fishing, Clochac was near enough to the sea to receive the Atlantic's gusts.

The bells rang then, the Angelus! Sounding like a warning at her back. She ought to be heading back. Instead she rushed headlong, along the track that had slurred now to a muddy rivulet, its walk-through soft as shit.

This slushy path piped her on, through the densifying forest. Here the air seemed green, as if illuminated by vegetation. She could smell the fresh water of the stream. Up ahead, where the funnel of lime green light opened out, she saw the trunk of an old oak, big as her house. A bundle of rough fur lay sprawled on the great coil of its roots.

Was it in that first glimpse of him that she discerned the human outline beneath the crust of wolfskin? Or, was it only when, emerged from the pergola, she'd gone up close to his face and seen him all at once as human, male, young? She was never able to recall crossing those last few yards between them. It was as if the whole trek, from cottage door, across yards and fields, through the herbal rim and into the interior - had occurred in a single trajectory, to bring her here: to this sight at the heart of the green's diffusion.

The fear that had dogged her departed. Abandoned by terror she stood sheepishly before him, aware of the fact she had no actual business being here. He had woken and was staring in her direction without seeming to register her presence. She felt obliged to explain herself to this stranger, to assure him of her purpose. Meticulous lies bubbled to her lips.

'I'm on my way to Gran's,' an extravagant arm flung towards the forest interior, drawing attention to the basket in the crook of her elbow; 'with some salad stuff.' She carried on, 'Usually I take bread or cake or pie or stuff. But today, it's just salad stuff.' She paused, as if registering a query. Was he taken in? Had he understood? He had sat up, with his back welded to the oak trunk and was compressing his mouth to rid it of the sour taste of sleep. He looked sallow and puny.

Egged on by his blankness, she dug a handful of greenstuff from her basket and displayed it, in corroboration of her words. He gave the sprigs a sharp, formal nod, as if scanning a hand of cards; then picked a bit of sorrel which he gnawed on with grim concentration. When she saw how he poor-mouthed, she bit her lips, regretting having conjured up loaves and pies and so forth. In speaking of his lack she had bound herself to remedy it.

'Tomorrow,' she promised. 'I'll bring you some bread.'

For most of the following night the girl lay awake in her box-bed, in the dread he would rebuff her offering. Providence, now alerted to her relative fortune, would be watching to see if the vagrant accepted her gift. If not, then that Dame would abandon her, as She had him: and all her insurance against the ragged winds be blown away.

There was a strong expectation that this coming harvest would give the first decent yield in ten years.

'Let not the curse enter via the blessing's door,' she murmured to Our Lady, whose effigy hung over the bed's foot. *'Because we are due fortune, Let not the Hound of Misfortune come among us.'* The exhausted prayer ran on through the dark, grinding itself down, until it was bone - bare of all but the torsion of its articulation. *'Because of this - therefore that,'* the syntax of superstition, both statement and supplication: *'That it will befall / That it will not.'* All night she lay flattened under the weight of its formula.

* * * *

Next morning she flew through her tasks then, while her mother was out in the yard, took a hunk of stale bread from the pantry and went to the oak. There, she watched as the boy dunked the crust in the stream to soften it, and ate it.

When she got back, her mother was stood in the doorway, hands on hips and face a study of suspicious puzzlement. Her daughter braced herself to be questioned. Not that she'd thought for a moment that her mother would fail to remark the missing crust. For she knew how her mother counted household stock. How she could break a vegetable stew down into each ingredient, and itemise the very spot in the yard from which each root, pulse and leaf derived. She nodded at her daughter and continued scanning the fields from the doorway, then went into the house asking:

'Where have you been all this while?'

'Getting some salad for our supper,' her daughter replied.

'What took you so long?'

'I saw that dog. You know? That one?' The mother responded with a short, vigorous nod. 'It was in the outfield,' the girl elaborated, 'and followed me, into the woods ... and I thought it wanted to follow me and didn't want to bring it home with me and I had to hide, so you see I had to hide in the woods, until it lost me -'

'That figures,' her mother's eyes flickered shrewdly. 'It must have been here anyway, earlier on, while you were gone. Must have got into the house earlier. It took that crust, you know, the crust I was saving for our soup thickening ... '

'Well, it gave me a fright and a half,' the girl said, with the air of one making light of her pluck.

'So it's back: that dog. Under our noses. Now be extra sure not to leave food lying around.'

'Of course.'

From then on the girl spread the thefts about the whole village: filching a loaf here, a string of sausages there, as she stood, passing the time of day. Because suspicion fell on the dog, the girl was able to feed the tramp in the woods every day with impunity. Remarks were passed on the wily nature of this dog which could thieve without ever being seen to do so...

Meanwhile, the boy grew stronger with every meal. By the fifth day his cheeks had lost their pallid hue and his limbs their lassitude.

On the sixth day, she reached the oak to find him not there.

She called his name. Silence, except for the birds and the stream. She called again. This time the branches of the oak tree shook and she looked up to see a hailstorm freakishly blossom from its boughs. He was up there throwing bread crumbs in her face! The doughy pellets flecking her upturned cheeks, she put her hands on her hips and mimicking her mother's stern stance, called up, 'Chuck the bread-of-my-charity back in my face would you?'

151

He jumped down, landing in a crouch before her, then, straightening up, slung the fur mantle cape-fashion over his shoulders. His eyes were the oily green of an Atlantic she had smelt all her life, but had never seen. The tatty shirt he wore gave her glimpses of flesh, pale and live as whitewood meshed deep within the trunk. It occurred to her then that she had never seen him without the wolf skin. That stiffly-matted hide clung to him like a carapace of bark.

The following day, being Sunday, the bells regulated her every hour; so it was the day after when the girl next managed a visit to the oak tree.

She arrived to find the boy coiled up in the same posture she'd first seen him in. His eyes were shut, though when she squatted beside him he smiled, as if knowing she was there. She peeled the husky mantle from his shoulders and gently turned him so he lay on his back. She pulled the shirt away from the belt and two rugged brown nipples stared up at her, like apple pips from the pale platter of his chest. His eyes had opened during this operation and his grinning mouth tasted of streamwater. Their kiss released a tearing sensation in her breast; of some tiny bird at last torn free, into real time.

He was pale and luminous like the plump vellum of those mushrooms that spring up overnight; his flesh gave an impression of absorbency. As if one day all her embraces might be inscribed there. One day: but for now, couched in the eternal present of the wood's heart, he was this plant she could pluck again and again without detracting one whit from its plenitude.

Every day, except for Sundays, he would be waiting for her, embedded in the base of the oak, playing dead. After the ritual peeling of the wolfskin he would sit, trustfully bare before her. Sometimes she might remove her high, highly starched white coif which, like the bell tower of Clochac, was pierced with airholes - and set it on his head. Then he would clown for her, rolling his neck with the arch grace of a village virgin on hearing herself named May Queen for the year.

* * * *

The villagers could not help but comment on the dog's increasing boldness, which they found all the more remarkable for the fact that no-one had seen hair nor hide of the animal for several months.

The last reported sighting had been the widow's daughter. And that was back in the early spring.

They kept nightwatch over their yards and larders, but to no avail, as the food did not go during the night, but disappeared in broad daylight. It was as if, caped in a darkness all of its own, the dog could go in and out under their very noses: as if its diet of stolen meat endowed it with the capacity to render itself unseen. By the pump the villagers would gather to compare notes on losses; every day except for Sunday somebody lost something. This exception proved the rule, for in recognising the holiness of the seventh day, the dog must know itself a miscreant.

* * * *

Around early summer, as if to give weight to the dog's growing reputation for ungodly mischief, it stopped taking food, and began taking objects instead.

A rosary

A single pot

A linen shirt, from the washing line

A pair of bellows

A crucifix, that used to hang above a bed

A broken axe

A votive candle

It was nearly harvest time and for once, too much rain had not rotted the seed in the ground, nor drought withered the ears on the stalk. For the first year in ten, the harvest promised much. Now the dog's shadow lay over the fields, turning the promise of its largesse into a foreshadow of even greater scarcity to come. *'Because we have been blessed we will be cursed,'* was the underlying litany of Clochac, that tolled out from the bell-tower, that bubbled up in the water of gossip from the pump.

All that summer it seemed the entire portable content of Clochac might disappear down the hound's maw. A vacuum on four legs stalked among them, gulping the space it occupied. And, the more it swallowed, the less substantial did it become. Throughout the whole summer not one of the villagers caught sight of the dog - yet it was everywhere apparent. It was in the tear the raven made as it flew through the sky. It was in the baby's mewling as it asked for milk. It was in the neighbour's sidelong glance accompanying the first exchange of the day. It was in the wind that parted the ripening barley.

By then the boy had long since left the woods by Clochac.

He'd gone around the early summer, when the wild strawberries turned ripe. The girl had eaten some as she walked along the stream; discarding the blossoms as she went. Fruit and flower grew so densely packed she could not pluck one without the other. Idly examining a blossom she saw a tiny rose with a hollow eye; the palest of pinks, the merest tinge of blood in the milken petal. And the berry itself, flecked with minuscule yellow pips - was just a sponge for the true fruit to cling to.

She'd taken her time that day, dawdling among details, lost under the microscope of the forest's eye. In her basket she had a whole boiled chicken for the boy.

He was not at his usual post, by the oak tree, but she did not think he had gone far. Knowing his predilection for fooling up trees, he was probably off climbing one. Looking about she saw his fur mantle slung over the lower branches of a beech. She peered up into its foliage, but he was not there. She wrapped the fur round her shoulders and went to sit by their oak. While she waited for him to reappear, she passed the time by remembering how, arriving one day, ragged with nettle stings, she'd popped into the stream for a bath. When she'd driven her heel into the water, it had risen up, a refreshing necklace around her collarbones. All that week, walking around the village, she'd had the sensation that water drops still gleamed on her; and that all who saw her saw how her skin was studded with jewels of pleasure. It occurred to her then, as she sat under the tree, that she had no more dreams of visiting the charcoal shack since her assignations with the boy in the forest had begun. Little Red now seemed a childish tale ... fetching and carrying along her allotted path ... to stray from it was all *her* freedom. Lying with the boy she had entered another realm completely. Where was he anyhow? She had to admit it seemed unlikely he would reappear in time for her that day. Disconsolate, she wrapped the offering of the chicken in his fur, and deposited it at the oak tree before going home.

She returned the next day to find a raven pecking away at the tattered carcass of the chicken. At the unwholesome sight of fowl eating fowl she felt her stomach explode. She lay by the oak, puking until she was empty of everything except the knowledge that he had gone.

When she felt able to stand again, she buried her vomit, using a twig to turn the earth. Then putting the remains of the chicken, and the wolfskin in her basket, she slung it in the crook of her elbow and climbed the oak. As if in vanishing the boy had imparted his agility to her, she ascended with the rapid ease of a cat. Once up, she draped the branches with fur; then broke the chicken frame down into its bony components and arranged them in the forks of the twigs. On the ground again, she took off her rosary and wrapped it around the bole, the wooden beads clicking as she worked the twine.

Since then she had returned to the oak tree nearly every day to decorate the tree with some object filched from Clochac.

Soon the tree resembled a haphazard museum of the village. As if some determined wind had combed this random collection of things from their keeping places and whisked them, through the forest, to land in the rustling head of the oak.

Her days were chains of purpose, culminating in the oak tree. Organising the thefts and decorating the altar of the oak absorbed her completely. She grew terrifically calm. While all around her were consumed with the matter of the dog, she alone went briskly and unobtrusively about her private business. At times it seemed to her she was all that held Clochac together. As the leaves of the oak tree filled out, the acorns bulged and the tree grew weighted with its wooden fruit. The objects she stowed amongst its foliage were woven together by the green and brown background. The things she put there appeared like products of the tree - as if the tree had breathed them out, as the fruits of its exhalations.

* * * *

It was just before the harvest. The sun was shedding the last of its rays on Clochac and the villagers stretched their faces gratefully towards it, like children reaching for a ball as it brightly disappears over the garden wall.

One day, at noon, when the light was at its glassiest, clarifying each particle; spinning from every detail a consummate form - the dog was finally sighted. The priest saw it, crouched over the pump, lapping at the wet skin of the basin. He carried straight on, to the church, where, climbing the belfry he sounded the tocsin.

Soon the entire village - with the exception of the girl, who was busy at her tree - had downed tools, and was gathered by the pump; where the dog stood greeting them with its terse, piercing bark.

It followed them happily as they began to wend their way towards the church. The children, thrilled as much by the break in routine as by the dog's return, prodded it on with sticks. Catching their festive mood, the dog raced with the sticks and nipped the children's ankles with excited yelps. Once, these same children had tormented the dog, finding a limitless world in the body of its pain. But now all malice had gone from their ribbing. There was only the stern levity with which the prodigal scamp is welcomed back into the fold. The children were suddenly older now, as if the dog's return had turned them into arbiters of the peace; into distributors of incentives and goads; into Little Elders.

They were met by the priest at the church door. He took the dog into his arms and nursed it all along the aisle. The narrowness of this path regulated the procession so the village, becoming aware of its own constituency, fell to a formal hush. Seeming to register this new solemn edge, the dog fell quiet.

They started up the spiral stairway, towards the belfry. The dog's four legs pointed upwards, in docile ecstasy at the priest's embrace. The priest could feel the creature's pumping heart, joining with his own in a single system of blood. It seemed to grow heavier with each upwards step and soon the priest found himself staggering under the dog's incandescent weight. The four men nearest to him moved in with their shoulders and like pallbearers ranged in the corners of the casket, they went up.

In the belfry, the dog was placed on the ledge of the embrasure. It stood there, its tan fur showing gold against the turquoise lead of the sky beyond. Stamped by the communal gaze, the dog was flat as a brooch, pinned against the air. Sunrays speared the airholes of the belfry and the air scintillated like a barn replete with its wheaten haul. The villagers inhaled, as if to gather in the odour of the golden weal that they would reap: as they breathed out, the dog gave a sneeze. Its frame buckled in the molten sun and it was gone, the blue's emptiness perfected in the drop.

Nona's Letter

Kirsty Gunn

I see Nona standing at the sink, her kitchen door wide open to the morning sun. Light falls, clean and square, onto her grey lino floor, and without shadow, the pale room seems weightless, its thin walls frail as shell.

This is all right.

No pain this morning and Nona feels fine about the weather. Early summer is always a good time for her. Something to do with not kidding yourself, she thinks, like you do in springtime, hoping any time now the warmth will come. Instead you're picking off the rusted tops of flowers, even while others are in full bloom, just waiting for the grass to turn yellow, the earth to dry...

At her age, what is change, growth? The roses push their pale pink tufted heads against her bedroom window, rustle their stiff leaves, but the loveliness of them has nothing to do with next year, next year. Whether the thorny branches lengthen, whether the petals become thicker, softer... It's this present scent of them she has, a cluster of them in a vase on the kitchen table. It's all she needs.

And yet...

Soap suds in the sink where she's doing the washing-up pile about her arms. What is this new feeling in her? For the past weeks, maybe longer, it's been growing up inside her, unformed, unspoken, a bereaved feeling that has no partner, only the dark gap where loss is. What is it? She still takes the

159

tablets for heart pain but it's not a thing of the body she sickens after, it's within her deeper than that. Sunlight plays across the trembling froth of bubbles in the sink, catches the side of a pan left drying on the rack. For a second the light around her is piercing in its intensity, a white glare across her face, but Nona doesn't notice. It could be like death, this feeling, a life held in check and nothing to mark it when it's gone. For some time she stands there, hands submerged in the soapy water, but unmoving. Then the light passes from her.

It's so quiet in here.

The radio isn't turned on yet and the warm, airy room seems to unfold, larger and larger, into silence. Usually the sound of the local station would be playing off Nona's sideboard now: farm news, the weather report fine and dry, school fairs for the end of term, country shows. Why should this morning be different? In the silence she feels the heat of the day, feels it through her cotton dress, through the soles of her bare feet on the kitchen lino.

What day is this?

She looks out of the window above the sink, across the garden.

Tuesday?

She draws her brown hands from the water, creams the bubbles from her arms, pulls the plug. As the water drains away she brings out knives, forks, serving spoons, rinses them briefly under the cold tap and lets them all clatter onto the draining board. That's last night's dishes done, so yes, it must be Tuesday. Yesterday, Monday, T.T. brought Alice and Bobby down from the pub.

'Stay for tea?'

'Yeah, that sounds all right.'

'No bother for you, Nona?'

'No bother, honey. It's all here ...'

With Alice there, she'd set up the table to be really special: the white cloth with the blue edging, six of the pink roses in the small cut-glass vase. Ever since she'd first met her, when Alice was just nineteen and Nona more than twice her age, she'd wanted to please her.

'I've got a nice piece of ham, the coleslaw's all made - and there are my new potatoes.'

I would always want to please her.

'You finished the ones I gave you?' T.T. cut in with his bright stare. 'You got through that sack full?'

For reply Nona said nothing. He would always be her little brother, even now he was seventy and bent on a stick, half the time he spoke it was only for the sake of it. Instead she turned towards Alice.

'So what you been up to, love?'

The younger woman lit up a cigarette, straight off the back of her last. She was too thin, Nona saw. Her arms and legs were like rope, and the fingers, fiddling with the match, had become stained and yellow. Too many smokes during the day, that was the trouble, too many vodkas in the pub with Bobby. In her fifties now, Alice looked old - when she used to be such a pretty girl. The kind, Nona remembered, people in her day may have likened to flowers. Pale, gentle like she may blow over in a wind. Soft breasts like the roses on the table there.

'I haven't seen you for a while.' She took a seat beside her. 'Been busy?'

Nona had the feeling then too, even with company it hadn't left her. Not the sense of her own solitary life building up, not the lack of marriage, children ... She'd never wanted those things anyhow, the rub of them - look at Alice and Bobby. What had their life together come to in the end? Dark after-noons in the pub, a farm that would never break even. One daughter born to Alice too late to ever make up a real family for her. It seemed to Nona that by serving a man's life Alice's had been uprooted, had been faded away by his needs. And now that child of hers was growing up a strange girl, staying alone in the house all day ... And Alice not like a mother ... Or a lover.

All right, all right.

Damn Bobby anyhow, a drinker. How dare he take any woman, let alone this one? How dare he take her from the light, set her inside?

That's enough ...

Still, Nona stands at her drained sink. She can't stop her mind running on and she's dazed by the speed of it. Months and days and years all spin and turn: a girl, a woman, a daughter growing up alone in a dark house - and which one of them is she? All three? Seems to her like three generations wheel in circles in her mind, youth and age caught up in each other's arms. Alice's child could be Nona herself, could be Alice ... Growing up alone, each one of them, but brought outdoors at last into the garden there for all three. Then seasons change and turn, and the clasped hands around the neck unfasten and though she cries out, *Please don't go!,* it's too late ... The circle is broken. And there she is now, the dishes dry as bone in the warm air, and Nona's blue eyes look clear through the window, out past the path, past the tall bamboo hedge at the edge of her garden, to the sky.

After some time her gaze turns away. She takes a dish-towel and dries her hands, her arms. The table is already cleared, the cloth in the laundry to be washed later. No-one stayed late the night before. T.T. had gone up the hill to his own house and Bobby had pushed back his chair soon afterwards.

'Come on girl. We're on our way ...'

'Yeah, guess so ...'

How tired Alice looked then, brought to her feet by the man she'd married. How fallen in step. As Nona had seen

them both to the front door, she'd wanted to cry out to her
again down through the years, *Wait! Stay!* The feeling in her
wanted it. To keep what little there was left to them, *Please
don't go!* Her hand had touched the small of the other
woman's back as they walked together down the hall and she
found herself saying instead, 'Just take care of yourself, that's
all.'

She crosses the kitchen now and gets a cup down from the
shelf, measures coffee into it, two spoonfuls, so it will be
strong and thick as oil when she drinks it. She can't tell anyone
how she feels. Even T.T. her own brother she couldn't ask for
help from, both of them alone, unmarried, but still that doesn't
give them a blind thing in common. After all these years of
looking after him, giving him his tea every night, listening to
his chatter as he sits on her table while she clears up around
him ... She's never asked for his comfort in return. And if she
did, he would just take fright it was her heart trouble again.
It's not his fault he only knows his sister by her silence.

Anyway there's no physical pain.

She takes the kettle to the sink, fills it with water, then
idles by the stove while she waits for it to boil. It's been over
two years since she was in hospital, and it doesn't seem that
long ago. Nothing seems that long ago.

And it's a good day for the garden ...

She might even walk up to town later on, pick up the
hyacinth bulbs she's ordered from Farm Supplies, always this
time of year she gets them in. What is it about hyacinths when
they flower, so like a ritual for her, those purple and white and
yellow heads? Something about her girlhood, in the sweet,
closed-in smell of the blooms, the bright sugary colours
brought out in the dark heat of the room where they're forced
to flower.

*Who is any man to take a woman from the light? Set her
inside?*

The kettle hisses. Nona turns off the gas, pours the boiling water into her cup and stirs it. Takes it over to the kitchen door and sits there on the step, the bitter steam from the coffee rising in the sunshine.

As she sips at it she looks over her garden, over the wide green lawn clipped close as velvet and the flower beds piled up at its edges in massed rows of yellow, white and crimson. The full bushes of roses down the side of the house, by Nona's bedroom window, promise a long summer, all the leaves on the hydrangeas promise it.

And yet, and yet ...

Already the stocks are in flower, standing up in ranks before the trellis that marks off the vegetable patch, soon even the trellis will be woven loosely all over with honeysuckle, sweet pea.

And yet ...

When she watches over her garden like this, Nona feels busy and crowded as if she has whole families to tend, flourishing loves, the whole place needing her. At seventy five she thinks, all this colour, this beauty ranged along her path, heaped up in raised beds, the vegetable garden in embroidered rows ... All this should be enough for her now. Why then, does she set her cup down beside her on the cracked wooden step? Why fold her arms tightly around her broad belly and feel tears come into her blue eyes? Even the warm sky, throwing a shawl around her, can't comfort her, or the breeze through the bamboo like a love's sighing.

Hush, hush, it whispers through the thin cane rods.

Hush, hush, it whispers across the flowers.

Through maidenhair and lily of the valley, *Hush, hush.*

All through the pale roses, a love's sighing.

Here then is how I see Nona, her story's ending, beginning. Her china cup set down, the warmth of the morning, bright garden. Minutes pass. There is a feeling in this old woman like

164

something might escape, be lost to her forever. For this reason, after weeping, she will rise. She will go back into the kitchen, to the sideboard where she keeps the radio. Instead of turning it on she will open a drawer, find an old notepad inside, a pen that works ... And in her quivery hand unused to writing letters she will start to write one now.

Dearest Alice, it begins.

I have the letter. The day Nona writes to my mother I am nine years old yet feel the isolation of all our girlhoods acutely as a flower forced to bloom indoors. When, finally, years after it's written, I open it, the letter will show me what silences there can be in the lives of women, what unspoken words, uncommitted acts. Yet also I will find in it, in Nona's words, a kind of love that is not unrequited. It's there in the fresh earth piled up round the stems of her dahlias still in bud, in their yellow petals closed squint against the bright light. It's there in her tall bamboo hedge, the rafts of pale cane shifting in the breeze. I have all these words now, her life, played out like shadows and sunlight across leaves and flowers. Three women, three generations, form a circle when I smooth out the pages and read.

Two Women on a Bus, 1940 - 1994

Hilary Bailey

It's midday, the sun's high in the heavens and Mrs Black-Leather-Jacket, or Mrs B-J as we will henceforth whimsically call her, is on the lower deck of a big, red London bus, heading South over the river, over Lambeth Bridge, to Kennington, the Oval, Brixton, Herne Hill and Crystal Palace. She's going to visit her mother, hoping this time they will greet each other with mutual pleasure, cordiality, love and appreciation. She doubts if this will happen. She doubts if it can happen between herself and her own daughters. Probably, it's nobody's fault. Women have been involved in a hundred year war conducted in public - in Parliament, on demonstrations, at meetings, in committees - about the vote, maternity rights, equal pay for equal work. The other half has been played out at home, behind closed doors, one to one, mother and daughter.

'If I grow up to have your life I'll kill myself.'

'Are you going out like that?'

'It's not like it was in your day.'

'It's not that different - you'll find out.'

Mrs B-J has on her knee a wicker basket, for her mother. It contains a bag of tomatoes, a crab, some red onions and a bottle of wine. She feels like little Red Riding Hood in her black leather jacket.

She thinks: of all the women on this bus (there are only three of them on the lower deck - herself, the woman across

166

the aisle from her in a fawn mac and a young black woman near the front, with a small child on her lap) - if each of us who has not had a kind word from her mother for one year suddenly came out in purple spots, which of us will be without them?

None of us, Mrs B-J. thinks. None of us. Except the baby, if it's a girl. 'That's a clever girl.'

She, and the woman in the fawn raincoat and the black woman with her baby would probably be well splodged, purple-poxed from neck to eyebrows.

What if these spots spread to all the women in the nearby streets? They are going past Parliament Square. How many, of the women rushing with briefcases to the Arts Council, the Houses of Parliament, the Treasury, the worse off ones, serving in snack bars, hurrying home from the cleaning jobs - how many would be covered in purple spots? Lots.

They're passing the Houses of Parliament now. How many of the legislator-women would be spotty? What about Mrs Virginia Bottomley, Secretary of State to the Ministry of Health?

Maternal love, where daughters are concerned, is a fierce desert. Sand, sand and still more sand. You stagger on over the burning dunes, eyeballs burning, tongue swollen with thirst, sun beating down on your head, searching for an oasis - all too often a mirage.

You can't blame them really. They're tough. They've had to be. Hundreds of years of sending their boys to populate and patrol the British Empire, then two generations despatched, one after another, to fight in world wars, bringing up the girls to put up with it. Slumps, strikes, too many children, too many wars - no world for weaklings. Mrs B-J wonders if she's brought her girls up in the same harsh tradition. She probably has. Mothers, like generals, are always fighting the last war. Between mother and daughter it can be a nasty, covert, dirty

Balkan war too, full of lies and treachery, spying and changing sides, alliances made and broken. It's a job of work being a mother. It really is.

'You've always been silly that way.'

'What can you think you look like?'

'I told you so.'

They're W.P.C.s, upper servants teaching the new maids their places.

'Fair? Life's not fair.'

'If that's the worst you ever have to put up with you'll be lucky, believe me.'

'What do you want as well - the fairy off the Christmas tree?'

Who binds your feet? Who holds you down for the clitoridectomy? Who decks the bed for the unwanted arranged marriage? Mother, that's who. Mother's scared not to. Society needs mother to do it so society can go on in the same old way. Mother's had to put up with it, so why shouldn't you? What will happen to you if mother doesn't maim you? What will happen to mother if she doesn't do it?

As the bus creeps over Lambeth Bridge Mrs B-J finds herself looking with intense dislike at the woman across the aisle from her, the woman in the fawn mac. She's innocent enough in her raincoat, shopping at her feet in a Marks and Spencer plastic bag, another thick, black, plastic bag on her lap. She's harmless. Mrs B-J just imagines she's the one who's keeping the system going. Because she knows no better. Because it's not her place to think.

She went through the Blitz in that mac, she's saying, with her string bag, gas mask and identity card. She was the Home Front. She's got a picture of a bloke in uniform on the parlour wall, glass broken, a bit skew-whiff because of the bomb that fell two doors up. She didn't of course. This one's much the same age as Mrs B-J. The woman with the string bag was her mother.

Dressing like your mother is the solution to the older woman's fashion problem - always has been. The trouble was, the mould broke in the fifties when Mrs B-J and, for all she knows, Mrs Mac lay in cooling, blue baths, dressed in jeans, very uncomfortable, shrinking them to fit. At that time you were nothing and nobody without a crisp shirtwaister, matching bag and shoes and 'little' white gloves.

Jeans made a difference. Nobody's mother had worn jeans as a girl. Jeans favoured youth, they were all the same price, they were unisex in a confusing way (you 'couldn't tell the difference' from the back, from the front they were tight enough to make it obvious). Class, income and sex distinctions all abolished in one big kerflump, leaving only age (and weight) as determinants.

Hard to turn back after those jeans, really. Mrs Mac has solved it - she's wearing her mother's raincoat and the perm she had when she got married. Mrs B-J's confused in her black leather jacket, a snip at Oxfam at £9.95, a rebel without a cause. Still, if the purple spots of the Madonna, Our Lady of Rejection, descended now both their faces would be blemished. Mrs Mac's been young once.

'What! You little fool! Now you'll have to get married. Don't look at me like that. You've made your bed, now you'll have to lie on it. You'd better put your name down for a council flat.'

Not much fun after a childhood spent with sweet rationing and no toys but Golly, made out of spare blackout material.

It probably wasn't much fun even if Mrs Mac's hadn't been a shotgun wedding. Going to the jewellers to pick out an engagement ring. No sight more melancholy than that of a young couple in the '50s standing in the High Street in the drizzle staring into the jewellers' window. Thrilled? They didn't look it. The ring was the first thing he paid for with his money, start of a new life, where he paid for everything and she was paid for. Growing up. *Ouch!*

Does Mrs Mac look back on those days with nostalgia? Think things aren't like they used to be, more's the pity?

What they didn't have in the '50s ... The pill, tights, legal abortion, illegal drugs, central heating or fridges (much) or washing machines. Black people and foreigners unless they were Irish or refugees from the war.

Women doctors and lawyers (hardly). Women practically anything.

What they did have in the '50s ... National Service, bomb sites, suspenders and girdles, full employment, black and white T.V., laundrettes, ballroom dancing, Norman Wisdom and Frank Sinatra and the Coronation. Wives and mothers at home all day. Waitresses and secretaries. Consenting males could get two years in prison for having sex. Back street abortions, open fires, working pits, Korea, Cyprus, Malaya. Posters of women doing housework in crisp shirtwaisters as if they hadn't come in contact with any dirt at all, waving their new mops with smiles of delirious excitement on their faces.

Those were the good old days for any woman with a taste for hand-washing, wearing more underwear than outerwear, peeling turnips and falling for a baby. In the rain.

Of course there weren't the hooligans about that there are today. You could walk from Land's End to John O'Groats in your knickers without fear of molestation. If over seven feet tall and carrying a machine gun. Otherwise you'd get raped and not dare tell anybody. There were no yobs, just teddy boys with razors and bicycle chains. There was no graffiti - there weren't any spray cans. You had to make do with chalk.

Crime was decently organised and only a certain kind of person got beaten up by the police, who didn't do it anyway. Police evidence was always accepted because the police knew the accused had done it. The old-time criminals were professionals, qualified men, so to speak, with a strong sense of professional ethics, administering crime with justice and impartiality - a privilege to be burgled by them. Where the men with razor scars on their faces, or the girls on street corners and the men who took their money fitted in - who can tell? The past is another country and we've lost the snapshots.

They're passing the Imperial War Museum now. They've tried to pretty it up with the Wartime Kitchen Garden but nothing can prettify that huge cannon outside, with its five foot barrel like Lord Kitchener, Pointing At You.

Mrs Mac, like Mrs B-J, must have spent a good few months of her life in air raid shelters, unless she was evacuated, along with another three and a half million city children, away from a threatened invasion and bombing. Later, you were nobody at school if you'd only been bombed out once. Distinction came with having been bombed out of your house twice - or even three times. Everybody at school knew some children who'd been quietly walking home from school, minding their own businesses, when a German fighter had swooped down and machine-gunned the lot of them. They were all dead, of course. Had this ever really happened? Was it a myth? Mrs B-J doesn't know.

Three and a half million children sent away from home. Many came back soon. Others didn't see their own homes and families for three or four years. A family visit brought a stranger to the rural door. When the father came back from fighting and the kids from being evacuated nobody in the household can have known anybody else. Mother, in the meanwhile, might have turned into a bus driver. You'd get Lambeth Social Services now, helping you to adjust.

Mrs B-J had spent some months in 1940 sitting in the shelter at the bottom of the garden with her mother and her granny. Her grandfather, who had been in trenches during the last war had been out as an A.R.P. warden. *(He's not brave. He just has no imagination.)* Her father had been fire watching on the roof of his office in central London. Because of lack of space in the air raid shelter Mrs B-J's grandmother had been in her wheelchair in the cellar. So had her brother, in his pram. (*He never woke up.- How do you know?*)

At six every morning Mrs B-J's mother would run up the garden path, raid or no raid, to give the baby his bottle.

Mrs B-J's ex-husband, whom we will call Mr B-J, had a granny who had flung herself across his cot during an air raid crying, *Take me, God! Take me!* God took neither of them but Mr B-J certainly grew up with a strange and tender love for the bangs, thuds and sound of breaking glass which had characterised his childhood. Mr B-J must have broken more windows than the Luftwaffe. It seemed to satisfy something in his soul. Let's be honest, a handy milk bottle and a pane of glass had been known to tempt Mrs B-J in her time. Made her fingers itch. A nice overarm, the arc of the bottle through the air - bingo - *crash, crash, tinkle, tinkle*. Oh joy! My client, Your Honour, is suffering post-war traumatic stress disorder. She has frequent Battle of Britain flashbacks.

Mrs B-J has a greedy excitement about brightly lit skies. Skies aren't what they were in her childhood, full of big, white barrage balloons, lanced by searchlights going to and fro. Fires on the horizon and the big black birds droning overhead.

They're passing that park by the Oval. Legend has it that just inside those railings there was a direct hit on an air raid shelter. They never dug it out. Hundreds of people are there, buried under the turf. Is it true? Mrs B-J doesn't know.

Back to Mrs Mac's family values. Mrs B-J herself doesn't quite believe in them. She thinks they are something they dreamed up in the U.S.A. She knows from films it means some very young-looking parents playing snowballs in their back yard in Connecticut, then going into a nice house to decorate the Christmas tree - then there's a homicidal prowler or ghostly hands from the graveyard below coming up through the well-polished floorboards. The children are screaming - everybody's screaming.

Mrs Mac who looks as if she's paid her debt to society in the family business may find it difficult to square the family values dream with her own reality.

What happened to her? Her children? Her son? In business on his own? Doctor? Works at the Town Hall? Married with two lovely kiddies? Thrice divorced with four children? Assistant Manager, Woolwich Building Society?

Whatever else she's doing, it's a pound to a penny Mrs Mac's daughter has a job. That was something Mrs Mac didn't bargain for in her youth. She had no choice. Pregnant women left work. Mrs B-J overstayed her welcome at work, got in the lift, bulging, frightened the Director General and a colleague. They didn't like it, perhaps they were scared they'd have to deliver her on the lift floor. Anyway, the writing was on the wall.

That may be where Mrs Mac's heading off to. To do a spot of child-minding for her daughter. A spot? Who called it a spot? She's probably run off her feet, Mrs Mac. She has a little job, then does a spot of child-minding, gets back, does a spot of cleaning then cooks up a bit of dinner. Men don't do a spot of conveyancing, a bit of steel-erecting or a tiny bit of briefing-for-the-Minister. They don't get run off their feet, either, as if they'd caught their coats in the bus door and had to pelt along or get carried off. They've been busy, they're knackered, they're dog-tired.

Small wonder, with a job description like Mrs Mac's that her daughter has probably got herself a proper job with a proper salary and a proper title, like Assistant Manager, Woolwich Building Society.

After Mrs Mac had picked out the ring, curtains, carpets, wedding dress her next engagement was, no doubt, in the maternity ward. National Health, baby boom, no husbands allowed then and perhaps, in the rush, no staff there either. No drugs, no choice and probably no cup of tea afterwards.

There were two schools of thought in those days. According to the older one, the woman really suffered - there was day on day of labour, the doctors despaired, the lives of mother and baby hung in the balance. Then there was the more modern school - perfectly natural happening, not an illness after all, no problems, peasant women have a baby in the corner of the field, pick up the sickle and go on reaping. Does Mrs Mac's action replay of her confinement follow one model or the other? Mrs B-J, as you'd perhaps expect, nearly had her baby in the street. Her husband had to run into the pub to phone an ambulance and all the men at the bar laughed at him. He hasn't forgiven (nor has her daughter who's had to hear the tale again and again) but he came closer to being present at the birth than most men did at the time.

Mrs B-J, let's be frank, believes herself to be more hep, hipper, cooler, trendier and generally more safe, more wicked - anything - than Mrs Mac. She's calling her agent, their lawyers are talking to her lawyers, she hasn't a penny to bless herself.

So she is surprised when comes a ringing tone on the bus and more than surprised - shocked - when from the pocket of her fawn raincoat Mrs Mac produces a mobile phone.

A mobile phone! What! What? Mrs B-J thinks hysterically. Mrs Mac has a mobile phone. She is one of that élite who can say casually, 'You can get me on my mobile.' If Mrs Mac has got a mobile phone why hasn't she got one? What is there in Mrs Mac's drab and dismal, sad and sorry life demanding this luxurious toy? Why isn't she at home, listening to something about Disability on Radio 4 and getting on with a spot of ironing?

As Mrs B-J struggles to hear Mrs Mac's part of the conversation, she catches the word 'contract'. What contract, she thinks wildly? A film contract? What's she doing - playing the part of a boring woman on a bus in a major Hollywood movie? A book contract? Mills and Boon? A beautiful novel burning with a gem-like flame about a woman on a bus going towards Brixton?

Mrs Mac's getting firm now, on the mobile. She's not pleased. Someone's made a mess of it, whatever it is. She's sorting it out. Perhaps it's a building contract. Mrs Mac's going to build a block of flats, a sports' centre, a private hospital. Perhaps she's going to host a phone-in on L.B.C. - bringing you, today, at ten on L.B.C. - Grousers. If you have any complaints about check-out queues, post office closures, mountain bikes being ridden on pavements, truant schoolchildren, phone Mrs Mac on 0171 something-or-other.

Mrs B-J is earwigging madly, can't cross the bus and deliberately sit down behind Mrs Mac to hear what she's saying. But her ears are adjusting to Mrs Mac's side of the conversation.

'You'd better tell him to drop what he's doing and get over to Balcon Avenue. Tell him to stop at Stockford's on the way and see if he can pick up what he needs for Linden Road. That way he can finish at Linden Road first thing tomorrow morning.'

What? goes Mrs B-J, screaming internally. *She* lives in Linden Road. That's where she lives. She left the plumber behind two hours ago, her central heating in pieces all over the floor.

'I'll call Vaillant and check it out with them. But better if he can get it at Stockford's.'

'I should say so,' thinks Mrs B-J. 'If he can get the part at Stockford's he might be able to fix it tomorrow.'

She's been bathing next door for a week, boiling water for the washing up. The weather's going to get colder.

Oh, bugger. She, Mrs B-J, is Vaillant, Linden Road.

The other woman has moved on to another topic.

'I'll ring Henderson from home in about half an hour. I've had enough. Either he gets his finger out or forget it. It's a lot of money, agreed, but it's been too long and I've heard on the grapevine he's having trouble with his financing. It may be just a rumour but - ' But Mrs B-J is thinking about her central heating, Stockford's, the plumber, the spare part.

Now Mrs Mac has rung off. Mrs B-J is wondering whether she should cross the bus, confess to eavesdropping, throw herself on Mrs Mac's mercy, beg and plead for early attention. She could tell her about having to bath next door. This woman, Mrs Mac, has her future in her hands. If it isn't fixed she'll go on bathing at Mary's, boiling up water. It could turn cold. Something holds her back. Perhaps it's the recognition that both she and Mrs Mac were brought up in uncentrally-heated houses, where people jostled for a position near the fire and bath water came from dodgy, explosive gas geysers or kitchen boilers which had to be stoked.

'Cold - you don't know what cold is. When we got up in the morning we could scratch our names in the frost inside the bedroom windows.

Hot water? You don't know what no hot water is all about. We used to have a bath in the same water, all six of us. By the time it came to my turn it was jet black and icy cold.

Cold? Our breath used to steam out in the dining room, we got frostbite in the kitchen and hypothermia in the bathroom. We used to break thick ice on the dog's bowl every morning. We slept in all our clothes.

Cold? You don't know the meaning of the word.'

They're stalled going up to Brixton. There's a crane ahead in the middle of the road, loading on portaloos, by the police station. Don't ask why. The bus crawls.

Another woman, in a pale blue mac, also with two bags of shopping, gets on to the bus. She greets Mrs Mac, 'Hullo, Rita,' and sits down beside her. They talk.

'Why don't they do these things at night, when the traffic's lighter?'

'She's got Cherry in at Baymede Nursery and got herself a job. It's the only way.'

'A dozen lovely red roses. Wasn't that a lovely thought? I was overwhelmed.'

'Brian's fed up and no wonder. There's nothing for him here, what with the divorce. He reckons he might as well go back to the Gulf.'

'He said he was home all night but my neighbour saw him in the pub.'

'She rings the Council day after day but all she gets is an answering machine.'

'Eight 'O' Levels. His father still can't believe it.'

'He's on the mend, so the hospital says. He wants to get back full-time but the doctor says no. Too stressful. The trouble is it's stressful at home, for him, too. He wants to know every little thing that's going on. If I tell him, he worries. If I don't, he thinks I'm hiding something to protect him.'

'You can only go by what the doctor says.'

Well - it seems Mrs Mac, who worked as her husband's secretary at his building firm for twenty years, after the children went to school, has had to take over the firm after his heart attack. Until he's better. It's that or closing down completely. Mrs B-J can hardly advance towards her across the bus now, banging on about her central heating. Mrs Mac has problems of her own. ·

'He'll be thrilled if I get it but - ' she tells her friend. But if she gets the contract she was talking about on her mobile phone, although it will help the firm it might make her husband feel useless, replaceable, obsolete. And he's a sick man. We know, thinks Mrs B-J. On the left, ladies, is the rock and on the right - let's have a big hand for it - the hard place.

The bus gets past the portaloo/crane obstruction.

'They seem to be treating her very badly.'

'Probably six of one and half a dozen of the other.'

'At least she'll never have to worry about money.'

'Half past ten in the morning. They're still not sure about one of his eyes.'

'They can say what they like. My Eddie knows a reporter who says he's got shares in it.'

The driver's put his foot down. They must be doing a good six miles an hour. They creep past mighty, municipal Lambeth Town Hall. The women get off outside a row of shops in Herne Hill. Mrs B-J travels on. Then she gets off.

As she approaches her mother's house can she hear Vera Lynn singing *We'll meet again*? Or is it a jolly Cockney chorus of *Roll Out The Barrel*? or *Rock Around the Clock*? Or can this be the strains of some great symphony, soaring strings, throbbing cello, sombre drum, joyful flute - the strains of some great and complex music made up piece by piece by women on the bus in their macs, with their mobile phones, their shopping? Is it composed from their continuous stream of narrative, about jobs, babies, crimes, divorces, illnesses, births, weddings, funerals, war and peace, comings and goings, home and abroad, kitchens, curtains, rewirings, landlords, mortgages, bosses, promotions and redundancies, hardships, helping-hands and quarrels?

No that's not what she's hearing. You don't hear that sort of thing in South London.

Mrs B-J carries the basket up the path to her mother's house.

Mulberry Juice

Elisa Segrave

You've been coming to this village every summer since you were four. The rocks under the sea-wall are still 'your house'. You even remember which rock is the bathroom - the pale orange one with the little pool in the middle - and which one is the dining room - the slanting long grey slab.

Your mother's also been coming to the village since she was a child. Your mother's always boasted about how tough she was, how she was able to climb the enormous rock, Barneybank, bigger than two houses, on the Dirty Beach, with no shoes on when she was five, how she was able to outdo the local fishermen's sons with her rock-climbing.

Even in middle age, your mother goes out prawning at low tide and comes back triumphantly with her bag full of live prawns. She takes you surfing - a long drive over Dartmoor to North Cornwall then several hours in and out of the foaming sea; you don't have anything as sissy as wet-suits - and another time she buys a canoe and intrepidly tries it out first herself in the sea below your house.

Are you supposed to vie with your mother over these feats of daring?

Your mother doesn't have any womanly pursuits. Most summers Mrs L, a fisherman's wife from the village comes and cooks for you on the sea-side holiday. Your mother whispers a story about Mrs L; years ago she murdered her own baby, throwing it over the sea-wall when it was a few weeks old. You'd rather your mother didn't tell you this.

Your mother can't sew a hem, cook a meal, or even look after a baby on her own, despite having had four children.

Your mother despises her friend Pauline who often comes with you to the sea-side, accompanied by her two little girls and sometimes by her husband Stephen. When Pauline comes, Mrs L isn't necessary. Your mother laughs at Pauline for trying so hard with the cooking. She says she's sick of quiche and mocks Pauline for making enthusiastic excursions into the local town for more ingredients. She criticises Pauline for 'waiting on Stephen hand and foot' - bringing him cups of tea as he sits in an armchair reading from his book on wild birds.

Your mother always jeers when she sees couples kissing in public, on a park bench or in a restaurant. How silly they look!

It's forty years since you first went to the sea-side village. You've been bringing your own daughter here every summer since she was a blonde baby, crawling eagerly after other children on the beach like a little friendly crab.

This summer, your daughter's nearly thirteen. Already she can do things that you and your mother can't do - like use a sewing machine. When she was nine she designed and stitched a whole set of original clothes for her Sylvanian animals. She can also cook a simple meal, which you can also do, of course, but what's just as important, something you've never achieved, she can arrange the food to look pretty, decorate it with parsley, and serve it in small appetising portions.

Today a group of you have decided to walk to a nearby cove, where you'll swim and have a picnic lunch. You get there by walking along the cliffs beside the sea. It's a beautiful walk - there's pink thrift, heather, the mauve-grey hills of Dartmoor in the distance, buzzards and seagulls wheeling and crying over the terrifying rock face and across the cornfields the church spire of the neighbouring village.

Below is the sea with sailing boats bobbing about - one particularly pretty one, with three red sails. Could anything be more lovely, more wholesome, than this line of wild coast in summer?

You spend two pleasant hours in the cove, eating sandwiches and swimming in the sea. There are other families on the beach, mostly with young children, because along this stretch of coast the beaches are perfectly safe, ideal for babies and toddlers.

Your own daughter, however, will be a teenager in a month, and has suddenly begun to care more about her appearance. Her hair, which for the last two years she's scraped into an unflattering pony-tail, is now in a tidy French plait. How composed, how womanly your daughter looks.

With her neat blond plait, her clean white shirt and her long legs in denim shorts suddenly she seems to you, and no doubt to others, like a young lady.

At four o'clock you decide to start for home. Your daughter climbs purposefully up a steep path out of the cove taking the dog with her, while you, your son and the two men with you, take a gentler route which ends up on the same walk overlooking the sea.

All the time you can see your daughter ahead of you, striding along the path with her long legs with the dog, a little black and white spaniel, beside her. Suddenly for no reason, you become nervous.

'I'd like to catch her up,' you say. 'There might be some funny people about.'

The man beside you takes you seriously and you both go faster. Luckily there are no wooded areas and most of the time you can see your daughter quite clearly, striding ahead of you beside the sea with the dog.

That night on T.V. there's a news flash. A young woman's body has just been found near that same cliff walk.

By the next day it's clear she was murdered - and raped. She was dragged off the cliff path, down through bushes and brambles. The police ask tourists and locals to report any man they see with unexplained scratches on his arms and legs. The young woman's two brothers, distraught, appear on the T.V. news appealing for help.

That night at midnight your daughter comes into your bedroom. Can't she ever go for walks alone now in the fields near her uncle's cottage? Can't she go alone on the train to her grandmother's? Can't she even take the bus to school?

You try to be calm and sensible; you tell her you must both keep a sense of proportion. She must just be doubly aware, that's all. It's possible that the man who murdered the girl knew her already. Maybe she agreed to go for a walk with him.

'And she has every right to do that,' you add firmly, to scotch any notion that if a young woman decides to go for a walk with a man she gets what she deserves. (If that were the case, judging by your own rash behaviour as a young woman, you'd be dead at least fifty times.)

By the next evening more information is released. The murdered girl, from Scotland, had a holiday job in a hotel: it was her second summer here. The police stage a reconstruction of her walk. Some of this is shown on the news.

That night it's you who's worried. Could the murderer still be out there on the cliffs? The sound of the waves below the sea-wall, normally so soothing, now seems sinister and threatening. The protected bay, where you've spent so many happy summers among the rock pools, now seems vulnerable and cut off.

You recall how, when you were nine, your mother showed you an article in 'The News of the World' about a girl with your own name who'd been murdered in a cornfield. There was blood on her sock.

You remember how your mother covered her hands with mulberry juice from the mulberries in the garden and pretended she was going to strangle you. Her hands rose up at you, smeared red. You were afraid.

On Sunday, when you leave for home, the traffic's calmed down and the only person in front of you that morning at the road block is a girl on a Palomino pony. The policeman, with a strong Devon accent - this kind of crime must be horribly new to him - tentatively asks what your movements were on that Wednesday. Then he lowers his voice: 'I expect you heard about the young lady. Have you seen anyone like this?'

He shows a photograph. A girl with long red-gold hair, a narrow, sweet, silly excited face, trips up the path towards the camera, towards you. How full of life she seems, how trusting!

So as not to dismiss her too quickly, in deference to the awful thing that happened to her, you stare a few minutes longer at the photograph than necessary. Then you shake your head. 'No.'

You're silent as you drive on. Seeing the photograph has made it horribly real. The girl was only a few years older than your daughter, who would also be called 'a young lady' by the policeman.

You don't want to go on thinking about it but you do. Another girl was murdered, earlier this summer, in the North of England, in a street near her home. You were shocked to see her mother nakedly shouting out her hatred and fury on the television news.

Now, you think you understand her.

Was your mother right after all? Your mother, who, her hands covered with mulberry juice, made you aware of the terrors that awaited you? Was she right to boast of her tomboyishness, her ability to out-do the fishermen's sons?

Was she right to hate being female?

You still don't know. You still don't know what to tell your daughter.

You don't really know.

Return to England

Mizzy Hussain

She was gorgeous. I wanted her more than anything. Her face was as round as the full moon, and her hair was as dark as midnight. Her glassy eyes were like blue saucers! And her eyelids were fringed with, *I swear*, purple eyelashes. She was dressed in red satin and gauze with tiny rosebuds scattered over her veil and full gown.

Ummi and I used to pass the toy shop every day, on the way to school. I was tormented by that doll. I would stamp my feet on the ground, squeeze my eyes shut and plead with Ummi. 'I want that doll, Ummi, please, PLEASE can I have that doll?' But her answer was always, 'No, I am NOT buying you that doll,' and then she would drag me to school.

The first day at school Abu talked to the teacher while my brother Wakar and I took turns to ride the rocking-horse in the entrance hall. The teacher was older than Ummi and Abu. She had brown, wiry hair and wore a mauve sweater, a thick woollen calf-length skirt and black high-heeled shoes. Her stockings had seams running up the backs of her legs.

Ummi stood quietly next to Abu whilst he did all the talking. Abu spent a long time talking to the teacher. Sometimes he would make a joke and they would both laugh. Ummi would smile when he did this, but I knew she didn't really understand everything they were saying.

And then they deposited me in the classroom with about thirty other children. I howled all day until home-time when they came to collect me.

I cheered up then realising they hadn't deserted me for ever, and there was the happy prospect of catching a glimpse of the doll again. I resolved that if Ummi didn't buy me the doll, I would ask Abu. Abu was kind. He bought me chocolates.

As we passed the toy shop I stopped to look in the window. She was still there, still tantalising me with her glassy eyes. The expression on her face was alien to me. She did not look at me but above me, through me, beyond me to some place or time I did not yet know of. She wasn't a child like me, nor was she a woman, like Ummi. She was a womanchild. She knew my secrets. And yet more than this, she knew the secrets of the world.

Abu was also looking at the doll. Ummi guessed his intention and before either he or I could say anything she caught his eyes and said, 'There's no need ...'

The next day arrived and the awful knowledge with it that I had to go to school *again!*

'But I already went to school yesterday!' I protested.

'You have to go to school every day,' replied Ummi, throwing back my blanket.

Abu was asleep because he had done a night-shift, so Naeem Uncle was given the task of escorting me to school.

On the way to school, I told Naeem Uncle about the doll and asked him if he would buy it for me. Fortunately, for him, the shop was closed so he promised me he would buy it when it was open. And then, as we walked on he said, 'Anyway, you're a little big for dolls now, aren't you?' as if picking up a half-finished conversation that I didn't remember having.'You must play with other children, not lifeless dolls.'

'But I play with Wakar, don't I? And sometimes Suzanne, when her mother lets her.' Suzanne was one of our neighbours.

'Wakar is too young for you. And Suzanne is older than you. And anyway her mother is no good. She doesn't like us. Better you make friends your own age.'

I heaved a sigh. 'Where can I find friends then?'

'In your school of course.'

'But ... but,' in exasperation I struggled to put my case but couldn't find the words. 'But ... I don't understand them.'

'Then you'll have to learn English. That's what school is for.'

'Why can't *they* learn Urdu. Or Punjabi even?'

As we approached the school, I tried to think of a way to avoid having to go in. When we got to the gate I gave out a gasp of surprise. 'This isn't my school! You've brought me to the wrong school!' Naeem Uncle peered through the railings and spoke to the children in the playground, then as his hands were poised on the latch of the school gate, ready to open the gate, hoping he was right, I pulled on his bony fingers and pleaded, 'Uncle, this is the *wrong s*chool. You've brought me to the *wrong* school. Let's go home now.'

He blinked nervously and we turned to go home.

The toy shop was now open and as we passed it I reminded him of his promise. This time he turned out his pockets and said, 'Yasmeen, I don't have the money.'

I was horrified. He had broken his promise. I kicked his shins and pummelled him with clenched fists.

'Why did you say you'd buy me the doll then? Why did you promise? You PROMISED!'

'Yasmeen!' he begged, trying to grab my flailing wrists to protect himself. 'Yasmeen, I would if I could, but all the money I earn I give to your Abu. I can't buy you the doll.'

I knew he was telling the truth. I had often seen him come home late at night, produce a wad of bank notes from his jacket and hand it over to Ummi or Abu. Every single bank-note.

So I walked back home with Naeem Uncle, dreaming of the doll, of her coming to life. I imagined a heart beating just like mine, of her arms soft and warm, embracing me, her mouth smiling. I imagined her gathering the full skirt of her gown, making a swooshing sound as she did so, and dancing, laughing, her hair loose and glistening luxuriously like a newly-washed plum.

When we got home, Naeem Uncle apologised to Ummi and said that he couldn't find the right school. When he was asked to describe the school and the route he took, Ummi raised her eyebrows and narrowed her eyes. When she narrowed her eyes they looked like upside-down crescents of lime.

'That was the *right* school, Naeem!' But she didn't shout at him. She just looked at me and said, 'Tomorrow *I'll* take you to school!'

The next day we walked hand in hand to school past the toy shop and past the beautiful doll.

It was nice walking down the street, just the two of us. As I looked up at her I saw a woman who was still young, slim and beautiful with her long, black, plaited hair, and her green, cat-like eyes. She was wearing a headscarf, a white *shalwar-kameez* beneath a camel coat and chocolate-brown shoes. I felt safe and secure holding her warm hand like I had never been before. I felt like I'd been wrapped in cotton wool, or a hundred silk saris.

As we walked she was teaching me English. Abu had already instructed me to call the teacher 'Madame,' which she found quite charming I think, for the rest of the children called her 'Mrs Howard.' Ummi was saying that if you do something wrong to somebody, for example, if you accidentally step on their toes, you say, 'Excuse me.' I tried to twist my tongue around the words, but all that came out was 'Eskweez me?'

'Nahin, EkSCIUZe me!'

And I thought she was *so* clever to know such English words, and we walked on, I occasionally looking up and quietly adoring this beautiful young woman who was my mother.

As we entered the playground, we saw it was empty except for one girl a little older than me. She had dirty blonde, unkempt hair, cut in a bob. She was wearing a grey pullover, a tartan skirt, and her blue, calf-length socks had collapsed around her ankles, spilling onto her black buckled shoes. She was standing with one hand on her hip, her right foot occasionally scratching her left calf. Her small blue eyes were screwed up against the light, one eye more squinted than the other. Behind her hostile look, I could see the faintest of smiles. I couldn't reconcile the two.

I realised we were late. Ummi had forgotten where my classroom was so we walked warily across to the girl and Ummi asked her for directions. The girl pointed to a metal staircase which we proceeded to climb after thanking her. As we climbed the steps Ummi took the opportunity to tell me about the expression, 'Thank you.'

'When someone helps you, or gives you something, you must say: Thank you.'

'Thankiyoo.'

'Thank ...YOU. Or you can just say: Ta. You can say that can't you?'

I nodded, 'Ahum, TA!'

When we reached the top of the staircase, just as Ummi was about to clasp her hand around the handle of the black door, the girl shouted, 'No actually, it's over there,' pointing to a building downstairs. Ummi paused for a few seconds, looked down at the building and its door, and then we walked back down, Ummi's court shoes clicking loudly against the metal steps, one gloved hand holding onto the rail to steady herself, the other gently guiding me down. When we reached the bottom, the girl said, 'No, it's up there,' pointing up the stairs again. Once again, my Ummi smiled gratefully, but this time uncertainly and said nothing except, 'Oh ... thank you.'

As we turned and started up the stairs again, this time in subdued silence, I started to feel the first inklings of humiliation but I didn't know exactly what to say to help my mother out. I couldn't say anything to the girl because the only English words I now knew were:

'Madame,'

'Hello,'

'Excuse me' and

'Oh, thank you.'

The girl was clearly making fun of my mother and I hated her and wanted to cry.

Ummi squeezed my hand and said, 'Don't cry. Be strong. You must never cry in front of people like this.' I will always remember the feel of her gentle strength when she squeezed my hand.

As I fought back my tears I heard a friendly voice behind me. 'Are you lost?'

Ummi and I turned round to face a teacher we had never met before.

'Are you looking for Mrs Howard's class?' she smiled.

Ummi nodded.

Before she led us to my classroom, she raised her chin slightly and shouted to the girl, 'Haven't you got a class to attend, young lady?'

And then to Ummi, 'I was watching through my classroom window and wondering what was going on!'

As we made our way to my classroom, I turned and looked back at the girl. My eyes held her small blue eyes for a long time. What had been a paradoxical expression - a smile behind hostility - I now recognised as a smirk. And the smirk had got bigger, more covert, revealing itself like a fresh stain darkening on a clean dress. She stared back, without flinching.

As we passed the toy shop at home-time I stole a glimpse of the doll's face. I still wanted her. The evening light made her skin seem translucent and highlighted her eyelashes making them, *I swear*, more purple than ever. She seemed to be saying, 'You will see that look - that stain - many more times.'

She Loves Me, Yeah.

Vicky Grut

South Africa, 1968

Linda sat by herself at break time, looking out over the netball courts where the sun lay in merciless sheets. Behind her the six and seven year olds played in the big, fluffy flower bushes, hopping in and out and crushing the pink and white blooms underfoot until a teacher came past and screamed that they were not allowed in there. The girls and boys scattered like spilled beads.

Linda was nine. There were no more boys in her class now. They had gone on to the big boys' school by the river. Linda was sorry. She remembered Simon, all red and freckled, always making jokes; Ian, pale and dark haired - gone now. Last year she used to watch them swarming about in the playground and think about Ian falling and being hurt. She liked to imagine him with blood on his head; she saw herself stroking his hair. She had barely spoken to him but still she dreamed of his head on her lap, his quick, irritable eyes half-closed, his face, pale, pale, under the beating sun, like a soldier.

Sometimes Linda thought about the war - the great war and that American one - and she worried. Sometimes when a plane went by overhead she had the idea that they might not know that the great war was over and be coming down to drop bombs. There was a waste paper basket in her parents' room, where Ma threw her face tissues, smeared with lipstick and foundation and thick, white face cream. It had a picture of two

193

soldiers on the side: one man standing by a horse. This was how Linda imagined the soldiers in that American war, sad and young, hot sun on their tin suits. But Daddy said it was quite safe. The great war had been over more than twenty years, and even Vietnam, which had been going on for almost half of her life, was very far away. Down here in Africa they were quite safe Daddy said, absolutely, perfectly safe.

At school things seemed to get slower and more dangerous without the boys. There were more silences to be filled, more details to be noticed, smaller differences to be remarked on. Today some of the girls in Linda's class stood clustered into a knot near the music block. They leaned in with their heads close together, hissing to one another like angry geese, snatching sideways looks at Pauline Anderson. Linda caught scraps of it as she walked past to sit on the step. *('Disgusting, my mum says it's disgusting!')* Trudy's mother had heard about it from someone at the doctor's and she'd told Trudy and Trudy had told everyone else in the class: 'Disgusting,' they hissed under the bright, clear sun. 'It's ten years since she had the last one! Shame on her. She's old! She should know better, that's what my mom says.'

Prissy little Pauline walked alone in her spotless uniform: white ankle socks, the regulation blue shift neatly belted at her waist, short brown hair pinned back on one side of her head. She was pretending not to know what they were talking about. Only last week, she'd been one of the popular ones so it was probably hard for her.

Linda was neither popular nor unpopular. Linda kept her mouth shut and their eyes off her. She couldn't afford to stand against these puzzling, volcanic furies; they rose and fell without warning, always swarming about looking for a new object. What was this all about? Why was it so disgusting? It only meant that there was another baby coming. Linda didn't want to ask because not knowing might make her disgusting too.

Ma came to pick Linda up from school and they stopped off at Ouma's house on the way so that Ma could have her dress fitted. Ouma's house was like some long, dead animal. The door was its mouth and from there the corridor ran right through to the end like a spine, with rooms opening off, one either side. The left side belonged to Ouma: the unused front room, the long living room, Ouma's bedroom, the pantry. Everyone else lived on the right. First Auntie Adele looking out on the street, then Pops, then the bathroom, then Esther in the kitchen, banging pots and pans over the old coal stove, then Esther's bedroom, opening out onto the porch. The others left Ouma alone in her side of the house. She was always there, perched on the edge of the sofa in the living room, waiting for someone to come by. She even slept there sometimes. It was the biggest room; it was the centre of the house. Ouma sat in it like a heartbeat, listening to the muffled sounds of her family all around, watching as they walked past, always on their way to somewhere else, calling out to them as they went: 'I've got a nice little piece of lamb for supper now!' or, 'Don't forget your raincoat, my angel!'

It was funny to think of Ouma and Pops married. Linda hardly ever saw them together except when Ouma came in to Pops' room to bring him cups of tea or sandwiches. They looked like figures from two different sets of toys, even their names were from different vocabularies. Pops was tiny and rat-like, thin with dry, shiny-pink skin and no hair. He stayed in bed most of the time because he wasn't well. He sang songs and did tricks; Ouma didn't. She sometimes sang but only to get a child to sleep, she didn't know any jokes. But she smiled when you wanted smiling at.

Sometimes when Linda stayed overnight, Ouma would let Linda come into her bed and lie in the shade of her broad back. Ouma was three times as big as Ma and yet she could sleep balanced right on the very edge of the bed all night without falling onto the floor. She could knit a fancy pattern and talk at the same time; she could keep the keys down the front of her dress without losing them; and walk on the outside of her feet. Linda watched her now, sitting on the edge of the sofa with her great grey knees spread open and straining at the edge of her skirt so that she could lean forwards and work. Ma turned to and fro in the half-made dress rimmed with pins and white tacking while Ouma's hands travelled along each seam, letting out or pinching in the cloth as she needed to. Ma was talking about how they'd put up the price of bread again and Daddy thought that would mean trouble.

'I don't want to frighten you but I think you must lock the windows at night, okay Mommie?'

Linda lay on the carpet and studied its pattern. You could still see what a wonderful thing it had been once. There were leaves and grapes and curling gold patterns on a maroon background, dripping red roses, plumed birds, dull and worn down to a stump but still there, a storybook carpet. Linda scratched against the weave with her finger; little tendrils of dust caught at her nostrils. She sneezed: glory dust. Ma looked over and said,

'Don't put your tongue on the carpet Linda. It's full of germs.'

Suddenly Linda saw that the carpet wasn't that beautiful after all. It often happened like this. Just a glance from Ma and the light changed and Linda saw things differently. Linda thought that Ouma looked a little sad then.

'I wish you'd let me buy a vacuum cleaner,' Ma said, and now Linda saw the spiders on the picture rail, the beginnings of dust balls under the sofa.

'Turn a little,' Ouma murmured through the fur of steel pins in her mouth as if she hadn't heard. Linda got a sour, unkind feeling in her stomach. Ouma was so big; she didn't want to feel sorry for Ouma. It was all the wrong way round.

'Little more,' said Ouma and Ma lifted her arms and turned; the silk shift swung like a bell around her thighs. Light shone in through the leaves of the loquat tree in the yard, covering her from the top of her yellow perm to her gold-thonged sandals with the fake red green jewels. She looked like an angel, thought Linda. One day she, Linda, would be like that too, though it was hard to believe. Last week she'd been watching Ma put on her lipstick and Ma had said,

'I'll show you how to do this for yourself when you're a bit older. You've got a difficult mouth - no Cupid's Bow and too much on the lower lip - but I'll show you how you can make the best of it.'

And Linda smiled and put it straight out of her mind because it seemed so foreign to her now, but one day she was sure she would want to know about such things.

'Keep still Baby,' Ouma said, through her mouthful of pins.

'Ow,' Ma snapped, rubbing at her leg, 'You scratched me.'

'Sorry,' said Ouma humbly.

In school assembly Mrs Gerber liked to read a passage from the Bible after she'd made the announcements for the day. Then they would all stand up and sing a hymn and say the Lord's Prayer and after that they would be allowed to march out, single file, following their teachers back to their classrooms.

'Today, children,' said Mrs Gerber, beaming at them kindly and distantly from the stage, 'Today I am going to read to you from the book of Genesis about the story of Abraham and Sarah. Do you know the story of Abraham and Sarah, children? I'm sure you older girls do. Abraham was the father of Isaac who was the father of Jacob whose twelve sons gave their names to the twelve tribes of Israel ...'

Linda shifted around a bit in her patch of space. It was going to be very hot later; already her legs were sticking with sweat, picking up tiny pieces of grit from the wooden floor. There wasn't much room to move. Her class made up two of the rows towards the front of the hall, looking over the heads of the babies; behind them stretched the rest of the school. Year by year they would move through these rows like a ripple until they got to the top of the school. The Standard Five girls were allowed to sit on chairs, their shoes pressing into the backs of the Standard Four girls.

'... so you see God made a covenant with Abraham. Does anybody know what a covenant is?'

The girl behind Linda leaned in and whispered very quietly, 'Can I play with your hair?'

Linda kept her head straight to the front as if she hadn't heard. The hands came anyway, lifting the weight of Linda's ponytail away from her neck, fingers combing gently through her hair, accidentally making needle-pains in her scalp now and then. There were certain girls who always wanted to do this, little hands clutching and stroking in the dark as they watched films or listened to stories. They weren't even girls she liked much, or girls who talked to her at other times; it was just a kind of compulsion with them, like chewing gum or picking scabs. Sometimes they undid the ribbon and elastic on her ponytail and then Linda felt in a kind of panic as if she was falling down, coming unravelled. She hated it. If the teachers saw you talking or fidgeting they would dart in from their seats along the side walls, or they'd pull you out of line afterwards and then you were in trouble.

But the teacher wasn't looking at Linda. There was a current running through the two rows of their class, something electric and barely suppressed. The teacher knew it and was watching for the place that it would erupt; the leaky place.

'... And God said to Abraham, As for Sar'ai your wife, you shall not call her name Sar'ai but Sarah. I will bless her and moreover I will give you a son by her; I will bless her, and she shall be the mother of nations; kings of peoples shall come from her.' Mrs Gerber's kind, gravelly voice floated out over their heads. 'Then Abraham fell on his face and laughed to himself and said to himself. Shall a child be born to a man who is *a hundred years old?* Shall Sarah who is *ninety years old* bear a child?'

Someone started giggling in the row behind Linda; others were shuffling and nudging each other, all bare arms and legs, and shoes knocking against the wood. Linda turned her head carefully to find where Pauline sat.

'And Abraham said to God ...' Suddenly Mrs Gerber broke off in her reading and peered down into the hall. 'What is it girls? What's going on down there? Mrs van der Merwe could you ...?'

Their teacher picked her way along the row until she came to Pauline. She hauled her up, limp and sobbing, like a drowned bird, and took her outside. Now the whole class would get into trouble, Linda thought gloomily, for shaming themselves in front of the school.

'Dear me,' said Mrs Gerber. 'Face the front please everyone. Face the front and pay attention. You're not at the circus.'

For some reason Linda had the feeling that Ouma was a bit sad that day. When she opened the door to them she seemed to be sagging more than usual in her big, flowery satin dress. Ma was brisk as usual, glancing at her watch just after she kissed Ouma's cheek.

'I can't stay long today Mommie,' she said. 'I've got the carpenters coming this afternoon and the traffic is terrible.'

'Just a few minutes, that's all I need,' said Ouma, shuffling ahead of them in her slippers. From the front room came the bright blare of Adele's transistor radio.

'Did the man come to fix that window then? I told him to come.'

Ouma nodded. 'Are you hungry my chookie?' she said, smiling over at Linda. 'You want to go and get a sandwich from Esther in the kitchen?'

Linda shook her head. Ma stepped out of the dress she was wearing and put on the half-finished one, zipping it up as she walked across the room to inspect the window. She lifted away the curtains and frowned.

'He hasn't painted it!'

'Ag, my darling, it doesn't matter,' said Ouma. 'No-one can see it.'

'It does matter,' Ma said irritably. 'I paid him to do a proper job. I'll tell him to come back and finish it properly. You've got to keep an eye on these people, you know that Mommie!'

Ouma sighed. She sat down on the sofa and rubbed her knees, veined and swollen from the rheumatism. She smiled weakly at Linda.

'Pauline Anderson's mother is having another baby,' Linda said. Both Ma and Ouma were looking at her now. Linda examined their faces for signs of disgust but there were none.

'That'll be a big gap. Almost like me and Adele,' Ma said.

'Anderson?' said Ouma, frowning with the effort of re-membering. 'Anderson? Isn't that Hennie le Grange's daughter? The one who was chasing after Lawrence like that before you were married?'

Ma waggled her eyebrows like she did when she didn't want Linda to hear something. 'A new baby, eh?' she said. 'That'll be exciting for Pauline.'

'It's not,' said Linda. But Ouma and Ma were busy on the dress again. *('How does it feel under the arms? Is it pinching you?', 'Don't pull Mommie!')*

Linda went to sit on the window ledge. Imagine, she thought, if Pauline's mother had married Daddy instead of Ma, would she still have been herself but just a bit different? Pauline on the outside and Linda inside, or a bit of both all the way through, like some kind of two-coloured ice-cream? It was almost too difficult to think about.

From Adele's room came the sound of the record player going at full blast: '*I wanna hold your ha-a-a-aand. I wanna hold your haaaand ...*'

'Can I go and talk to Auntie Adele then?'

'No,' said Ma.

'Why not?'

Adele was exciting. She had a candle in a wine bottle on her mantelpiece and a box with a hundred different kinds of beads. Once she'd been over to the petrol station across the road and got a can of petrol to put in her room because she liked the smell. Sometimes she wore a coloured band around her head.

'She's supposed to be studying for her exams,' said Ma. 'Though how she can work with all that row...' and then to Ouma squinting down at the hem, 'You can take it up a little bit more I think.'

'More?' Ouma shook her head. 'You'll get a cold on your kidneys my darling.'

Ma rolled her eyes and laughed. 'Get with it Mommie!'

Linda looked away.

'*I wanna hold your ha-aaand ...!*'

Sometimes Linda wished for a mother who wasn't 'with it'. She thought it would be nice to have one like everyone else's: a mother who wasn't always in a hurry, who didn't go out to work but sat at home knitting cardigans, darning socks, making cakes and bread for her children; a mother who would never dream of wearing trousers or mini skirts, whom no-one looked at twice in the streets. Sometimes it made her throat go tight when she saw other children in their hand knitted cardigans, wearing their mothers' thoughts around their shoulders all day. But Ma would never be like that. She was always in a hurry and machine-knitted was so much neater she said.

'What a life!' she said. 'What do they talk about at the end of the day?'

Esther stood in the doorway, wiping her hands on her apron. 'What must I buy for tonight?' she said to Ouma.

'Shall I get Esther to fetch us some nice pork chops?' Ouma looked over at Linda, pretending a certain casualness. 'Linda always enjoys a nice little chop don't you my angel?'

'For heavens sakes Mommie, I've told you, we're going in a minute!'

There was a silence. Ouma took another pin out of her mouth and slid it into the cloth at the hem.

'Why don't you leave Linda here with me? She can stay the night. Would you like that my chick?'

'I don't know. She has school in the morning...'

'Esther can walk her over. It's only five minutes from here.'

'Do you want to stay Linda?' said Ma. They were all looking at her now: Ouma, Ma, Esther.

'Stay with your old Ouma tonight,' Ouma smiled, soft and wobbly as oil. 'We've still got some of that *melktert*, haven't we Esther?'

Esther nodded. She shifted her weight onto one foot. She pushed one finger under her head cloth and scratched at her scalp, waiting for them to make up their minds. *Krik-krik-krik-krik-krik* went Esther's nail on her head.

'You can have a nice piece of *melktert* for dessert. Or Esther will make you some jelly, won't you Esther?'

Esther nodded without smiling.

'Do you want to stay?'

Linda clenched her teeth. Outside the wind was rising. Sometimes, when she was at home and it was really windy, she climbed the tree in front of the house and sat as high in it as she could. Whenever the leaves fell back to rest, the wind would dive in and clutch at her as if it would pick her up and fling her for miles. She imagined how it would go: out across the town, past the hospital where people climbed the front stairs with stiff flowers and others sat waiting shabbily at the back, past the university, over the patch of green with its marked out benches, past the black church and the white school and the powder house that the Dutch built and the rugby ground where they sometimes played cricket, past the ugly little modern church where people got married and brought everyone there to see it, and beyond even this to the farms with their fields of grapes, laid out in solemn rows and given so much space, where the people walked barefoot on the dirt roads and women tied their heads in little rag cloths and the children walked miles to the two-roomed school because this was how it was; this was how it was.

For Ma, Ouma must have been that other kind of mother, Linda thought. Ouma would always have been there; never criticising, never busy when Ma needed her, always making time. Linda had that hot and scratchy feeling again.

'Linda?' said her mother.

'No,' said Linda suddenly and she turned and buried her face in her mother's skirt like a baby. 'No. I don't like it here. I want to go home. I want to be with Ma and Daddy.'

Ouma watched with soft eyes. Even this, thought Linda, even this won't make her not love me. What is the point of love like this? Anyone could have it.

'So what shall I get then?' said Esther, still standing, expressionless in the doorway. Ouma jumped as if she had forgotten about Esther.

'Ag,' she said slowly, 'just see whatever he's got cheap.'

Grandchild

Geraldine Kaye

extracted from a novel in progress, ***Late in the Day.***

'I think ...' Lottie's sad down-slanting eyes widened like lakes and seemed to fill her entire face.

'Fran, I think you'd better phone the hospital.'

'All right, if you're sure ...' Francesca said.

The ambulance slid to the kerb and Lottie walked along the passage and across the pavement with an air of concentration.

'There's a good girl then,' the ambulance man said cheerily as he opened the back doors. Francesca followed with the plastic bag which served as a suitcase.

'Oh, where is Hugo?' she murmured looking over her shoulder back along the road.

'Bit pressed for time, love,' the ambulance man said nodding her into the ambulance where Lottie was bending forwards, her belly clutched in the circle of her arms. 'Can't hang about with number four, know what I mean?'

'Sorry,' said Francesca, clambering in. 'It's my son should be here. Hugo.'

'Oh!' Lottie whispered and grabbed Francesca's hand, twisting hard as the contraction rose through her body like a ring of fire.

'Easy does it, love,' said the ambulance man.

Going up in the hospital lift, Lottie still held Francesca's hand but she seemed scarcely aware of her surroundings. As if her eyes as well as her consciousness were turned into her body. The waters broke as they got to the labour ward.

'Do you want me to stay until Hugo comes?' Francesca said tentatively - Lottie must know about the abortion she had suggested ... well, recommended and offered to pay for privately; Hugo chronically unemployed; three skimpy little children reared on Social was enough, surely? Perhaps Lottie would feel her presence was an ill-wishing one. Unlucky.

'I'd rather have you here anyway,' Lottie said, staring at the white mountain of her belly. Francesca was touched. Why was she so reluctant to be there, she wondered? Why had she felt so strongly about this baby anyway?

As a young woman her own fecundity had thwarted both her and Freddy's attempts to control it. Freddy had ultimately accepted the two boys with indifferent grace but he had refused absolutely to let her continue her three subsequent pregnancies. If she did, he said he would leave her. The doctor was no help under the old law. She had wandered down a mean back street with an address scribbled on a bit of paper but even that was more than they could afford. Francesca had got a book from the public library in the end. She was ignorant but had never been frightened by the intricacies of her own body.

'Oh!' said Lottie twisting suddenly. 'Oh-oh-oh!' Her cries rose like a seagull's and died away.

'Shall I get someone?' Francesca said.

'Not yet,' said Lottie closing her eyes. Limbo, Francesca thought, there was nothing to be done but wait.

Squatting on the bathroom floor she had studied the diagrams and soaked her hands in Dettol. She had felt the tiny sac, pulled at it with her fingertips hard as she could. Nothing happened but two specks of bright blood on the bathmat. She had had to fetch Hugo from infant school at half-past three. Spilt milk streamed across the supper table.

'I've had enough,' Freddy had said picking up his chop and two vegetables and striding away to his study. 'We have both had quite enough. Too bloody much.'

'Another one coming,' Lottie panted, trying to smile. 'Did they ever give you raspberry leaf tea?'

'Won't be long now,' Sister said burrowing briskly. 'You're fully dilated, Mrs Smith. We'll get you up to the delivery room in a jiffy.'

'Oh, where *is* Hugo?' Francesca said desperately. He should be here - whatever Lottie said, a husband should be there. Freddy might have liked his children better if he had seen them born.

'Please stay, Francesca,' Lottie murmured. Her face looked drawn and grey against the white of the hospital gown. 'Please come up with me.'

'Only husbands and mothers in the delivery room, if you please,' Sister said, her blue eyes inquisitorial. She resented the fashionable invasion of what had once been her private domain. 'Are you Mrs Smith's mother?'

'Course she is,' Lottie said tilting back her head as the trolley slid away down the corridor. 'Come on, Mum ...'

'Coming,' Francesca said. Lottie needed her, needed Sister and the little pink-faced nurse too.

Francesca had needed someone that night. They had gone to the Odeon Cinema which was a breakthrough. Having made his views on further children known, Freddy had not spoken to her for two weeks. In the middle of *Look Back In Anger* the pains had started, hot blood trickling and then gushing against her thighs. She had had to run out to the

Ladies, sat there in the urine-scented gloom, hearing the blood plop out of her and trying to stuff her pants with toilet paper until she passed out on the floor. Freddy's name was flashed on the screen.

'For God's sake why didn't you tell me?' Freddy said afterwards. How she had bled - they had called an ambulance.

'A deep breath, Mrs Smith, take a deep breath,' Sister said, pulling on her rubber gloves. Above, the mirror stared down like a round silver eye. 'Hang on a moment, dear.'

'Can't,' said Lottie huskily, but her voice was lost as her body took control, shaking her violently. Francesca stared at the mirror hypnotised - Lottie's knees and the black patch of pubic hair and the scarlet rush. A long, low moan, a cow-like bellow. Too bloody much.

'*Push*, dear, *push*, Mrs Smith.' A round head shot out, yellow hair, flat against a palpitating scalp. Another loud bellow and the whole length of blood-stained child slid from between her legs swinging in Sister's hands.

'There you are,' she said. 'A lovely little girl.'

'A girl,' Francesca breathed. What had that other child been, she wondered?...the Odeon was a Bingo Hall now.

'Francesca,' Lottie said as she closed her eyes. 'We'll call her Francesca.'

Charity

Michèle Roberts

I have a young erotic mother. Her hair, shiny and black, curves round her face and flops forward into her large dark eyes. She has an olive skin, olive eye-lids, straight black brows. Her mouth is big and wide, her lips plump and rosy as cushions over her large white teeth. Today she's wearing a long dull green mac buttoned down one side and tightly belted around her narrow waist, high-heeled ankle boots, and a red beret, and she's slung her bag diagonally across her front like schoolchildren do.

It's raining. Neither of us has an umbrella, so we walk along arm in arm under the colonnades, up and down, up and down. It's lunchtime. Most people are inside eating. The yellow and grey city seems empty. Except for us. Talking as we pace, exchanging stories as fast as we can. Months since we've seen each other, so many words to turn over in our hands and offer each other like pieces of new bread torn off the still warm loaf. Then she makes up her mind, and invites me home.

We shake ourselves in the hallway like two wet dogs. She pulls me after her into the bedroom to find me some dry clothes. We watch each other undress. Slither of a rose-coloured slip, of seamed black stocking. She turns down the blue quilt on the bed, and I slide in next to her. My mother's flesh is warm. The sheets are cool and smooth. I lay my hands on her hips and pull her close, kiss her soft mouth, her

shoulders, stroke her hair, the wet silky place between her
legs. The storm drums on the roof. She kisses and caresses
me. Her smell grows stronger, like a garden after the rain. She
offers me her breast, round and white and fat, ardently we lie
in each other's arms, touching kissing sucking biting, then my
swollen cunt boils over and I come.

I wake up from the dream disconcerted, still fizzing. I'll tell
it to Gabriella tomorrow when we're having breakfast together
at my kitchen table, and she'll laugh. She'll be dipping a sweet
biscuit into her little cup of black coffee, her feet tucked up
under her, comfortable amongst the cushions of the basket
chair, her profile alert against the white wall, and then she'll
light a cigarette, impatient to tell me *her* dream. Her presence
unleashes our words. We're off. Each time we see one another,
this jostling at the start, glad galloping down the track of
stories. After knowing her for twenty years.

[2]

Auntie's kitchen smelled of the damp washing which we hung
on a pulley above the fireplace and on racks in front of it. Our
woollen jumpers, the sheets and towels, made a moist tent
over our heads. The floor was brown lino, bruised and dull.
The sink and draining-board were tin. We had a cupboard for
food and crockery, a tea-trolley on which we kept the iron and
the radio, and a table at which we ate, read, played cards,
filled in the football coupon. It was a crowded place, things
everywhere: saucers full of cigarette stubs and ashes, piles of
old magazines, piles of clothes ready for ironing, our
wellingtons stood against the back door and our two bicycles
leaned against the wall nearby. We didn't have a garden shed
so we kept the spade and rake in a corner, together with a sack
of compost and a pile of wooden seed-trays.

The kitchen was dark, as though it was always winter. We had a standard lamp with a flowered shade that stuck out like a skirt, and a smaller lamp on the table for reading by. Auntie was a great reader, starting with the morning paper and going on to the magazines people gave her, Whitaker's Almanac, a dog-eared gardening book, and crime novels from the library. When it rained we set a bucket to catch the drips. We were quite cosy, jammed up together by the fire, Auntie in her chair with an ashtray balanced on the worn arm, the dog on her feet, and me on the old leather pouffe holding the toasting-fork. Sometimes we had toast with pork dripping for tea, if it was a Monday. The best was sausages, which Auntie taught me to fry over the open fire. There was a perfectly good cooker in the corner, but we both preferred this sort of cooking, like camping. The sausages were beef, tight and shiny they rolled in their spluttering fat. We liked them black and charred, then we clapped them between thick slices of white bread and butter. The softness of the white bread, the heat of the sausage melting the butter to gold puddles that dripped down my chin, swallows of warm tea alternating with bites of sausage sandwich, this was a banquet. The dog got the crusts.

The little estate of council houses near the railway line was built to look like cottages grouped around a central green. Low brick houses, with plain front doors with little wooden porches over them, plain windows with sashes and sills. Built in the twenties I think. Cramped inside, but not ugly to look at, not like the modern blocks and high-rises, and, out the back, gardens that ran gaily into one another, separated only by low withy fences. At the bottom of the gardens was the railway line. Auntie showed me how to leave pennies on the track for the trains to flatten. Sometimes they struck sparks. That was the best route home from primary school, along the little embankment thick with rose bay willow herb and cow parsley. I learned the names in nature study. It was a wild place. I could lie hidden in the long grass, its purple fringes waving above my head, and stare at the sky and listen out for the trains. If it was raining or snowing I came home the short way, by the road, and Auntie would hang my socks and gloves to dry in front of the fire and let me have hot Marmite.

Auntie was not what you would call a good-looking woman most of the time, except in the afternoon when she got tidied up for her visitors. She was tall, with a jaunty face. She didn't look anything like the other children's mothers, the ones who waited for them outside the school railings and wore bunchy blouses and full flowered skirts. Auntie wore men's jeans, thick and straight, in heavy indigo, big sweaters. She put her hair up, morning and night, into a turban, and brushed it down in the afternoons when she put on a frock. She always wore bright red lipstick and could talk with a cigarette in her mouth. Sometimes she seemed very old to me, and sometimes more like a boy. She let me play with her curlers, pierced metal cylinders with loops of black elastic, and with her big wrinkled hairpins. One of my treats, when I'd been good, was going into her handbag to see what she'd got, another was helping to wash her hair in the bath, carefully tipping jugs of water over her head until she was done.

That was the same jug Auntie used for me when I had colds, enamel, with stains inside. She put a brown capsule, thick and squashy, in the bottom, then covered it with boiling water. I sat by the fire with a towel over my head and inhaled the steam of the melted capsule, so rich and hot I almost choked. Then she made me go to bed early with Vick rubbed on my chest and a mug of hot orange. She made me take cod liver oil and halibut liver oil and gave me boiled sweets afterwards as a reward. My other great reward for being good was being allowed to go by myself to children's cinema on Saturday morning, with three pence extra for a bag of chips on the way home. Being good meant not getting home from

school until four o'clock each day in the week, by which time
the last of the visitors would have gone and Auntie would be
putting the kettle on for tea. Nor was I allowed to disturb
Auntie early on weekend mornings. We never had dinner on
Saturdays and I liked this. I was free to eat my chips while
dawdling along the High Street, and then to play all afternoon
on the embankment. Auntie would come from the pub, have
her sleep, and then we'd have tea together and listen to the
radio.

Before she went to the pub Auntie would do the shopping
in the market. Tea on Saturday was always a good one. We
both loved fried potatoes with onions. Or we'd have a rasher
of bacon, or mushrooms on toast, or sausages. I always made
the cocoa last thing, she said I made cocoa better than anyone.
If it was a weekday I had to polish my shoes ready for the
morning, then I'd read comics or a book in bed until it was
time to turn the light off. Have you said your prayers she'd
ask. And I'd say yes. Then she'd pull the blankets up round my
ears, kiss me, and go. Her kiss tasted of cigarettes. If I had a
nightmare or if I couldn't go to sleep she let me come and
sleep in her bed. It sagged a bit. We slept together in the dip in
the middle. Under the thick warmth of her pyjamas she was
both bony and soft. I'd wriggle to get into a good position,
she'd grunt at me to quiet down, she smelled of face cream.
She didn't put her curlers in till the morning, she said they hurt
too much to sleep in.

She was a mixture of easy-going and strict. I could fiddle
about in her make-up drawer, or the box of old clothes she
kept for dressing-up, or her envelope of photos of when she
was young. As long as I didn't break anything through care-
lessness she didn't mind. When I was small she perched me on
the crossbar in front of her on her bike and rode me round and
round the little green at the front of the houses. Then she
taught me to ride my own bike. She got me some roller-skates

from a jumble sale, with small metal wheels and worn leather straps, and waved me off. But she didn't much like me mixing with other children and never let me bring friends home to tea. I went to other children's houses for tea at first at primary school, then less and less because I couldn't invite them back. We'll keep ourselves to ourselves, she always said. She took me to Mass on Sunday evenings, and we sat at the back. Once when the priest came to visit she slammed the door in his face. The first and only time I forgot not to come home straight from school and walked into the house without knocking and went to find her in her bedroom she yelled at me and threw me out. When she came to find me she slapped me. She was very firm about washing hands after the toilet, please and thank-you, things like that. But she didn't mind me getting filthy in the garden digging in the patch she gave me next to the sweet peas, or trying to cut my own hair like I did one time, or re-peating the rude words and rhymes I learned in the playground. When she laughed it was a hoarse sound because of all the cigarettes. When she washed my hair for me in the bath she made it stiff in a soapy spike before she rinsed it with the jug. If I didn't cry with the soap in my eyes I got a boiled sweet, then I'd sit on her lap by the fire until my hair was dry and she would talk about winning on the Premium Bonds or on the pools, or the Grand National. We placed our racing bets through the milkman, but we never won anything.

There was an old clock on the mantelpiece, with a soft regular tick. When it chimed, Auntie always exclaimed: ten o'clock struck at the castle gate! If I disagreed with her about anything she would retort: what girl, you dare to thwart me thus? Me making a noise was a schemozzle, mess was a pile of tack, me complaining was a performance. Twelve noon was the sun going over the yard arm and meant you could have a drink. A suit on a woman was a costume. She said I kept my eyes in my stomach and that enough was as good as a feast.

When she burped she said *pardon*. I loved the way she smoked, moistening her cigarette in the corner of her mouth between her red lips or holding it between her thumb and forefinger. She kept her cigarettes in a little silver metal case, held down by an elastic, like a row of babies in bed, and she had a silver lighter she showed me how to fill with petrol. Strike a light darling, she would say, holding up her cigarette, and I would rush to light it for her. She could blow perfect smoke rings, she said she learned how in the army.

It didn't occur to me to question her much about her life before I lived with her. Not until I was forced to become aware, through other children's gibes and rhymes, that she was odd and therefore bad and so I too because I lived with her. She had a brother and sisters, she told me once, all older than her, all emigrated now to Canada and New Zealand. One died of scarlet fever when he was little. A long time ago, well before the war. Then she'd give me a shove: stir a stump. And I'd get off her lap and make the cocoa with the half-pint of milk carefully saved from tea-time. By now the fire would be sunk to a low red mass. Auntie would consider it, frowning as she made her decision, then tip on just a few more coals. To any further questions on my part she'd retort: what you don't know can't hurt you. And that was that.

[3]

Who made you?
God made me.
Why did God make you?
To know, love and serve Him in this life, and to be
happy ever after with Him in the next.

Those are the words printed in the books in front of us on our desks. We know them by heart. It's hard to believe God made us, really, because we can't see Him. Whereas everywhere in the school we've got statues of the Virgin Mary in different outfits. She's far more real. Our nuns belong to the Order of Our Lady of Perpetual Succour. Sister Boniface, known as Ugly Face because of her mole and her moustache, has explained to us many times that perpetual means everlasting, never-failing, while succour is a form of the virtue of charity and means giving and sustaining. The words are written up all over the school in curly script, in here too, over the blackboard behind Ugly Face on a sort of gold banner. Alice, sitting just in front of me, raises her head to look at them, then whispers loudly to Mary, her neighbour: perpetual suck; perfect sucker; and they bend giggly faces over their catechisms.

Ugly Face has been repotting the spider plants she grows on the high tiled windowsills of our classroom. She's forgotten to take off her gardening apron, thick blue cotton tied around her waist with blue strings. The colour of Our Lady's robe, the colour of Nivea Creme tins and the little salt wrappers in packets of crisps. Sitting at her desk like a pulpit she picks earth from under her fingernails while she drones us through our little books. God has no colour because He's an invisible spirit, but everything connected with Our Lady is blue.

Perpetual blessed suck, Alice whispers. Her mouth nuzzles at the words. Mary goes red in the face and coughs. Miss Barney, the biology mistress, complains girls of our age are awful, always whispering and giggling. She's trying to teach us to be good citizens who'll go on to be teachers and lawyers and doctors and she gets cross when we go into fits during her lessons when she says words like breast. She was teaching us respiration and she said: You can feel your heart beating, it's just under your left breast. We all laughed, we were so ashamed she should use such words. Also she asked us how many entrances there were into our bodies and none of us

216

knew. She was shocked. But she's a Protestant so she doesn't count. Mary and Alice and I all chose desks together at the start of this term. Mary's been my best friend up till now, but I'm thinking of asking Alice to be instead. Alice is friends with me but she's friends with the bad girls too, the ones like Karen and Janice who know the name of the sin St. Maria Goretti died rather than commit. A boy stabbed her with a knife because she wouldn't do it. I don't know what it was. The bad girls, Karen and Janice and the others, they talk about things like this in corners, then they look at me and laugh. They whip off their hats the minute they're through the school gates and unbutton their macs, they eat sweets on the street and wear nylons at weekends when the nuns can't see them. They talk to boys too, the black-blazered ones from Haberdashers up the road with long grey flannel legs and broken voices and spots.

This term I've been made form captain. That means having to keep everyone quiet before morning and afternoon assembly and in between classes and when we line up for dinner. The bad girls make a row and I have to report them. They hate me and laugh at me, it makes me very unhappy. Anyway, it's lower-class to be bad. Alice doesn't understand that because her parents are foreigners, her grandparents didn't come to England until the start of the First World War. Alice has got hairs under her arms and at the top of her legs. So have I. Once when I was staying the weekend at her house she pulled out one of her hairs in the bathroom and then showed it to me in the bedroom. It was long and black and curly. Mine are pale. I didn't dare show her one. She laughed at me. That Saturday her mother took me to buy a bra, she said I needed a proper one. The little draper's shop in Golders Green was dark and hot and smelled of scent. The Jewish lady assistant came into the cubicle with a handful of bras and actually touched me. Bend forwards from the waist, dear, she said: bend into it from the waist. She put her hands on my bosoms and pulled them up so they fitted. Very nice dear, she said: very nice.

Ugly Face gets bored listening to us recite the answers from the catechism. I watch her gaze wander over our desks, each one with its sloping wooden lid, inset china inkwell. Like the little houses in packed rows, all the same, down the hill where Mary lives. We're not really all the same of course. Mary's parents are quite poor but definitely not lower-class. They don't have to pay fees for Mary because she's so bright, she won a scholarship after she passed the eleven-plus. On the other hand there are girls here whose parents are rich enough to pay the fees but lower-class. Lots of money but badly-educated. That's why they want their daughters to have a good education. You don't have to pass the eleven-plus to get in here, you just have to pass the entrance exam and be able to pay the fees. I got a scholarship too, like Mary.

The bad girls are lower-class of course, but some of the good ones are as well. You can tell by the pictures they paste on the underneath of their desklids: highly-coloured pictures of the Sacred Heart, big soppy birthday cards of pink kittens and puppies. They're the ones who wear scapulars under their blouses, and cords jangling with tin miraculous medals, all identical. I've got a real Italian mantilla, black lace, that Mary's mother gave me when she came back from holiday, and I've got a picture of Our Lady feeding Jesus stuck under my desklid. It's from the Middle Ages so it's not rude. Modern pictures of women with bare bosoms are rude, that's why Mary's father hides his at the bottom of the wardrobe where he thinks no-one will find them. But we found them that time when we were playing Sardines. I've also got postcards of women dancing in fields by an Italian artist called Botticelli, okayed by Ugly Face because they're art.

Not all art is okay. Sister Wilfred the librarian has pasted little black strips of paper over the rude bits of naked men in the Greek art books. She lets Alice and me use the library because we don't make a noise. We're doing a project on Charity this term in R.E. and we have to do research. We found a book with pictures of the Virtues, who were women from olden times. Justice had a pair of scales, Faith had a sword. Charity was a lady with no clothes on her top under the black bit of paper, feeding four babies at once. I saw a lady do that once in the dentist's waiting-room. She pulled up her jumper, quick as a flash, and I saw her floppy white chest before she pressed the baby's head to it. The waiting-room was small, with a high ceiling and a gas fire. It was gloomy and dark. It was cold, it smelled of leather and dust and gas. I was sitting there praying the drill wouldn't hurt too much and thinking about what the martyrs had to go through and there was that lady with the bare fat chest. All year long I dread the next visit to the dentist and the terrible pain, it's never out of my mind. The minute it's over I start dreading the next time. The drill grinds away, slow and noisy, and you wait for when it will go on a nerve and make you want to scream. I don't scream. I bear it for the Holy Souls in Purgatory. The lady's baby screamed and she pulled up her jumper just as though she was in her own home. The Virgin Mary on my desklid isn't like that. She's far more beautiful than the stupid plaster statues all round the school. When I'm crying my eyes out she's the one I pray to. She knows how much I wish I was thin and popular and pretty with long straight hair and not so clever. She understands all this and she still loves me. She knows why I'm praying so hard the bell will ring for the end of school. Before Janice and Karen can say anything.

The sunshine is like polish on the red tiled floor that the postulants have to wash every week. The postulants have to help the lay sisters with all the heavy housework round the school as a test of their vocations, then some of them, once they're through the novitiate, go on to Catholic teacher training college up in London, and the others become lay sisters. Sometimes the postulants get the laundry muddled up and send us back nuns' bras, huge and loose and floppy. I know a lot about nuns' lives partly because of being a boarder and being closer to them than the day girls are, partly because of reading all the books in the cupboard at the back of the classroom. Lives of the saints. Most of the women saints were nuns. You can't really be a saint if you have a husband. Ugly Face hopes that some of us, once we're in the Children of Mary, will develop religious vocations and join the Order. The best and highest thing a girl can do, is become a nun, but if she hasn't been called by God then she'll become a wife and mother. It's not so high, but it's what most girls end up doing when they leave.

Ex-pupils come back as Old Girls to Parents Day and the Christmas bazaar. Alice's mother is the most stylish. She wears chiffon and silk, big hats, and she has red fingernails. She has a curvy figure and good legs and a crocodile handbag. She told Alice she still makes love with Alice's father, at least once a week. When I go to tea there we have bagels and cream cheese, black bread and gherkins. Once we had pickled herring and another time smoked salmon. Alice's house is full of thick white carpets, armchairs covered in gold plush, cabinets that light up full of grey and blue figurines of ladies dancing, big oil paintings, very modern.

Alice is Jewish but her parents think a convent education can't harm a young girl. All the other schools in the area are either Protestant or secondary moderns. We do elocution and deportment as well as all the other subjects, and next year we'll start ballroom dancing with Sister Agatha. For deportment we have to walk round the hall with books on our heads and curtsey to Ugly Face without dropping them. Then she inspects our fingernails and our white gloves. Last summer we had to kneel on the floor and she measured down from the hem of our tennis-dresses to make sure that they were not too short. Two inches above the floor was all right but no more. Alice sits in on religious education and comes to Mass and Benediction, she's in the choir too, but of course she can't become a Child of Mary. Or a nun. The girls who become nuns have a wedding-day after they've been postulants for six months, then they die to the world. It's very beautiful and sad. They glide up the aisle in their white dresses with their hair spread out down their backs, then the habit and veil are fitted over them and they disappear.

But if you get married and have children you disappear as well. Housewives stay at home all day and talk about recipes and babies, they read women's magazines, they go to the hairdresser's every week and have their hair cut off and have perms. I shall never get married and have children. I might try and go to university, but after that I'm going to become a nun. I shall take a vow of silence and never speak. When the time comes I'll just do it. I wouldn't dream of telling Father Dean. It's bad enough having to go to confession to him and have him call me by my name when he gives me my penance. I'd never tell him what I thought about anything. I tell him the same sins every week, quarrelling with my school friends and talking in the classroom, and he always gives me three Hail Marys.

Ugly Face closes her catechism with a snap. As well as her blue gardening apron she's still wearing her blue over-sleeves, heavy cotton gathered at wrist and elbow. Arms folded in front of her now, hands clasped, blue eyes burning in her white face under their heavy black brows that almost meet. She looks very young, she's got a really peaceful face. Mary's mother says nuns look so young because of their sheltered lives with no responsibilities. By that she means her own work of running the house and bringing up her children and giving piano and dancing lessons. Ugly Face is sorry for Mary's mother because she has to go out to work and can't dedicate her entire life to her family like other girls' mothers do. Only lower-class mothers work. Mary's mother isn't lower-class of course. Ugly Face said we should be charitable. Some women had to work for the good of their families and we shouldn't judge them. They had to get up extra early in the mornings to clean the grates and light the fires and get the children's breakfast. Mary put her hand up and said that her mother didn't do that, she lay in bed with a cup of tea.

In her own way Ugly Face isn't bad. Like now, in her blue gardening apron, when she leans forward with flashing eyes telling us about charity, which means perfect love. Mary's father says that in some countries, like he saw in the war, they think moustaches on women are attractive. That was how he met Mary's mother, in Italy in the war. She came back to England with him and they got married. He became a Catholic to please her and now he's really keen on it, he's Secretary of the Knights of St. Columba and he organises all the parish trips. Ugly Face's moustache is just a thin line above her upper lip. Mary's father noticed it at the school bazaar when he was helping her pack the bran tub. I watched him talking to her, teasing her until she went red and burst out laughing. He was treating her like he treats all us girls. He's quite handsome, Mary's father, with wavy black hair and a little black moustache. Nuns aren't supposed to be like women but Ugly face is. Moles too, Mary's father said, are not unattractive.

Mary's mother was beautiful when she was young, you can see that from the photographs. She says having six children has ruined her figure. Her black hair has a bit of silver in it, at the front, and she wears it in a low bun behind, like a ballerina. She always wears lipstick. She puts it on after lunch, thick and red, and she re-powders her nose, she uses the little mirror of the powder compact from her handbag. I hate women doing that in public, they should do it in secret. But I like seeing the inside of the handbag. And its perfumey smell. Mary's mother can't afford nice clothes though. She makes the children's clothes on her machine and she buys her own clothes from Marks and Spencer. She tries to do things the English way, because Mary's father hates all foreigners except for her, but she's still got a strong Italian accent, especially when she's angry. Foreign food is very oily and greasy but Mary's mother is a really good cook. She says they don't have tinned spaghetti on toast in Italy. She's learned how to cook English food and she's really quite good at it. She can do carrots in white sauce, cauliflower cheese, steak and kidney pudding, scones, lots of things.

That day when they were talking about Ugly Face and whether she was attractive or not I was there for high tea. High tea is lower-class but Mary's father likes it. We were having cold ham and lettuce, beetroot, spring onions, tomatoes and chutney. We have salad cream on our salad and Mary's mother has olive oil, she's not allowed to pour it all over everyone's lettuce, only on her own plate. It was all served in little glass dishes that fit into a round wooden tray. When they bring people back from High Mass for drinks before Sunday lunch Mary's mother fills it with peanuts, cocktail olives, cheese balls and twiglets. Mary and I have to keep offering it round while the grown-ups have gin and tonic and cigarettes. Then we have to lay the table for lunch and wash up afterwards. It's very boring so I offer it up for the Holy Souls in Purgatory. I only hope someone will do the same for me when I am dead. Mary's mother said how sorry she was for Ugly Face, denied her natural fulfilment and knowing nothing of real life. That was after Mary's father said that about women with moustaches. In England you buy olive oil at the chemist's, it's used for earache. After tea, we had to do the washing-up again. The saints had to put up with things like that. The Little Flower had to work in the laundry with a nun who kept splashing her. She offered it all up. It's called the Little Way. It's one of the hardest roads to holiness. Sometimes I think that after I've left university I might put off being a nun for a bit. Alice and Mary and I want to live in London and be bohemians and meet beatniks. So I might put it off.

When I'm staying at Mary's house I can play with her dolls. The best one is Anya. She's got long blonde hair and blue eyes and she's very slim. Mary's garden is quite big, because they're on a corner, it goes round the house on three sides. At the back there's a little sunken lawn with trellises of fruit trees and long thin beds underneath them filled with marigolds and nasturtiums and forget-me-nots. There's a gap in the low brick wall holding up the trees and flower-beds, it's Anya's cave. She gets kidnapped by brigands and kept in the cave, they take all her clothes away and just leave her covered with a rug. She's very brave but she can't escape. The brigand chief says to her that she's his favourite slave. He takes the rug off her and looks at her with no clothes on for a long time. He stares at her breasts. Very quietly he tells her that she's got the most beautiful breasts he's ever seen.

Another of my favourite places is under the soft fruit bushes, under the black netting. You can wriggle in to the far end and it's a completely secret place, black earth and grass and weeds and the raspberry bushes meeting overhead. Anya gets lost in the forest. She's in medieval times, she's run away from her parents' castle dressed as a boy, she's following the robbers' army. She's supposed to hate the robber chief but secretly she's in love with him. He finds her in the forest and makes her his page. Then she has to sleep in his tent. One night he discovers she's not a boy after all but a woman. He sees her with no clothes on, with her top all bare. That's one of my favourite stories. I play it over and over again. Nobody else knows about it except Mary, most girls think dolls are for playing mothers and babies. Grown-ups are stupid. They can't remember what it's like to be my age. I've sworn to myself I'll never forget what it's like to be ten, and now eleven. I don't know why.

I don't remember my parents. Auntie told me they died in a plane crash when I was two, coming back from holiday. I was lucky they left me with my aunt or I'd have been dead too. I don't miss them at all because I can't remember them. I'm lucky because first of all Auntie adopted me, then when I got too much for her the nuns let me be a full time boarder. They want to give me the best possible chance. In olden times orphans had to live in the workhouse and were dependent on charity, the same as the African children are dependent on us nowadays. Charity means people giving loose change. Catholic orphans had the worst time because the English hated Catholics and didn't want them to get good jobs. The Foundress started the Sisters of Our Lady of Perpetual Succour especially to care for the Catholic girls and their babies, her nuns rescued them and put them into their orphanages. They brought them up to be good Catholics and not to be afraid, they got some of them fostered or adopted in good Catholic homes, and they looked after the rest of them in the orphanages. Some of the orphans had mothers but the mothers knew it was in the children's best interests to leave them with the nuns so that they could find jobs and make a fresh start.

Being illegitimate is the worst thing you can be. Another word for it is bastard. It means you haven't got a father and that your mother isn't married and that she did something really terrible and lower-class. It is very shocking and dirty. It's like an extra dose of original sin and it never rubs off. People whisper and point when they see an illegitimate person. Janice and Karen said I was but it isn't true.

Very soon I should think the bell will ring for the end of afternoon school. I hope it does, so that there's no time for the

question and answer session. Janice and Karen have told me
what question they are going to ask and I'm praying the bell
will go before they've got a chance to say it. I'm praying to
Our Lady not to let me down.

The classroom has its own special smell, chalkdust and
polish. It's like being on a ship, sailing along high above the
garden, we're so high up, on the third floor, with the air
blowing through. Sometimes at school I'm very happy, like
when we're all sitting quietly reading our set book and no-
one's torturing me. Last summer, my first year here, we had
some of our lessons outside, sitting in a circle on the grass.
The big lawn has oak trees on it, with benches. That's the only
part we're allowed in, except for the tennis courts below.
Further down is a sort of wild part, with very long grass, and
a pond, and a little path winding in and out of the trees, and a
hut with a statue of Our Lady. I went down there once with
Mary and Alice, it was private and hidden, like being under
the raspberry bushes, only even better because it was
forbidden. We lay in the grass and told secrets.

The thing about the convent that really fascinates me is all
the places we're not allowed. I long and long to know what it's
like inside the nuns' part. It's there so close you can touch it,
but you can't go in. You can't see what it's like. It's dark, and
invisible, you can only imagine it. It's a secret house side by
side with the one you know, like in the story when the girl
walks through the mirror into the world beyond it. The day
girls' houses are ordinary sized and modern, with lots of windows and no dark places or secret places. When I'm staying
with Mary and Alice we can go wherever we want in them.
We know them inside out. There aren't any surprises. Whereas
the convent is over a hundred and fifty years old, the main bit.
You come into the round entrance hall, it's all white pillars
and a carved white fireplace and pictures on the ceiling.
Opposite is the library, done by a decorator called Adam, with

another big white fireplace and more pillars. To the left is the Red Passage, dark and low with red tiles on the floor, which leads to the school part, and on the right is a narrow black corridor, more like a tunnel really, which leads through into the cloister. We turn right into the cloister and get into chapel, into the main part. We're not allowed to turn left, because that's the nuns' cloister, it goes into the convent. More than anything I want to be able to walk around that corner and see what's there. But of course I can't. It's completely impossible. It's a forbidden place. So there's this whole half of the building I'll never be able to see inside. Not unless I become a nun. We're only allowed through the white entrance hall on the way to the chapel. There's a separate entrance for the school, in the big yard, that leads straight into the classrooms. I often pay a visit to the Blessed Sacrament at lunch time so that I can go down the black tunnel and along the cloister.

Ugly Face says the nuns' food is much worse than ours, she says we're lucky to get such good food. We find that hard to believe. We get thin grey meat full of gristle and fat, carrot dice tasting of soap, watery cabbage, lettuce with no salad cream. The chips are best, we get those on Fridays with fried fish which is mostly thick batter. When we have blancmange, which is white and wobbly with a glacé cherry on top, the big girls call it an Agatha. They laugh quietly so Sister Agatha won't hear. St. Agatha was a martyr who had her bosoms torn off. When it's your turn to be a server, you eat after everybody else and you get more food, the kitchen nuns keep it back for you. At table the big girls serve out the food and always give themselves the most. We're not allowed to talk until Sister Agatha rings her little bell, and it's like waiting in the mornings for assembly to begin, it's almost impossible not to talk. Then you have to stand up and own up to talking and everyone looks at you. If you stand up too often you get sent to Sister Superior. She has a terrifying face, white, like a cat's, she has gimlet eyes and a cold quiet voice. Getting sent to see her in her office is the worst thing that can happen to you, apart from being expelled. Two of the boarders got expelled last term, they were found in bed together. I didn't understand why that was so disgusting, Karen and Janice were giggling about it in class, those two girls did something we aren't supposed to know about. I wish I knew what it was. Alice and Mary both knew but they wouldn't tell me.

I am praying and praying to Our Lady that the bell will ring. Ugly Face is looking at the clock and remembering that because of what Pope John has said in the Second Vatican Council she has to encourage us to ask lots of questions in R.E. So she stops talking and tells us to make comments. Karen and Janice look at each other, then Karen puts her hand up.

It's about Charity, she says, it says in the book that Charity means loving everybody but loving men is wrong Sister isn't it unless you're married and even then you can only love one well Sister is it true what everyone says that Marie's auntie went with men for money she was a whore everyone knows that it's true isn't it?

[4]

I always liked the long way home from primary school because striding along the top of the railway embankment I could pretend I was a pirate chief sailing over rough seas in search of booty. That day hunger filled me, the wind in my sails. It drove me through the long sharp grasses between low coils of bramble, nettles and dockleaves, the froth of cow parsley. I skimmed along a narrow path worn by others' feet before mine. Our route was the same. It led home.

I was in a hurry because I wanted my tea so badly and because I wanted to ask Auntie to get me some new plimsolls for Sports Day. Mine were a disgrace, apparently, I had been told off for looking so scruffy. It was my last term at primary school, my last Sports Day. I felt I might stand a chance of winning the hundred yards sprint if I had some new shoes to run in.

The kitchen was empty. I threw my satchel on the table. The dog didn't bother barking a welcome, she was too old and fat, and she was dozing by the grate full of cold ashes. I called out for Auntie as I ran upstairs, and again as I went in through her bedroom door.

The room was dim, the curtains drawn against the afternoon sun. Auntie was resting on the bed. Her eyes were open. A burning cigarette balanced on the ashtray next to her. She was wearing her afternoon frock, the one with mauve and blue flowers on it. It was unbuttoned all down the front. She and the man with her, lay very still, like in a photograph. Perhaps they were not still, perhaps that is the way I choose to remember it. I looked at her bare white bosom, at the man who curled in her arms and sucked at one of her breasts like a baby.

I fled back to the embankment, to my hideout in the long grass. When I reappeared later, at the proper time for tea, she slapped me, angrier than I'd ever seen her. Her hand caught me on the cheekbone and left a bruise. We had sardines on toast. Quite soon after that she decided that since I'd won a scholarship to the convent school I might as well be a boarder. That was after the two ladies from the council came to see her. She said I would have to understand it was all for the best. She sat on the stairs and cried. I'd never seen her do that before. It was then that I realised that something was broken, and that I'd done it.

[5]

I fell in love as fast as possible at university. I chose one of my teachers, because he was a teacher, because he was older, because he was powerful, because he was kindly, because he was glamorous. He took me to Italy. I thought I'd fallen in love with him but it was Italy that captured my heart. I didn't know the difference.

I bought myself a red satin mini-dress with the last of my grant, and gave myself cheekbones with the aid of blusher. Auntie would have called it rouge. She never met my lover because I didn't invite her to. She came up to Cambridge to visit me once and I was ashamed of letting my friends see her. Her old stained mac and her untipped Woodbines and her out of date slang. I punished her for all this, and more, by keeping aloof, not bothering to write. By then she'd moved to Manchester, anyway, and we met rarely. I preferred it that way.

I left my lover on that first trip abroad together. We went to Rome, so that he could attend a conference on linguistics and Renaissance poetry. By day he attended seminars and lectures and I went sightseeing. I kept company with saints, virgins, sibyls, hermaphrodites, angels, madonnas. It was the long vacation, Alice had gone to Switzerland with her parents, and Mary was in Greece with her boyfriend, I knew no-one in Rome. In the evenings we had dinner with my lover's colleagues from the conference. Understanding little of their talk I was mostly silent. I concentrated on the food. At night my lover worked and I read novels.

One day, bored with being a tourist, I accompanied my lover to the Herziana Library at the top of the Spanish steps. Waiting for him to finish work, I flicked through an old book of engravings I picked at random from the shelf. Allegories. The battle of the soul. The Virtues. There she was, Mrs

Charity, feeding four babies from her bare white breast and no black square stuck over it. For some reason, that evening I rang Auntie in Manchester from the hotel. I learned that her funeral had been the week before. Lung cancer. She'd never mentioned it.

Next morning, having made my phonecall to Mary's mother's niece in Vicenza, I left my lover a note, got on a train and fled north. In the hot steamy weather of mid-August we stuck to the fake-leather seats. The carriage was packed with young men on military service going home on leave, talking and laughing, sharing bottles of beer. Sweat rolled down my armpits and my forehead, disguised my tears. Outside the scratched window the tightly-strung vines were pale with heat, the hills a blue blur.

Opposite me, wedged in between the soldiers, sat a plump country woman and her plump daughter. The latter wiped away great drops of perspiration from her face, wriggled and sighed. I could see that she felt her clothes were too many and too tight. Finally she leaned aside and whispered in her mother's ear. The mother nodded and busied herself at her daughter's back, lifting, searching. The daughter blushed and held her head high. She moved one big shoulder, then the other, then shook herself. Triumphantly the mother slid the daughter's bra from out of the back of her clothes. The daughter laughed in relief and pleasure. The soldiers had noticed nothing. I saw Auntie's impassive face as she lay on the bed holding her man-baby. Behind my copy of *Middlemarch* I was still crying but I was laughing too. The daughter slept, head on her mother's arm.

Once we were beyond Florence and had emerged from the tunnels cut through the mountains, the weather broke. Freak thunderstorms tumbled into each other high above our heads. At Bologna, the station was flooded, the underpass was blocked. People waded ankle-deep across the railway lines to clamber onto their trains. We reached Vicenza in the early evening. Gabriella met me at the station. She seemed quite unsurprised by my phonecall, without fuss invited me to stay until I decided what to do next.

We walked through the warm rainy streets under her umbrella. Once in the centre of the city we went along under the colonnades over gleaming grey paving stones. She took me into the Caffè Garibaldi, bought me black coffee and a brandy, sat next to me at the little round marble-topped table while I finished crying. All around us smartly dressed women lit cigarettes and gossiped. Gabriella's head was close to mine. I looked at her big, rosy mouth, her flopping dark hair, her square amber ear-rings, and gulped down my brandy. She began to smile. She nodded at me, waited for me to speak.

Blurting out my story in faulty, childish Italian, I discovered that I could make myself understood. I was alone and separate now, no kindly academic lover to translate for me, mediate between me and the world. Talking in Italian felt truer than my usual English speech. Because another woman sat there, delicate and solid, and listened to me with interest and wanted me to go on. Opening my mouth I tasted ash, I bit into shards of glass, I swallowed dust. The word Auntie meant a warm flannelette back in bed, a tobacco kiss, yet the bed was empty and her mouth gone. I stumbled along, finding Italian words one after the other, rolling them, sour milk, over my tongue: Mrs Charity has had to turn her back, Mrs Charity has had to shut her bedroom door, Mrs Charity has had to go away. I grabbed one of Gabriella's cigarettes and sucked on it.

We crossed the Piazza dei Signori in the steamy drizzle, arm in arm under the umbrella again, Gabriella talking to me about her childhood in the south. Her small flat, high up in a shabby palazzo just round the corner, had a chipped-marble floor and was walled with books. She showed me the shower, the bed, and left me, propping the door open. A shaft of golden light slid in. Wrapped in a quilt, fenced round with pillows, I dozed in the half-dark, listening to the mutter of her typewriter, the soft gaiety of *Don Giovanni* on the record-player. Soon, she'd told me, she'd come in to wake me. We'd have a glass of wine, think about dinner. Her friend Filippo was coming to take us to a restaurant. Until then, rest. The darkness held me like a pair of warm strong arms.

Our Lady of Perpetual Succour Mrs Charity Auntie my young erotic mother.

Biographies

Hilary Bailey spent her early life between two Kent air fields during the Battle of Britain then moved to London in time for the start of the bombing. She attended eleven schools, the reason, she alleges, why she never learned to spell properly or use the semi-colon. She is divorced and has three grown-up children. From 1972-5 she edited the science fiction magazine *New Worlds,* and from 1979-87 was a regular fiction reviewer for The *Guardian.* Her first novel was published in 1975 and was followed by ten others. Her most recent novel, a return to science fiction, is *Frankenstein's Bride.*

Sally Cameron was born in 1961 and grew up in Leeds. She now lives in East London where she divides her time between writing and developing a community garden. Last year she was short-listed for the Ian St. James Award.

Betzy Dinesen worked in publishing for many years before becoming a freelance editor. She compiled *Rediscovery* an anthology of short stories by and about women covering 300 years, and recently started writing fiction and poetry herself. Born in Denmark, she grew up in Surrey and now lives in South London.

Souad Faress was born and brought up in Accra, Ghana, during the struggle for Independence. Her father was Syrian and her mother is Irish/English. They moved to the North West of England when her brother became seriously ill, and as soon as she could she moved to London. She has built a career in acting, while writing for herself ever since she moved to England. *The Lost Bus Stop* is her first published short story.

Chrissie Gittins was born in Bury, Lancashire. Growing up meant realising that her brother got paid more on a Saturday for being a petrol pump attendant than she did for dropping milk jugs into shopping baskets at the Alpine Coffee Lounge. She changed jobs. Then studied at Newcastle University and St. Martin's School of Art. Her poetry has been published in magazines and anthologies, and her feature *Poles Apart* was broadcast on Radio 4 twice in the summer of 1994. *American Tan* is her first published short story.

Bonnie Greer says, 'When I was told at the age of four not to ask why the fat lady's dress stuck out in front because it wasn't nice, I knelt down and poked my head underneath to find out for myself. I've been trying to find out for myself ever since.'

Vicky Grut was born in South Africa in 1961 and lived in Madagascar, Italy and Denmark before moving to England to study Fine Art in 1980. Since that time she has worked in the independent film/video sector, for a small academic publisher and for an international scriptwriting programme. She has completed a collection of short stories (not yet published) and is currently at work on a novel. She lives in London with her partner and four year old son.

Kirsty Gunn grew up in New Zealand, studied English at Oxford and hung about in New York before coming back to London. She has had stories published in *Borderlines, The Junky's Christmas, Obsession,* and *Death and Bereavement* (Serpent's Tail) and a novel *Rain* (Faber, 1994). 'My sister and I both grew up having very close relationships with our grandmothers - something that has continued to interest and inspire us all our adult lives. There is something in what we have of them, I think, in *Nona's Letter.* My starting point was there ...'

Brigid Howarth was born in 1969 and grew up in Dorset. She studied in Manchester and Massachusetts, then came to London and worked in publishing. She is now a freelance arts administrator. She says, 'Many people look back on the place where they grew up with nostalgia, but I only feel a loathing for Britain's Deep South, where Maxine has the misfortune to find herself.'

Mizzy Hussain was born in 1964 in Blackburn, Lancashire where she lived throughout her childhood, apart from two early years in Pakistan. After studying at Robert Gordon's Institute of Technology in Aberdeen, she began to work as an arts administrator. She has been co-ordinator of the Aberdeen Women's Festival and Theatre Coordinator for the Oval House, London. She is currently working for the Mán Melá Theatre Company.

Geraldine Kaye has spent much of her life in London and studied at the London School of Economics. This was followed by eight years spent living and working in Asia and West Africa. Her first book was published in 1958 and she has since written about a hundred books for children and young adults which have been translated into 13 languages. These include *Comfort Herself* which won The Other Award 1985, *Snowgirl, A Breath of Fresh Air,* and *Someone Else's Baby. Forests of the Night* is due out in 1995. She has three adult children and three grandchildren.

Carolyn Partrick was born in Texas in 1951. She emigrated with her family to England in 1964 and has lived in London since 1978. She has trained as a carpenter and as a teacher, and has worked at both of those trades, among others. A lesbian, she has two grown children and a grandson in whom she takes great delight. She has written a radio play which was short-listed in the 1993 London Radio Playwrights' Competition, but which has not been produced. *The Gulf* is her first published short story.

Ellen Phethean was born in South London in 1952. She is a writer and performer with the women's performance poetry group The Poetry Virgins (as heard on Radio 4's *Loose Ends.*) She has had her work published in two Poetry Virgins collections, *Modern Goddess* (Diamond Twig) and *Sauce* (Bloodaxe and Diamond Twig 1994) and broadcast on Radio 4's Poetry Please. She teaches Creative Writing. *War Games* is her first published short story.

Kate Pullinger grew up in British Columbia, Canada, where she dreamed about the world that lay beyond the trees. At 17, she left for Montreal and the Yukon, eventually reaching London where she has remained. Her books includes a collection of short stories *Tiny Lies,* and 3 novels, most recently, *Where does Kissing End?* and the novel of the film *The Piano* (co-written with Jane Campion.) Her new novel *Between,* set in London and British Columbia, marks a profound longing for the forests of her childhood.

Stella Rafferty was born and grew up in Lancashire and moved to London when she was 19. In 1994 she won a prize in the Sheffield Thursday Short Story Competition.

Ravinder Randhawa was born in India and came to England when she was seven years old. Those years of sand, dust, sun, space and sky live like magical motes in memory. She now lives in London. She has published two novels, *A Wicked Old Woman* and *Hari-Jan* and has contributed short stories to numerous anthologies.

Máire Ní Réagáin, born in 1963, entered the academic world at the tender age of 3. In 1967 she gave up 'a promising career' (Máire's mother) when she failed the Babies' Ballet Examination. During the course of her many schools her most notable achievements include a Religious Studies Medal (engraved) and a Major Sporting Award (Egg and Spoon, 1976). She lives in Fulham, can't type, or hold more than 2 pints.

Michèle Roberts found growing up complicated: two cultures, two languages, two religions, two countries to be negotiated; plus being a twin; plus dealing with all the sexual guilt enforced by Catholicism. She has survived to write novels, poems and short stories and to get them published. She has discovered growing-up continues all your life.

Daphne Rock was ten years old when the War began and sixteen when it ended, so that the inevitably changing emotions of those years were augmented by death and disaster, vengeance, fierce patriotism and finally, 'the pity war distilled.' Topsy turvy years which made her both stoic and fighter-for-just-causes. Loves teenagers whom she worked with for many years. Appalled by current educational / law and order policies. Writes plays, stories and poems: a collection of poetry will be published by Peterloo.

Elisa Segrave spent her early childhood in Spain. After leaving her convent boarding school in 1966 she was introduced to 'Swinging London' and as a result dropped out of Edinburgh University and went round America collecting underground newspapers. She is author of *The Diary of a Breast*, an account of having breast cancer, and has edited an anthology of stories, *The Junky's Christmas*. She has had stories and articles published in The *Observer,* The *London Review of Books,* The *Guardian,* The *Independent* and various Serpent's Tail anthologies including *God: An Anthology of Fiction* and *Obsession.*

Kirsty Seymour-Ure was born in 1965 and grew up in a village near Canterbury. She read English at Durham University and has lived in London since 1988. She has worked as an editor in illustrated publishing but has now taken the plunge to go freelance so as to spend more time writing. She has had poems published in various magazines and a story in *Smoke Signals* (Serpent's Tail), a collection of the winners of the first London Short Story Competition.

Susanna Steele was born in Ireland in 1948 and now lives in Hackney. She works as a teacher, lecturer and storyteller.

Karen Whiteson was reared in Northwest London and in the coastal region of Spain. She has written a libretto for a chamber opera about Joan of Arc, which was performed at the Riverside Studios. Her poetry has been published in *Frankenstein's Daughter* and her short stories have appeared in The *Edinburgh Review* and a Penguin anthology. She lives, writes and teaches in London.

📖 Six Plays by Black and Asian Women Writers

editor: Kadija George

A landmark collection of plays for stage, screen and radio demonstrating the range and vitality of Black and Asian writing. Featuring work by:

WINSOME PINNOCK MEERA SYAL MAYA CHOWDHRY TRISH COOKE RUKHSANA AHMAD ZINDIKA

"... showcases a wealth of talent amongst Black and Asian communities...often neg-lected by mainstream publishers ..."
(Black Pride Magazine)

"... a minority within a minority. Reading about their fears, hopes and aspirations in this entertaining way is an education in it-self."' (Artrage Magazine)

"... the strength of the collection lies in the fact, that it brings to readers plays that do not rely on stereotypes ..."
(The Weekly Journal.)

PRICE: £7.50   ISBN 0-9515877-2-2

📖Seven Plays by Women: Female Voices, Fighting Lives

editor: Cheryl Robson

A bumper collection of award-winning plays by a new generation of women writers. Features work by:

AYSHE RAIF APRIL DE ANGELIS
CHERYL ROBSON   JAN RUPPE
NINA RAPI EVA LEWIN JEAN ABBOTT

"A testimony to the work and debate that is going on among women, artistically, theoretically and practically. It is an inspiring document "
Clare Bayley (What's On)

"... these plays provide a forum for exposing the continuing discrimination against women ... they offer directors new material, actresses strong and challenging roles and audiences good theatre."
(Theatre Magazine)

"... likely to become much used texts in community-based theatre."
(The Guardian.)

PRICE: £5.95   ISBN: 0-9515877-1-4

📖 The Women Writers' Handbook

eds: Robson, Georgeson, Beck

An essential guide to setting up and running your own writing workshops. Featuring work by 15 new writers and:

CARYL CHURCHILL JILL HYEM
BRYONY LAVERY AYSHE RAIF

"A gem of a book. Everything a woman writer might need in one slim volume"
(Everywoman Magazine)

"... plenty of practical advice and information including detailed suggestions for a series of sessions."
(Writers' News)

"... gives practical inspiration for all of us unrecognised novelists and hidden poets."
(Spare Rib)

PRICE:£4.95   **ISBN: 0-9515877-0-6**

Mail Order: C/o The Women's Theatre Workshop, Isleworth Public Hall, South St, Old Isleworth, Middlesex. TW7 7BG.
Distribution: Central Books **Tel:** 081 986 4854